QUEEN SACRIFICE

TONY RICHES

COPYRIGHT

This book is a work of fiction. References to historical events, real people or real places are used fictitiously. Other names, characters, places and incidents are the products of the author's imagination and any resemblance to actual persons, living or dead, events or locales, is entirely coincidental.

Published by Preseli Press

ISBN-13: 978-1479357178
ISBN-10: 1479357170

ABOUT THE AUTHOR

Tony Riches is a full-time writer and lives with his wife in Pembrokeshire, West Wales. After several successful non-fiction books, Tony wrote *Queen Sacrifice*, followed by *The Shell*, a thriller about present day Kenya. A specialist in the history of the early Tudors, he is best known for his Tudor Trilogy. Tony's other international best sellers include *Warwick ~ The Man Behind the Wars of the Roses* and *The Secret Diary of Eleanor Cobham*.

For more information please visit Tony's website www.tonyriches.com and his blog at www.tonyriches.co.uk. He can also be found at Tony Riches Author on Facebook and Twitter @tonyriches.

To my wife
Liz

PREFACE

10th Century Wales is a country divided, with the kingdom of the south becoming Saxon and the north violently defending the old ways. The inevitable civil war is brutal and savage in this tale of divided loyalty and revenge, treachery and love.

Kings and queens battle for control of the country, with wealth and glory for the victor and death and ruin for the loser. The bishops of Wales struggle to keep the faith while knights and war lords turn events to advantage and the lives of ordinary people are changed forever by the conflict.

Queen Sacrifice is also a legendary tactic in the ancient game of chess. Russian chess grand master Lakov Neishtadt describes the sacrifice of the queen for higher interests as 'a source of continuing fascination for the chess novice and master alike.'

The narrative faithfully follows every move in the queen sacrifice game, known as 'The Game of the Century' between Donald Byrne and 13-year-old Bobby Fischer in New York on October 17th 1956.

The Gwyn (Welsh for White)

White King: **Gwayne**, son of the old king
White Queen: **Elvina**, sister of the Saxon King Athelstan with handmaiden **Bethan**
White King's Bishop: **Renfrew**, Archbishop of Llandaff
White Queen's Bishop: **Cledwin**, Bishop of St Davids, with housekeeper **Anwen**
White King's Knight: **Sir Padrig** of St Fagans
White Queen's Knight: **Sir Gwynfor** of Picton
White King's Rook: Caerphilly Castle
White Queen's Rook: Pembroke castle
White King's Pawn: **Delwyn**, of the Royal Household
White Queen's Pawn: **Owen** of the Royal Bodyguard
White King's Bishop's Pawn: **Cade**, bondsman archer
White Queen's Bishop's Pawn: **Elfred** the farmer
White King's Knight's Pawn: **Kane**, the longbow master
White Queen's Knight's Pawn: **Hayden**, trainee Knight
White King's Rook's Pawn: **Afon**, longbow archer
White Queen's Rook's Pawn: **Neb**, man of Pembroke

The Du (Welsh for Black)

Black King: **Gethin,** father of Prince Evan

Black Queen: **Rhiannon,** mother of Prince Evan and sister of **Ceinwen**

Black King's Bishop: **Deniol** of Flint

Black Queen's Bishop: **Emrys** of Bangor

Black King's Knight: **Lord Vorath** of Flint

Black Queen's Knight: **Lord Llewelyn** of Ynys Mon

Black King's Rook: Flint Castle

Black Queen's Rook: Ynys Mon Hill Fort

Black King's Pawn: **Idris,** Commander of the King's Guard

Black Queen's Pawn: Hywel, Queen's Bodyguard

Black King's Bishop's Pawn: **Rhys,** bondsman of Flint

Black Queen's Bishop's Pawn: **Madoc** the thief

Black King's Knight's Pawn: **Tristan,** swordsman

Black Queen's Knight's Pawn: **Bryn** the blacksmith

Black King's Rook's Pawn: **Dafydd,** acting Commander of Flint Castle

Black Queen's Rook's Pawn: **Cadell** the mercenary

Map of Wales

CHAPTER 1

*H*is destiny was to be the greatest king to ever rule Wales - or to die, defending all he valued in the world. As he waited in the late autumn sunshine for the riders to approach, the king felt a stab of regret.

His father had proudly named him Gwayne, the white hawk, the future defender of the people of the Gwyn. He'd always known he would one day take his father's place but was completely unprepared when it happened so brutally. Gwayne swore an oath to avenge his father and keep his lands safe, at any cost.

Gwayne's kingdom now extended over the whole of the south, from the most westerly point of Wales in St Davids, all the way to the border with the English and half way to the north. While the people of the north had clung to the old tribal ways, those in the south had done well through trade with their neighbours.

Saxon merchants had safe passage by boat up the channel to Brycg Stowe and had brought wealth, trading pottery and fine cloth for Welsh livestock, grain and the black coal. The last year had been good and the royal treasury was richer than ever before. Most importantly, the Gwyn had a plentiful supply of well crafted armour and weapons, as well as new ideas on the strategy of war.

He personally supervised the building of the Royal Llysoedd at Pennard on the Gower peninsula, a site he had chosen years before. Well placed to reach the garrison outposts at Pembroke and Caerphilly, Pennard was beautiful, with sweeping views to Three Cliffs Bay and the sea.

Gwayne planned to rebuild it with local stone but for now the palisades and curtain wall meant it could be defended well. The only entrance was through the gatehouse and it was here he stood, looking out at the small settlement growing around the Llysoedd. The year had not been without its challenges but the news they were waiting for could mean the hardest challenge was yet to come.

The king dressed in the English style, with his dark hair and beard trimmed and a heavy engraved silver buckle fastening his fine white cloak. He had the confident manner of a king but would never be mistaken for a Saxon, as he spoke with the distinctive deep accent of south Wales.

His bare arms had the firm muscles and scars of a battle hardened fighter, yet his eyes flashed with the sharpness of a well educated mind. The tough exterior hid a sensitivity that made him vulnerable but he tried to live up to the legacy of his father and the legend he had become.

On his left was Sir Padrig, his loyal and trusted knight. They had grown up together, drinking and gambling at St Fagans, the home he'd given to Padrig with a knighthood for saving his life. It was a hard debt to repay but formed a special bond between them.

Padrig was putting on weight but still moved like a fighting man and dressed as one, with an expensive white painted breastplate and flowing white cloak the sign of his nobility. He had a coarse sense of humour that went down well in the taverns, where he would challenge all comers to arm wrestling and always won. His keen eyes now scanned the distance as they waited for the visitors. Padrig enjoyed the friendly rivalry of his fellow knights and was glad to have the advantage of arriving early.

To the king's right was the love of his life, the youngest sister of the Anglo Saxon King Athelstan and now his queen. His marriage to Elvina had not been for love. It was arranged to turn the uneasy truce with the English into a permanent alliance.

He noticed she'd chosen to wear her best white dress to greet their visitor. She smiled mischievously at him and desire flashed through his mind as he remembered the first time he undressed her. She looked beautiful as the autumn sun shone on her golden hair, tied back with blue silk ribbons. Gwayne caught his breath at the delicate scent of exotic perfume reminded him that he was married to one of the wealthiest women he'd ever known.

He wore his father's gold ring on his right hand and had a habit of turning it round on his finger when he was thinking. He did that now.

'Please don't be hard on him,' said the queen, her voice soft so only he would hear.

The king tensed as he remembered how Sir Gwynfor had amused his wife. He always felt their age difference an irrelevance until he saw her laughing with the handsome champion. He had thought long and hard about what he should do and decided that the smiling knight would pay the price for his disloyalty.

Not now though, the moment would come and the queen would never know. He looked into Elvina's deep blue eyes and was saddened to realise he could no longer trust either of them.

'He is ambitious. You would do well to remember that.'

Before she could answer him the group of riders galloped into view, the hooves of their heavy war horses thundering noisily on earth hardened by a long summer. They brought their horses to a controlled halt and dismounted with practised ease.

As well as the young knight there were two soldiers and an older man the king recognised as a mercenary from the other side of the Welsh border. The soldiers carried silver lances with flowing white pennants, the battle standards of the people of the Gwyn.

'Greetings, my lord,' said Gwynfor, unbuckling his sword and handing it to one of the soldiers. His voice was clear and strong, with a trace of a west Wales accent.

Gwayne missed his glance at the queen but she did not. Neither did Padrig, who was skilled at pretending not to notice things which may be turned to some advantage.

The knight was looking well from his travels. He wore fine new armour made by skilled craftsmen and looked tanned from the long summer. His hair was fair for a Welshman and he was clean shaven, a rare sight that drew attention to his good looks.

Gwynfor had become champion with ease and was their best hope for finally defeating the northerners. He was a master of the deadly longsword, having spent seven years in training, practising the strokes and manoeuvres until they were perfected.

The heavy weapon needed strength to swing but could slice off the limbs or head of an enemy in a single stroke. He was also a skilled horseman, tested in battle many times. Now he had been assessing the readiness of the men encamped along their northern border. He had built a strong following, a natural leader.

King Gwayne smiled, 'Welcome, Sir Gwynfor. We must talk, in private.'

'You've been busy since I was here last,' said Gwynfor, noting the palisades of freshly cut timber that now defended the entire estate. He grinned at the king. 'Let us hope your work has been wasted.'

Gwayne shook his head. 'The threat is not just from the north, we must be on our guard against raiders from the sea.' On his sign, two servants opened the heavy wooden doors to reveal the inner courtyard. 'Come in, there is much to discuss.'

The soldiers led the horses to the stables and the queen discreetly left them, but not before exchanging another meaningful glance with the young champion. The knights followed the king to one of the oak beamed rooms of the Royal Llysoedd, where a log fire was already blazing.

There was a strong smell of wood smoke but it was warmer than any of his castles. Light flooded in from the windows, which had thick but precious leaded glass, with the pale blue-green tint that showed its Saxon origin.

The lime washed walls were decorated with the antlers of stags and above the fireplace was a battered but elaborately crafted shield, once used in battle by the old king. It served as a reminder of the great man and of the need to protect their people. In the centre of the room was an oak table laden with food and wine.

King Gwayne sat at his throne, a high backed wooden chair intricately carved with his emblem of the hawk gripping a crown in its talons. He gestured for them to sit and dismissed the servants, who had poured them each a goblet of wine.

Gwayne studied the warriors. His kingdom was in their hands, as it was only a matter of time before they would have to defend their lands again. The two men were so different in character but bonded by their craft and worked well together. Padrig had experience and strength, Gwynfor youth, education and cunning.

Gwynfor took the seat facing the door. 'We are preparing well. Our men are ready from the coast at St Davids to the border at Chepstow.' He watched the king, waiting for some sign approval but none came. 'We have plenty of bondsmen but need more leaders,' he continued. 'I have chosen a few of the best for battle training. Some will go to the garrison at Pembroke and the rest are on their way to Caerphilly.'

King Gwayne nodded but looked deep in thought. He was remembering how the last men he singled out as leaders had died. Brave and loyal, they had given their lives for the Gwyn and the burden of responsibility weighed heavily on him.

'What news of the north?' asked Padrig, taking a large swig directly from a wine flagon, ignoring the now empty goblet in front of him.

'Our scouts report that the Du have not ventured from their lands,' replied Gwynfor. 'Yet we keep a close watch.'

'I don't trust them,' said Padrig.

The king grinned, then looked serious. 'It is just a matter of time before they invade, we must be sure they don't take us by surprise.'

'Or we could take the battle to them,' said Gwynfor, watching the king closely. He was confident of their strength. King Gwayne wanted to keep the peace but there had never been a better time to drive the Du from the north and take the whole country.

The men were preparing for battle and he was ready to lead them. At the very least, success would mean a share of the spoils of war but the real prize was the chance of succession. If anything were to happen to the king there was yet no heir, so the people of the Gwyn would look to a strong leader.

'We wait,' said the king firmly. 'Send scouts north and prepare a chain of beacons to warn of any attack.'

'There is another way,' suggested Gwynfor, his voice calm. 'I have with me a mercenary who knows the ways of the Du. He will spy for us in the enemy ranks,' he said. 'Pay him well and we will know their every move.'

Padrig laughed and clapped Gwynfor hard on the back. The good wine was starting to take effect 'You had this planned all along!'

'Only if the king bids it,' replied Gwynfor. For the first time he saw Gwayne look impressed.

'Bring him here, Sir Gwynfor, I think I know the man.' He walked over to the fire and threw on another log, sending a shower of small sparks into the air.

Gwynfor left the room and Padrig took the chance to speak to the king, his apparent drunken state forgotten. 'Mercenaries have no honour,' he scowled. 'It is a clever plan but feels wrong.'

The king nodded. 'You are right, as ever, Padrig. You will have to watch Sir Gwynfor and his accomplice as best you can.'

The heavy wooden door banged open. It was Gwynfor and the mercenary.

King Gwayne looked up as they entered. 'What's your name man?'

'Cadell, my lord. I am a freeman of England.' His dark eyes held the king in a confident gaze. He had the heavy leather jerkin of a soldier but wore an ornate dagger at his belt and in different times could have passed for a nobleman. What struck Gwayne most was his rich West Country accent, rarely heard in Wales since the border disputes.

The king looked thoughtful. 'What do you know of the northerners?'

'I have travelled through the lands of the Du for many years, my lord.'

'But where are your loyalties?' asked Padrig.

'To the coin of Athelstan,' grinned the mercenary without hesitation, 'I make no secret of my trade, pay well and you will find no more loyal servant.'

'Good,' said King Gwayne, 'I like your honesty - and I know you from King Athelstan's court?'

'You do sir. I am surprised you remember me.'

'A king has to be sure of who is at his back.' Gwayne gestured towards the door. 'Tell them you are to have food and lodgings in the barracks, we have plans to make.' They watched the mercenary leave.

Padrig helped himself to an apple from a bowl on the table and half of it disappeared in one bite. 'How did you find him?'

'It took a while,' said Gwynfor. 'I also saw him when we visited the English Court and marked him as a mercenary.'

'How will he get messages to us?' asked King Gwayne.

'He travels freely in the north,' said Gwynfor. 'I will tell him to wait until he has information of real value, then find a horse and come south as fast as he can. He is a skilled rider and has the makings of a knight.'

'What is a knight after all,' laughed Padrig, 'but a soldier who can ride a horse?'

The king smiled. Gwynfor resented that he had trained long and hard to reach his position at King Gwayne's side but Padrig had won his place easily. The truth of the matter was never spoken. His friend Padrig would do well not to make sport of the young champion, however.

Gwynfor stood and turned to the king. 'I have ridden long today, my lord. I need to tend my horse and get some rest.'

King Gwayne nodded. 'We will talk in the morning. You have done well.'

Gwynfor left and started heading for the stables when he saw an attractive young servant girl, one of the queen's handmaidens, lighting candles to brighten the dark hallway. She recognised him and smiled. He stopped and stared deep into her eyes, making a judgement.

'The queen,' he said quietly, 'Take me to her.'

~

Archbishop Renfrew knelt at prayer in his private chapel. It was one of the finest in Wales, being close to the Saxon border in the prosperous village of Llandaff. His church was one of the earliest

Christian sites in Britain, founded by St Dyfrig. Pilgrims called often to visit the relics of the saint and their offerings had paid for the stonemasons and artisans to restore the ancient building into the finest in the kingdom.

The archbishop had simple tastes and felt uncomfortable with the obvious display of wealth. His one exception was a gold crucifix with a large ruby set in the centre, which he wore on a chain round his neck. It had been given to him by the king and showed remarkable craftsmanship in the engraving. He was unaware that the crucifix, with its precious stone, marked him as a target. More than one ruthless thief would be waiting for an unguarded moment.

The golden crucifix was not his most treasured possession. The archbishop was also the proud owner of a Vetus Latina, the ancient priceless Bible of antiquity. Older than the Vulgate Bible of Saint Jerome and painstakingly hand written in Latin calligraphy, Renfrew's copy had been illuminated in gold leaf and magnificent colours. He never told anyone how he came by it and saw himself as a custodian of the work, dedicating his life to its study and safe keeping.

Renfrew was liked by all who knew him and had the dark eyes of the Welsh that shone engagingly as he spoke. He was not old but his once jet black hair and beard were turning grey, giving him an air of authority he found increasingly useful.

Fluent in many languages, he was a favourite advisor to the king and had introduced him to the young Queen Elvina. The power that came with his duties also brought responsibility. He had brokered the truce with their former enemies through the marriage, which had worked out better than he could possibly have hoped. Although the Welsh Church was outside the jurisdiction of the English Bishops, Archbishop Renfrew was well connected. He knew the Anglo Saxon King Athelstan faced opposition from Owain of Strathclyde and needed an alliance with the Welsh kings.

Athelstan had made a treaty with the Viking leader Sithric, King of York, sealed by the marriage of his sister, Edith, to the Danish king. When Renfrew discovered that Athelstan had four other sisters, an idea formed in his mind. He found out that the youngest of the English princess was unmarried.

King Gwayne could have had his pick of the eligible Welsh nobility, so it was fortunate that the king found Athelstan's sister Elvina attractive. She had her brother's striking blond hair and was well educated in matters of the royal court. It had not been easy to arrange the introduction but God was willing, and the Saxon Bishops had seen advantage in supporting him.

Allegiance with the House of Wessex was their best defence against the endless border struggles and the threat from Viking invaders. The problem of the northern tribes of Wales was quite a different matter. One which he feared would only be settled by bloodshed.

Renfrew was a man of peace and had slept badly for several nights, concerned about rumours of warriors rallying at Flint Castle. The king would surely be sending for him before long but he was at a loss to see how war could be avoided. He decided to write to the Bishops of the north. They were loyal to a different king but shared the same religion.

CHAPTER 2

Queen Rhiannon of the Du held her strong baby close and wondered what the future would hold for him. She felt overwhelming relief to have given her husband the son he longed for. She silently thanked God the birth had been without problems. She knew good women who died screaming in agony when babies could not be brought safely into the world. That was not her destiny, at least not this time.

The king smiled at his wife and child. 'We will name him Evan, after my Grandfather.' King Gethin was a striking figure, one of the strongest and best educated ever to rule over the Du. In the tradition of his people, his hair was long and dark. He wore the tribal tattoos and a heavy gold ear ring, yet it was his eyes that people remembered. They had an intensity that marked him as a natural leader of men.

Rhiannon looked into her new son's big dark eyes. 'Evan is a good name for a Prince.' She had dreamed of this day when she was a young girl, growing up by the sea at the hill fort in Conwy. Her parents were long dead, killed by the devastating plague that swept through the land more than ten years before. Her older sister, Ceinwen, had looked after her for as long as she could remember, teaching her the ways of a Welsh Princess.

She looked similar to Rhiannon, tall and athletic, with the same raven black hair worn free flowing and long. They both turned heads wherever they went, for different reasons. Rhiannon's dark eyes saw deep into a man's soul and left him enchanted. Ceinwen's good humoured approach to life made her eyes twinkle attractively although she seemed unaware of the effect of this on the men she met.

The queen called for her sister now. She had been helping her throughout the birth and looked tired but happy. 'Ceinwen, thank you. You have been so good to me. Let it be known that the new prince is to be called Evan.'

Ceinwen laughed. 'It means fortunate one,' she said. 'He is indeed fortunate!'

Rhiannon smiled. 'We have all been fortunate, that we live to see this day.' Ceinwen left to spread the news. Everyone in the kingdom would hear before the day was over.

King Gethin had never been happier but knew that dark clouds loomed over their future as a family. He had been sent worrying news that in the land to the south the people of the Gwyn were preparing for battle, training their men and readying defences. He had summoned his lords and warriors to talk about what they must do, but for now tried to put it out of his mind.

Rhiannon was too excited to notice the change in his mood. 'We must have a royal feast. All the tribes should be invited.'

Gethin grinned. 'The tribes are already here. They are waiting for me so I must go to the arena and start the celebrations.' He left Rhiannon alone with the baby and she noticed her son was still staring at her, with his father's intense, all-knowing gaze.

She held him to her swollen breast. 'Little Evan, my prayers have been answered by you.'

The Palace of the Du was simply furnished, with sheepskins on the floor and a big stone hearth to keep them warm. The

Du were nomadic, moving with the changing seasons, so it suited Rhiannon to have few possessions, apart from one she kept close wherever they travelled. It was a dark oak chest, with an ingenious iron lock. King Gethin thought it held her dresses and trinkets, which it did, but the old chest had another purpose for Rhiannon. To keep her precious papers safe.

She was the first Du queen to learn to read and write the Welsh language, thanks to the patience over many years of her teacher and mentor, Bishop Emrys. The king had made it clear they must follow the tradition of handing down the stories by word of mouth but secretly, when she could, Rhiannon was writing down the ways of her people.

It had been a slow, laborious process. The bishop lived in Bangor, so his lessons were limited to his visits when the king was away. More than once they had nearly been discovered but Rhiannon was ready to confess that she was learning the religious texts.

The key was always on a chain around her neck, so after making sure she was alone, she unlocked the chest and slid open a secret panel where her papers were safely hidden. One day she would share her writing with her son, Evan, who she would also teach to read and write the language of their people.

She unrolled the parchment Bishop Emrys had provided and taking the sharpened quill began slowly writing about the birth of her son. The black ink dried slowly and her hand was a little unsteady but she knew in her heart the value of a written record of their times.

∾

The men of the tribes assembled in the open arena. Unlike the Gwyn, who had united under a single flag, Du warlords were loyal to the king but ruled vast lands of many tribes. To the east, the tribal warlord Vorath kept the peace in the lands to the border with the English at the old Roman town of Chester.

To the west, Lord Llewelyn did the same for the territories up to the furthest tip of the Isle of Ynys Môn. King Gethin had worked hard to bring them together as the people of the Du. It had not been easy to win the respect of all the tribes.

There was a hush as the king entered the arena. It was a clear autumn evening and he felt a gentle sea breeze. The sun was setting and the arena was lit by the flames of dozens of brightly burning torches.

The king carried the sacred dagger, a finely crafted weapon with a handle of carved black obsidian and a curved, savagely sharp silver blade. He held it high, signifying his royal command. He could see there were more men gathered than usual.

King Gethin looked around their faces, recognising many and bringing them to silence before he spoke. His strong voice resonated clearly across the arena. 'Today is a special day. I have a son and have named him Prince Evan!' A deep cheer of approval rang out into the night and Gethin felt an overwhelming pride in his people. It had been an emotional day. He had feared he could lose his beautiful wife or his precious son, or both, so it was with a huge sense of relief that he addressed the assembled tribes.

Warlord Vorath watched from the side of the arena, surrounded by a group of young warriors. An impressive figure, with a dark beard, his bare muscular arms were encircled with tattoos of sacred symbols from the old days. His father had died of wounds in a battle with the Gwyn and he harboured a need for vengeance that made him sometimes reckless.

King Gethin noted that Vorath wore his black cape with his fighting sword and dagger at his belt. They had fought together many times, against the Vikings, the English, Irish raiders and the ruthless southerners, the Gwyn. He smiled at the memory of the stories they shared. There was no better man to have at his side.

Vorath stood and faced the king. 'We wish you well, my lord, and your son too.' He paused while they cheered in agreement. 'We pledge our support if there is trouble from the south.' Another cheer went up. Vorath held up his hand for silence. 'I pray that no more good men will die defending our land - but we are ready to do so!' Men started rhythmically thumping the hard ground with ends of their spear shafts, an old tradition that warmed the heart of the king.

Next it was Lord Llewelyn who stood. Vorath sat down and waited to hear the legendary orator. The traditions of the Du passed from one generation to the next, so much importance was placed on oratory and there was no greater master.

The king was surprised to see his old friend Llewelyn looked thin and frail. He was recovering from illness and carried a long fighting staff which he leaned on for support. Dressed in black, as was the custom of his tribe, the elderly lord counselled peace with the Gwyn.

Now he looked round at the torch-lit faces of his countrymen and shook his head dramatically. 'Many of you think it is time to drive the Gwyn out of Wales.' He paused for effect, waiting for a reaction to the question in his words. 'Even those who advocated talks with the king of the Gwyn must admit he is now a puppet of the Saxons!' Llewelyn enjoyed stressing the word puppet and was rewarded by a deep murmur of agreement. 'Marriage to the foreigner's sister had sullied the blood of Cymraig.' At this the men all stood up and cheered.

King Gethin was used to the posturing of his lords and waited for the noise to settle down. Once they were all seated, he addressed them again. 'We have learnt that the people of the Gwyn are preparing for battle.' He had their full attention now. 'You say you are ready but we must also prepare, we must give them no advantage, spare them no quarter.'

The roar of approval echoing around the arena was interrupted by a loud and sudden bellow behind him. He turned to see two strong warriors, each with a firm hold on the horns of a large black bull.

The king approached them, swiftly drew his dagger and with a deep and deadly stroke slashed the throat of the powerful animal, ending its life in a spurt of red blood across the hard packed earth of the arena. He paused, watching the reaction of the men. 'The time for talking of peace is over,' he said, holding his bloodied dagger in the air defiantly. 'We will take the rich lands of the south and make them ours.'

This was the signal the men had been waiting for. Their king had not disappointed and the celebrations for the birth of his son turned into a celebration of a new beginning for the people of the Du.

~

Bishop Deniol slept badly and woke before daylight with an unhappy dilemma, his mind on the letter he had received from Archbishop Renfrew of Llandaff. As the king's counsel and spiritual advisor he knew his duty but as a man of the church he should not be talking of war.

Deniol had few friends, partly due to his abrupt manner and tendency to lapse into long silences, lost in his own thoughts. He was, however, a gifted scholar and would have much preferred to see out his days reading in the library of Basingwerk.

He dressed and went to his study to read the neatly written letter for the tenth time. He trusted Renfrew and had to acknowledge the archbishop's skill at setting out a persuasive argument. He had heard the king speak about the Gwyn and knew it would be impossible to get him to agree publicly to any kind of truce.

Now there was a son there would be more at stake. Bishop Deniol knew he must seek an audience with the king to discuss the letter. His duty was to at least present the archbishop's idea before it was too late.

The bishop rang a bell to summon his servants and told them to make ready his carriage for a journey. Unable to ride a horse any distance, he'd paid the village carpenter to modify a sturdy farm cart, with a cover to keep out the rain and a comfortable seat.

He had been all the way to the Island of Ynys Mon in his cart and now he rarely travelled without it. He also told them to track down his bondsman Rhys to travel with him. As well as being experienced at taking the cart over the unreliable tracks of the northern coast, Rhys was company on a long journey.

Rhys was short, with dark hair and a secretive manner, so gave little idea of how he felt about anything. He was quietly pleased when he was told he was going on a long journey with the bishop. As a bondsman he was little more than a servant, so had no choice but to obey the bishop's command, but a visit to the king would mean he would hear all the latest news.

His father had been a famous warrior, so Rhys should have inherited a good living, but he was the youngest son. When his father died his older brothers shared the land and money between them, leaving him to find his own way in life. They had sons of their own, so he was never going to inherit.

Rhys had a plan, however. He'd seen a crossbow when some mercenaries from England visited Basingwerk and took an interest in how it worked. He was good with his hands but tried several times to copy the design, only to be disappointed.

It was only when he used wood from a sacred yew that he achieved the results he wanted. Rhys took it as a sign and practised with the crossbow whenever he could, hiding it amongst his few possessions. At first, he had found it hard to draw, but he made a lever and a simple ratchet. The small bolts, fashioned from salvaged cut down arrows, fired with deadly accuracy, so fast that the eye could hardly follow them.

If there was a war, he had a way out of spending the rest of his life as the bishop's man. He would not be fighting hand to hand, with swords and daggers. With a crossbow he would become an unseen assassin, his victims only aware of the hiss of the bolt when it was too late. Rhys smiled to himself at the thought and remembered how firmly and deeply his crossbow bolts lodged into the trunk of a tree he used for practice.

The cart was making good progress on the coastal track, as work had been done over the past year to widen it and fill the worst of the holes. Rhys wondered what had happened to make the bishop need to see the king so urgently. They were travelling light, so he knew it would be a short visit.

Bishop Deniol looked up at the sun, trying to judge the hour. 'I need to get to the king before nightfall, if we can.'

The track was straight and level, so Rhys encouraged the horse to break into a trot, saying nothing but casting a furtive look at the bishop, who looked tense and worried. When they arrived at the king's encampment Bishop Deniol was fortunate, as the king agreed to see him straight away.

The king was alone in his meeting room. The only light was from candles of tallow, which smoked and cast long shadows as they flickered. The walls were decorated with a collection of finely made swords and spears, reminding any visitors that they were dealing with a warrior king.

Deniol had been in the king's meeting room many times but still eyed the weapons nervously. 'My Lord, you are blessed to have a son,'

'Thank you Bishop Deniol, but I doubt you have come all this way...'

'You are right lord. We need to discuss a letter from the archbishop of the Gwyn.' He handed the letter to the king, who was well versed in Latin and studied it for some time before answering.

'This could be a trick,' he murmured to himself, deep in

thought. He suddenly turned his penetrating gaze on the bishop. 'Your counsel, Deniol?'

'There is no deceit, my Lord, he replied, 'The archbishop is a good man, I have known him for many years.

'You know the Gwyn are readying for war?'

'Yes. I fear they may have spies among us even now but you ask my counsel. I say we should talk. Many lives may be spared and you will be remembered as a man of peace.'

The king looked at him darkly. 'Do you truly believe Athelstan will treat us as fairly as a king who is married to his own family?

'No. I do not.' The silence hung in the air and they both knew the truth. Bishop Deniol struggled with his conscience. 'My lord, if war cannot be avoided, the Church has an obligation to ensure it is just.'

'So what would you have me do? Am I to stand by and watch as the Gwyn take our lands?

Denial looked uncomfortable. 'I have made a study of the writings of Marcus Cicero, my lord. He wrote that men owe each other obligations even in times of war, especially not to kill the innocent.'

The king up held his hand to show he wanted to hear no more. 'You are to reply to the letter, Deniol,' said Gethin quietly. 'Tell the archbishop we are also readying for battle. They will not take us by surprise!'

~

Bishop Emrys would also have been consulted on the reply but, as the queen's personal cleric, had been with her throughout the birth and celebrations. He had now returned to his church in Bangor.

An athletic man, he had risen to high office through his many gifts. Bishop Emrys was possibly the brightest of his generation and the youngest ever to reach the rank of bishop. He'd learned to read and write in several languages, including Greek and the Nordic text of the Vikings, as well as absorbing the nuances of Latin and was an acknowledged master of the Welsh language.

Emrys was also a man of many secrets, most of which involved the queen. Rhiannon had pleaded with him to teach her to write the language of their people and to provide parchment, ink and quills to practice. One of his secrets was that he had planted the seed of the idea in her mind when she first became queen.

He appreciated her gratitude, so continued the pretence that he was teaching her against his better judgement. It also meant that he could spend much time alone with her. Another secret was that he knew of the compartment where she hid her writing and therefore why it was so important to her.

Of all the secrets shared between them the biggest and most dangerous was that he'd fallen in love with her. Not simply the loyal love of a subject for his queen but a love that grew from the deepest sexual attraction any man ever felt for a woman.

From the first moment he saw her, his life changed completely. His first thought on waking would be of Rhiannon, and he would be distracted from his prayers by improper thoughts of her. At first he had tried self flagellation, lashing his own back until it ran with blood in a futile attempt to drive such thoughts from his mind.

He wondered if he'd been possessed by a devil or if a witch had cursed him with an evil spell. The more time he spent with the queen, the deeper his feelings for her became and he finally realised it was no spell, but a love that could not be denied.

He knew that if the king ever found out, his life would be forfeit, so he had accepted that the best he could hope for was to be her confidante and counsel. He suspected that she knew of his feelings for her but it was never spoken of. Bishop Emrys would give his life for his queen.

~

Lord Vorath returned home from the celebrations fired up with a new sense of urgency. He had feared that he would never get the chance to avenge the murder of his father without taking things into his own hands. Now he summoned his men to the great hall and told them the news. They were going to drive the Gwyn from Wales.

'The Gwyn have an alliance with the English,' shouted Dafydd, one of the younger warriors from the castle at Flint. A skilled swordsman, he made little secret of his ambition to take over leadership from Vorath one day. 'We will need to guard our border to the east.'

The significance of Dafydd's words was not lost on the gathered warriors. They were ready to take on the south in a fair fight but war with the powerful Saxons was a very different prospect. To take on both at the same time could only have one outcome.

Vorath stood and surprised them all with the strength of feeling in his deep voice. 'This is our land!' He paused to control his emotion and continued in a more measured voice, stressing his words so none could fail to understand. 'It is our home. We fought off the might of the Roman empire.'

He looked round at their faces. 'We routed the Vikings when they tried to invade and we have held firm against the Saxons.' It was true and they all knew it. 'If it is my destiny to die protecting the people of the Du then so be it, but we have right on our side. We can win this battle. We will defeat the Gwyn.'

Lord Vorath remained standing as the warriors cheered and noted that Dafydd was also cheering loudly. Vorath smiled as he realised that of all his warriors, the troublesome young Dafydd was the closest to a son to him. He would avenge his long dead father and help the man from Flint learn to become a great leader. Or he would die fighting.

CHAPTER 3

*B*ishop Cledwin of St Davids had built a personal fortune through his good stewardship of the land he managed in the name of the church. Fond of good wine, he dressed simply but furnished his Lys as well as any palace.

Cledwin was a heavily built man, with a booming voice to match and retained a small army of servants. More like the Lord of the Manor than a man of the cloth, he tended well to the local communities, so earned their loyalty and respect.

St Davids was the most important religious diocese in Wales and relics of Saint David brought wealthy pilgrims from all over the country. Bishop Cledwin had little interest in the Saxons, who were a long ride away from the west coast of Wales. Occasional ships from Ireland would raid the coastal ports but never troubled him. His wealth was mostly tied up in farmland, which pirates could hardly carry off.

The marauding Viking longships were a different matter. Viking sails had been sighted in the Irish Sea and they were known to target the lightly defended religious centres looking for gold and provisions.

There were reports of raids to the north where they had taken men and women, presumably as slaves. St Davids was well known for its wealth and close to the coast, so though Cledwin was glad to have royal protection, he worried about how long it would take for help to arrive from the king.

His relationship with King Gwayne was complicated. Bishop Cledwin was nearly as rich and powerful as the king and, in his view, better educated. This meant he had an important part to play in helping the king develop the Welsh Law that kept order in the south. Cledwin had been bishop and advisor to the old king and remembered Gwayne as a young Prince, so was the only person in the land who could really stand up to him.

Where Archbishop Renfrew in the east was a skilled politician, Cledwin was skilled at administration of the Church. He made certain that any laws passed were to his advantage and had developed stricter rules for the diocese under his care.

He had also been able to persuade the king of the benefits of extending the parish boundaries. As bishop he was entitled to enforce collection of tithes at one tenth of the income of the faithful, so he was keen to cast his net widely in the sparsely populated west.

Bishop Cledwin had taken to the habit of sleeping after lunch and was roused from his sleep by his housekeeper, Anwen.

'Archbishop, you have a visitor.'

'At this ungodly hour?' he grumbled. 'Tell them I am not receiving visitors!'

Anwen was well used to his blustering. It was early afternoon and she smiled. 'It's the tenant farmer, Elfred, your honour, he wishes you to plead his case.'

After Elfred's mother died she was the only person other than him who knew that Elfred was his son. Bishops were not expected to be celibate but the knowledge gave her a power over him. She had not yet felt the need to use this knowledge but was certain the day would come.

'Tell him to wait in my room,' said Cledwin, looking for any sign on her face and seeing none. His eyes followed her as she left. Attractive as a girl, she had grown more so with age. She dressed simply but well and had looked after him for longer than he could remember.

Anwen knew a great deal more about him than he would have wished, so he made sure he could rely on her loyalty. The bishop studied himself in an expensive burnished silver mirror. He was getting older and would need to think about his successor. Of necessity, his only son had been brought up as a farmer. He was a good one and Cledwin was secretly proud of him but he was not for the church. Another would need to be found to continue God's work.

He went into the room he used for less formal meetings and found Elfred standing there. It always took him by surprise to see the boy grown into a man but even more so today. Hard work on farms had made him strong and rugged but his eyes still shone with his mother's sensitivity.

Elfred had grown a beard that suited him well, although it made him look older than his twenty-five years. What surprised Cledwin was to see his son dressed as a soldier, with a new white tabard over a hide jerkin and a short dagger at his side.

'What's this?' Bishop Cledwin frowned, a note of annoyance in his voice.

'I need your help, my lord bishop,' said Elfred with a directness that again reminded Cledwin of the woman he once loved. 'I am to report for battle training at Pembroke Castle but there is much to do on the farms.'

'Nonsense. You are needed here. Who else would manage my estates?'

'If you would write to the king, I trust he would approve your request.'

Not for the first time the bishop wondered about telling his son the truth. Then a thought occurred to him. 'Why has Sir

Gwynfor chosen you, when there are plenty of bondsmen who would leap at the chance?'

'Sir Gwynfor's men were asking in the village for anyone who could write their name. It is well known you have schooled me well to help you manage the farms.'

The bishop nodded. He had been a good teacher, not just for his son but for the young knight as well. A new idea occurred to him. If Elfred could keep to the good of Sir Gwynfor, he would be able to ensure protection for St Davids, not just from the Viking raiders but, God forbid, if the warriors of the Du were ever to reach West Wales.

'Anwen!' he called, 'Wine for my visitor.' He sat down heavily in a large chair and gestured for Elfred to sit next to him. 'Let us discuss this.'

Elfred looked at him in surprise. 'I am not a fighter, bishop. All I ask is to see the harvest safe. I hope to marry soon and raise a family, not go off to a foolish war with our neighbours.'

'Sometimes, God's plans are not easy to fathom. Let us not decide such an important matter for the diocese in haste.'

Anwen brought wine and they watched in silence as she poured it into rare glass goblets Bishop Cledwin kept for special occasions. His eyes met hers and he could see from the twinkle of amusement that she knew the significance. He could have been angry but instead smiled as she left them. He would be lost without her now and although she knew it, the arrangement suited them both well.

Cledwin took a small sip of the wine and recognised it immediately as his best. He looked directly at the young farmer. 'It is your duty to look to the needs of the people,' he told him. 'Bishops are allowed to fight, if we have to, but we need to make provision in case we are ever attacked.'

'Who will tend the farms and the harvest if I am away fighting?' Elfred asked.

'You must find someone. Tell them to come to me and I will

train them in managing the estates, as I have with you.' He spoke with an air of finality and had clearly made his decision. Before Elfred spoke again, the bishop rose from his chair and crossed the room to a large oak chest. The heavy lid creaked as he lifted it and produced something wrapped in an ancient battle standard.

Elfred stood. He could see that the bishop was quite moved at the sight of the sword. He suddenly realised this was difficult for the old man.

'It was my father's sword. He was a great warrior and now you should have this, in honour of what you are about to do.'

Elfred knew better than to argue with the bishop. He took the sword and felt the easy way it balanced in his hand. It was a fine old weapon, the blade still sharp and true. If he had to go and fight for his people at least he would be well armed. 'I am honoured,' he said. 'I will serve you well, bishop.'

Cledwin watched him as he strapped on the sword. It suited him and Cledwin wished Elfred's mother could have known how well the boy had turned out.

He put his hand on Elfred's arm. 'God go with you, my son, keep safe.'

'I shall, with your blessing,' replied Elfred, missing the significance of the bishop's words or the emotion in his voice.

~

In keeping with tradition, the queen had her own household and the Royal Llysoedd had been designed so her chamber was set apart from the king's. Queen Elvina expected a long wait for the king's meeting to be over, so was surprised when her maid announced that Sir Gwynfor wished to see her. Better educated than any of them, she resented being dismissed at such an important time.

She was the sister of the English king but was being treated like a servant. She missed the English Court, where well-born women were treated as equals to men. Her brother Athelstan would praise her ideas, rather than exclude her from matters of state.

Elvina had studied the Welsh Laws and the status of the queen was clear but they never called her such, instead saying 'my lady'. It was important to her that she should be accepted by the people - but on her terms. This was her life now. Sir Gwynfor was the man who could make this happen and she was going to make sure he did not fail her. Elvina saw that her maid was waiting for an answer.

'I will see him, but first bring my new gown.' She looked quickly around the room. A stone fireplace dominated the room and the good blaze made certain that she would not be cold that evening. The flickering light of many candles reflected back from deeply polished wood and gold ornaments reminded visitors of the king's wealth.

Although richly furnished by the standards of the Gwyn, it seemed spartan to the queen but to her taste. She didn't miss the finery of King Athelstan's palaces and was learning to appreciate a simpler life by the sea in Wales.

She went over to the window and checked that there was no one in the courtyard. Bethan would have the sense to make sure they had plenty of warning if anyone approached through the door at the end of the long corridor. If she could be trusted. The flicker of doubt was quickly extinguished, the stakes were high.

Elvina dressed and, taking one of the candles, lit some rare incense her brother had given to her as a parting gift. It gave the room an exotic, eastern, other worldly feel, exactly as she wished.

When Gwynfor was finally escorted in he said nothing, just stood admiring her in silence. Her hair, like her brother, King Athelstan, was not blonde but gold. She dressed in the Anglo Saxon fashion, a pure white gown set off by a dazzling sapphire on a silver chain round her neck. It was the most brilliant he had ever seen but could not compete with the deep blue of her eyes, which were mesmerising him.

She smiled at him 'Sir Gwynfor, I am honoured.'

'Forgive me, my lady, I had to see you.' He realised he was staring and suddenly felt out of his depth. This was not a familiar feeling and it excited him.

'Tell me, are we ready for war?'

He had not expected the question and found himself responding honestly. 'In truth we are not yet ready. We lost good men in the last battle but have soldiers in training. If God wills it, we will be ready.'

'And you, Sir Knight?' she looked at him with amusement in her eyes. 'What part will you have in all of this?'

Now Sir Gwynfor smiled. 'I will serve you to the last. Soon we will defeat the Du and I will make you the true Welsh Queen.'

It was what she wanted to hear and he sensed that a new bond had been formed between them. Queen Elvina felt her pulse race. The risks were unthinkable. They would both be put to death if Gwayne discovered them, or worse. She looked into Bethan's eyes, wondering exactly how far her loyalty stretched. 'Leave us please Bethan,' she said quietly with a glance at Sir Gwynfor.

Sir Gwynfor didn't speak but stood looking at the queen until Bethan had quietly closed the heavy oak door behind her, then quickly crossed the room, swept her into his arms and gave her a passionate kiss. He had spent hours planning this moment, but had forgotten just how wonderful it felt to kiss a woman he truly loved.

Elvina laughed when at last he relaxed his grip on her and she could speak. 'It has been a long time for both of us. Too many lonely nights filled with dreams of you, Gwyn.'

He smiled at her use of the name only his mother had ever called him. 'Let me look at you.'

She lay back on the bed and pretended to shyly cover herself with a silk shawl, deliberately failing to do so in the full knowledge of how it would provoke him. 'What would you like me to do?'

'Show me how much you love me.'

She did, until they both lay exhausted and bathed in sweat.

Elvina cuddled into his strong arms, feeling safe and content. She would happily have gone to sleep but suddenly remembered how dangerous it was for them both.

'You will have to go. I don't want you to but we should not test our luck.'

Gwynfor gave her one last lingering kiss and quickly dressed.

She enjoyed watching him and loved the way his eyes never left her nakedness. 'Will this war mean that I will be able to see more of you?'

'I will make certain of it.' He looked at her one last time and left.

Elvina lay alone on the bed feeling sad, although she could never remember being happier. It was going to be harder than she had thought to be a good queen of the Gwyn.

Elfred had been able to find a boat in Porth Clais that was sailing in the direction of Pembroke. It was quite impressive, dominating the tiny harbour that served St Davids. The boat was a trader, with a large cargo hold and little in the way of accommodation.

Two sailors were making ready the lateen sail, which was flapping noisily in the light breeze. Keen to avoid a long journey on poor roads, Elfred looked for the skipper and found him checking sacks of local potatoes on the quayside. He was a sharp eyed weather beaten man with greying hair and the lined face of a man who has spent all his life navigating the treacherous coast of the Irish sea,

'Captain, can you take me to the castle at Pembroke?'

The captain looked him up and down, assessing his potential as crew. 'You will have to work your passage. Do you know your way about a boat?'

Elfred was not a sailor but had grown up by the sea and was a strong swimmer. 'I am a quick learner, he said.' I can read and write after a fashion and I can load those sacks for you. '

The captain nodded. 'You could,' he said, looking at the high water mark on the harbour wall. 'We are short handed on this passage and need to be ready for the tide.'

Elfred was used to carrying sacks and soon had them stowed below decks. He was travelling light and found a place for the things he had decided to take with him to the castle. As well as the sword, the bishop had given him a bag of Saxon coins. These were safely inside his jerkin, as he wasn't ready to trust his surly looking fellow crew members.

As he watched the tide filling the harbour, he wondered when he would see his farm again. His life had changed so suddenly he hardly had time to adjust. His hand fell subconsciously to the handle of the magnificent old sword. Not for the first time, he thought over his conversation of the previous day.

He had never thought before of Bishop Cledwin having a father and, if he had done, would have imagined he came from a long line of clerics. Some time, thought Elfred, he would have to ask more about the man whose sword he now wore. It felt natural and gave him the look of an experienced soldier, which he was not.

As soon as it was afloat the ship cast off and the sailors expertly caught the breeze in the sails and headed out to sea. Elfred had been out with the small Porth Clais fishing boats many times and was familiar with their course, but had never been as far as the port of Pembroke.

'A fair wind,' he said to the captain.

The captain looked up at the brooding sky. 'Just as well. The current favours us as well, so we should make good way before nightfall.' He produced a loaf of rough bread from a locker and tore off a piece, which he handed to Elfred. 'Do you know how to take the helm?'

Elfred shrugged. 'Show me and I'll learn.'

The captain smiled and gestured for him to take over the ships wheel. 'Keep an eye on the sail, if it starts flapping, bear up like this,' he said showing how lightly the boat handled. 'Stay close to the coast and keep a bearing on that headland,' he said, pointing to a shape on the horizon. He kept watch while Elfred manned the helm, occasionally giving advice but he seemed quietly impressed.

The sky darkened and Elfred noticed the sea had white crests of foam on the top of the waves. He tasted the salt spray and started to enjoy his new life. At the same instant he felt sudden sadness and a sense of loss for the life he was leaving behind.

He knew so much about how to get the best from the farms, but so little about the world. It had all seemed so clear, his life mapped out. A wife, some land of his own, a family and sons to pass his knowledge on to. Now he wondered if he would ever return to the life of a farmer.

The thought troubled him as they sailed through the night. The wind turned and the sea got choppy, so the passage through Jack Sound was thrilling and frightening in turns. Waves crashed alarmingly over the deck, drenching them all and more than once the boat was blown over to an impossible angle and struggled to right itself.

Worst of all were the jagged black rocks looming out of the foaming water. He remembered a saying from the fishermen of Porth Clais. 'It's not the sea that'll kill you, it's the land!' He said a silent prayer of thanks when they arrived safely in Pembroke and tied up at the old stone quay.

Elfred thanked the captain and continued his short journey on foot. He approached the garrison with mixed feelings. He was excited at the sight of so much activity as the town prepared for battle. The old wooden hill fort was being rebuilt with stone and was already being called Pembroke Castle.

He looked up in amazement at the height of the walls and saw how the river made the north side almost impossible to attack. He could hear a rhythmic cadence of stone mason's chisels, mixing discordantly with the random clang of swordsmen training to fight somewhere within the grounds.

The only entrance was through a tall tower with a lifting bridge over a deep defensive ditch. The wind changed direction and on the top of a tower the long white standard of the Gwyn flowed in the gentle breeze. Elfred saw it and felt a surge of pride in his country. He approached the tower with a new confidence.

'Who goes there?' called the guard at the entrance to the garrison.

'A soldier of the Gwyn reporting for training,' shouted Elfred, looking uncertainly at the guard. 'I am here on the orders of Sir Gwynfor of Picton.'

The guard viewed him with suspicion. 'Who are you?'

'My name is Elfred. I have come by sea from St Davids.'

The guard made no move to let him pass but at that moment a soldier arrived at the entrance to the castle. The man was about his own age, dressed in a heavy chain mail vest that looked too large for him. He was carrying a heavy bow over one shoulder and had a leather quiver, full of arrows over the other.

The soldier looked at him. He had obviously heard the exchange. 'Sir Gwynfor?'

'Yes,' replied Elfred.

'Then you are with me,' said the soldier. 'Another lamb to the slaughter!' He grinned at the thought and clapped Elfred on the arm. 'Ned's the name. Come in and meet the others.'

'There are others like me?' asked Elfred, surprised.

'Yes, and more over at Caerphilly I've heard. I've been here a few days learning how to use this thing.'

Elfred looked at the bow. 'We are to be trained as archers?'

'Archers, swordsmen, jack of all trades - and master of none!' said Ned, 'I plan to make the most of this war and you should too!' He led Elfred into the castle and took him to the garrison barracks. The room was surprisingly clean and tidy, with a row of simple beds and various weapons neatly placed in wooden racks.

'Where are the others? asked Elfred.

'Sentry duty. It's your turn tonight, so get some rest.'

Elfred was tired and gladly stretching out on a vacant bunk, fell asleep straight away.

~

Elvina woke alone in her comfortable bedchamber and wondered at the events of the previous day. She could not be in love with the young knight but felt a strange excitement at the memory of him. It was a feeling so far absent from her life with the king. It was, after all, a marriage of convenience, not a love match, until Sir Gwynfor opened her eyes to the truth of her situation.

She called for her maidservant Bethan. Elvina thought Bethan a classic Welsh beauty, with jet black hair and dark eyes. She had chosen not to bring her Anglo Saxon servants, as with Bethan as her handmaiden she would learn more about the people of the Gwyn. Bethan was teaching her the language of the Welsh and something of their customs. The queen had learned quickly.

Bethan appeared in the doorway. She had been expecting the call and bowed to the queen before speaking. 'My lady?'

'Where is the king?' asked Elvina

'He woke early, my lady' said Bethan, 'I think he has been meeting with Sir Padrig and Sir Gwynfor.' As she said Gwynfor's name she remembered the moment they had shared in the corridor.

An unspoken understanding. He would never know it was no

accident she was in the corridor at that moment. Now she had more power over them both than she had dreamed possible. One day her time would come.

Queen Elvina lay back in her bed. The sun was shining, lighting up the room. The small leaded glass window was open and a gentle breeze brought the sound of birdsong. If she listened carefully, she could hear the waves breaking on the shore at the foot of the cliffs.

She was happy with her life in Wales, but unfulfilled. She had wanted just one thing, to be accepted by the people of the Gwyn. Now she wanted more. To be the first Queen of all Wales and have her rightful place at her brother's side.

She knew she was a favourite of King Athelstan but he had used her as a convenient way of dealing with what he called 'the troublesome Welsh'. Soon, she thought, he would see her as an equal. Sir Gwynfor was the key and now he was hers.

Bethan had been waiting patiently for orders. She crossed over to the window and looked out on the courtyard below. 'The groom is preparing horses,' she said. 'They must be going for a ride.'

The queen sat up in bed. 'Prepare my bath, if you will,' she said, 'I want to look my best when they return.'

∽

King Gwayne and the two knights had been arguing about the merits of using the element of surprise by attacking the Du or waiting for their enemy to show their hand. Padrig had suggested a ride along the headland path and the King agreed.

It was good exercise for the horses and the fresh sea air was exhilarating. They galloped dangerously close to the cliffs, finding sport in expertly following the twists and turns of the narrow path through the dunes to the beach. The king reined in his mount and the others matched him.

'I used to come here as a boy,' shouted the king over the noise of the heavy surf that was whipping the water into white foamed crests, 'There is no finer ride in Wales!'

Gwynfor shouted back. 'Which is why we need to protect it, by taking the fight to the north!'

'We cannot attack the northerners without good reason,' said Padrig.

The king stopped and turned his horse to face him. 'Was my father's death not reason enough?'

'Would the old king have wanted us to start another war?' asked Padrig. It was an argument they had practiced many times, always with the same outcome. The king knew the answer.

'Let me test their readiness,' suggested Sir Gwynfor, swiftly drawing his sword and slashing it through the air to make his point. 'We need to know their strength - and show them we are stronger.'

'Yes, this waiting is hard for me to stand. It is time to make our destiny.' Gwayne spurred his horse back to the gallop and the others followed, racing hard across the long expanse of golden sand. The king led the way, following the line of the surf, the horse's hooves digging deep holes that were washed away with each crashing wave. Padrig would recall that moment in the months to come.

$\mathcal{I}$t was a short but dangerous journey across the fast flowing River Menai to the island of Ynys Mon. The water was dark and deep and good people of the Du had drowned attempting the crossing. There were good reasons for them to try, for as well as some of the best farming land in the country, the island was home to many tribes.

Reaching out into the Irish Sea, Ynys Mon had been invaded by the Roman army, marauding Vikings and Irish pirates but still the Du clung steadfastly on to their birthright. The legacy of several generations of relentless fighting could be seen in the land and the people. Old hill forts dominated the high ground and were still maintained by men who had learnt to stay prepared for invaders.

The largest of these wood and stone hill forts now brought Lord Llewelyn and his servant Bryn to Ynys Mon. It was Llewelyn's responsibility to protect the west of the kingdom, so he needed to be certain it was ready for any attack from the Gwyn.

Llewelyn was recovering from a long illness and carried a long fighting staff everywhere he went. He would lean on it for support but was also skilled in its use as a weapon and had killed men with it in the past.

It was clear from the practised ease with which he handled the staff that Llewelyn was not to be underestimated. Dressed always in traditional black, he was immediately recognised and liked by the people who lived on the island, as well as respected as a warlord of the king.

His follower Bryn could not have been more different, so they made an incongruous pair as they waited on the quayside for the boat that would make the crossing. Bryn was a giant bear of a man, with an unkempt beard and a deep, throaty laugh that belied his violent nature.

He had a weakness for the ale houses which were springing up in every town and would invariably end up in a drunken brawl, unable to account for his actions when questioned by his master. The two of them had been together many years now. Something of Llewelyn's skill as an orator seemed to have rubbed off on his bondsman, as Bryn was prone to offer an opinion on every subject to anyone who would listen.

Bryn pointed. 'The boat is on its way back my lord!' He had keen eyes, as Llewelyn could see nothing through the autumn mist that hung in the damp air. It was a short trip of about a thousand paces and he was pleased to see that the river was fairly calm.

He shuddered involuntarily at the memory of an earlier trip across the narrow straits of the Menai. The short sail had failed to catch the wind and, despite desperate rowing by the oarsmen, their boat had been caught in the current which carried them quickly down the coast at a perilous speed.

Bryn had enjoyed the experience, cheering and encouraging the rowers as they strained and sweated to keep away from the jagged rocks, but Llewelyn had never felt the need to learn to swim. Although he would not admit it, he had felt completely helpless and not for the first time had been in fear for his life.

They boarded the old boat and this time sailed swiftly across without incident, to be greeted by the wagon driver who was waiting to take them up to the fort. 'Good morning, my lord,' he said, smiling and touching his hat as a sign of respect. 'You are here for the Mabon?'

It was a poorly kept secret that the elderly lord followed the Druid religion. After a thousand years of tradition, it was barely surviving on the island as the power of the church took hold. His involvement was now reduced to celebrating the solstices and equinoxes, so the timing of his visit to the island to coincide with the autumn equinox was no coincidence.

Llewelyn looked at the wagon driver more closely and recognised him as a fellow Druid. He smiled back but it was a fleeting moment and he quickly looked concerned again. 'We will give thanks for the gifts of the harvest and prepare for the darkness of winter,' he replied. 'I fear it will be a long dark winter.'

The queen of the Du would make an excellent hostage if she were captured by any of their enemies. In the past, the Vikings targeted the royal house and very nearly carried her off in a daring night raid. The people of the Gwyn were also known to use cowardly tactics, so abduction of the queen was a very real threat.

Rhiannon therefore had a personal bodyguard to follow her whenever she travelled, an experienced warrior called Hywel. Hywel was a proud and careful man who took his royal duties very seriously. He was always immaculately dressed, with well trimmed ha
ir and beard and kept his sword polished and sharp. Before the war against the Vikings, he had been much like any other easy going warrior. The experience of battle had changed him,

however. Hardened by the ruthless savagery, death and torture he had seen, he withdrew from the others and had few friends.

The captain of the guard, an outspoken and less experienced warrior called Idris, was the king's personal bodyguard and there was always a tension between them. One evening Hywel was drinking alone in the king's alehouse when Idris, who had also been drinking, went over to him. 'What do we have here?' he said loudly.

Hywel looked at the younger man with thinly veiled contempt. 'You are drunk, Captain.'

'Maybe I am, but you must show respect.' Idris swayed a little, unsteady on his feet.

Hywel could see the captain was looking for trouble, so realised there was only one way out. 'I must be going. I am on duty early in the morning.'

Idris laughed and turned to his companions. 'He guards our queen closely, I think a little too closely?' The men laughed but their fun was cut short when Hywel struck him down with a single vicious blow.

One of the guards rushed to help Idris, who lay bleeding on the floor. 'Now you've done it! Grab him men, he will pay for this!'

Hywel didn't resist as they bore him off to the dungeon. There were many witnesses to what seemed an unprovoked attack on the captain, who was slowly recovering but needed to be carried home. Discipline in the king's guard was harsh and Hywel knew that there would be no trial or chance to explain.

Chained to a wall with no food or water, he'd been given plenty of time to regret his action. After the briefest consideration, a sentence of flogging and dismissal was agreed by the captain. His nose had been broken and he was in no mood for leniency.

When word of what had happened reached Rhiannon, she begged the king to intervene. He considered doing so but knew it could be seen as a sign of weakness. As a compromise, he agreed that the flogging should proceed but ordered that Hywel should then return to his post, having been taught a lesson. The outcome may have been different if he had known the accuser was right.

Idris chose one of his strongest and most ruthless men to administer the punishment, which was to be witnessed by as many of the guards as could be spared. Hywel was led out into the courtyard and his hands were tied high on a wooden post set into the ground.

Idris read out the charge, not without some satisfaction and much self importance, then stood back to watch as the hide whip was lashed across Hywel's exposed back until it was criss-crossed with deep red cuts. Hywel flinched with the agony of each lash, but did not cry out. He clenched his teeth and swore quietly to himself that one day he would be avenged.

~

Lord Vorath sent one of his most trusted warriors, a man called Tristan, to help Dafydd ready the castle at Flint for battle. Tristan had grown up in the household after his entire family were murdered one night by raiders from the sea. He had fair hair but the dark brown eyes of the people of the Du, which spoke of mixed parentage or possibly a Celtic background.

A quick learner, Tristan had been taught by Bishop Deniol and could read and write the language of the Du. At one point Deniol had hoped to convert the gifted warrior to following the church and even began teaching him Latin. There was a hunger for revenge in the young man's eyes, however, that marked him out as a fighting man.

Lord Vorath recognised this and spent long hours training him with the sword and dagger until the sweat dripped from them. For all his loyalty and energy, Vorath felt that Tristan lacked the spark of leadership he had seen in Dafydd, so he hoped that putting them together would be good for both.

Unknown to Vorath, Tristan was already planning to become his successor. He secretly thought the warlord was starting to lose his touch and made up for technique with brute force. Tristan suspected that in a battle against the well trained soldiers of the Gwyn, the old fighting methods would be the undoing of his lord and master.

In the meantime, he was glad of the opportunity to help prepare the men at Flint Castle. He already carried authority over them as Vorath's man and was well known amongst the lesser warriors of the tribes. Once they saw his skill with the sword he would start winning supporters of his own. Vorath had provided him with an old horse and provisions for the journey to Flint. He was grateful for the mount but arranged for it to be stabled at a smallholding out of view of the castle so he could arrive on foot.

Tristan entered the castle unchallenged. He was unimpressed, as it showed that they had a lot of work to do. 'Guard!' he shouted. 'Turn out the Guard!'

A small group of men hastily sprang into action but he looked at them disapprovingly. 'Where is the commander?'

'At his home,' replied one of the guards. 'He lives in Flint, so does not need to stay at the Castle.'

'Tell all the remaining men to assemble in the yard right away,' ordered Tristan. 'I will speak with them.' He went to the commander's building and, finding it unlocked, went in. The place was in disarray, and it was clear the commander spent little time there, but he found a bowl of fresh water and quickly washed away the grime of his long ride. Back in the castle yard he found about fifty men waiting for him. This was exactly what he wanted, the chance to show he was a leader.

He waited until they fell silent and spoke to them as he imagined Vorath would have done. 'The future of our people is in your hands,' he said, pleased to see he had their full attention. 'We must prepare the castle for an attack from the south. I want guards on duty night and day and a warning beacon to be readied at the highest point.'

The men looked relieved to have their orders. Tristan set them to work and sent a messenger for Dafydd to return to duty. The advantage of his time with Bishop Deniol was that Tristan had privileged information about their enemies. The English had their hands full with the Vikings in the far north and would not be troubling them. It was the Gwyn they were preparing for. If the bishop was right, it would be soon.

~

The mercenary Cadell had no difficulty joining the growing band of soldiers at the Ynys Mon hill fort. He'd enjoyed the long journey by sea from the south, working his passage as a deck hand on a trading vessel.

The coastal towns were well used to traders with Saxon coins, so when he landed he used a small part of the money he'd been paid by Sir Gwynfor to buy the rough woollen tunic he now wore. It would take time for it to be comfortable but it helped him blend with the warriors of the Du. He also invested in a sharp spear and a short but effective sword of the type preferred by the fighting men of the tribes. He examined them closely and was glad he would not need to use either.

Cadell explored the fort that was to be his temporary home, impressed by the scale of the earthworks. He guessed it must have taken many years of backbreaking work to carry the stones that made thick walls the height of two men around the whole area.

Unlike the smaller wooden forts of the south, this had enough room for an entire town within the defensive walls. Even the big space within Pembroke Castle looked small by comparison. The most impressive feature was the entrance, which consisted of out-turned walls forming a long narrow passage, overlooked by a raised stone gate house. Cadell realised that anyone attacking the fort would have to run a deadly gauntlet of arrows and stones, only to be stopped by a second line of defences.

The men of the north were very different too. In the south they had become used to seeing bondsmen pressed reluctantly into service, with little affection for the knights who ruled over their lives. His new companions were true warriors, who would fight instinctively, even if there was nobody to tell them what to do.

Most were armed with spears, which they threw with deadly accuracy, while others had the short swords or bows. Cadell began training with the spear every day at the hill fort on Ynys Mon, which had been made to look as disused as possible, with cattle grazing in the centre and some of the buildings party dismantled.

The warriors had been practicing rapidly 'retreating' into the fort to lead any attackers into the deadly entrance tunnel. They had no idea if these preparations would ever be needed but the practice had the effect of building up the warrior spirit. Cadell wondered if that had been Llewelyn's aim all along.

The spear was the main weapon of the Du, although many of the warriors wore a sword and several also had the traditional dagger on their belt. Unlike the bow, which could take months to master, skill with the spear could be learnt with a few weeks practice.

Spears were also easy to produce locally and the hills of Ynys Mon resounded to the clang of blacksmith's hammers, as they made more weapons and repaired any that were broken. The spears were sharpened to deadly points and metal strips were riveted on to the shafts to strengthen and reinforce them.

Cadell quickly developed a new respect for the spear as a versatile weapon of war. The most common spear had a thick shaft that served well as a fighting staff at close quarters, with a razor sharp, pointed steel blade fastened to the tip.

The second type was the version Cadell had chosen when he first landed in the north and was called the 'Angon', a slender throwing spear as long as a man, with a barbed head that was the legacy of the pilum used with great effect by the Romans in their invasion of the Island.

The warriors were trained in the use of both, over and over again, learning to hit moving targets representing mounted fighters, or to strike, slash and thrust as hard as they could, with bales of straw acting as the enemy in hand to hand contact. It was also traditional for the Du to shout a bloodcurdling yell as they charged with spears, to gain advantage by alarming the enemy and causing them to panic.

Cadell joined the warriors as they lined up to be addressed by Lord Llewelyn. He had already heard of the Lord's exploits from the other men, so was surprised to see the man before him leaning heavily on a stick.

Llewelyn spoke, his voice barely carrying across the open ground in the centre of the fort. 'It is good to see you have prepared well.' He looked around them, recognising many and quickly winning over those he did not. 'Any invader can see we are ready for a fight, so that is what I need you to work on. I want to make it look as if we have neglected the fort. Hide your weapons close at hand and bring livestock into the grounds. If anyone makes it as far as here, they will not live to tell what they found.'

The men cheered loudly. Cadell could now see why they spoke of Llewelyn with such pride and wondered if he would ever be able to pass this information back to his paymasters.

∼

Bishop Emrys had never liked Madoc. His previous assistant

drowned at sea and he had agreed too hastily to the surly replacement. He also suspected Madoc of being a thief but as yet was unable to prove it. Small trinkets, coins and once a gold plated cup had all disappeared without trace.

Emrys considered setting a trap but then regretted even having such un-Christian thoughts. Madoc was oblivious to all this, as he was concerned only with himself, complaining loudly if he was asked to do anything without direct reward. A solution had occurred to Emrys, however, which could rid him of the man once and for all.

Madoc appeared in the doorway. 'You asked for me bishop?' His reedy voice always seemed to sound questioning, making Emrys think the man looked guilty about something. He couldn't help wondering what else he would find missing.

'You are to report to the captain of the guard for duty.' He watched Madoc's face closely and thought he saw a flicker of interest before the usual dour expression returned.

'Why, your grace?'

'We need every able bodied man ready to defend the king,' replied Emrys with some satisfaction. 'I must learn to cope without your services for a while.'

Madoc looked worried. 'I am your servant, Bishop, and must do as you ask, but I have no skill with a sword, or bow, so would be a poor guard for the king?'

'You can be a lookout,' said Emrys. 'There is to be a line of men right across the country to alert us to any attack from the south.'

Madoc could see that the bishop was in an uncompromising mood and went to pack some belongings for the journey. He wondered if the bishop knew what it was like to go hungry for days, living only off what he could forage or steal from the fields.

Madoc had no education and had been cast out by his family when he was barely old enough to fend for himself. He had learnt some important lessons along the way, however, including that everything in life could be turned to some opportunity, in time. It was therefore with cautious optimism that he reported for duty at the guard house of the king a few days later, having been in no hurry to make the journey from the bishop's house in less time.

He asked to see the captain and was shown into a surprisingly well appointed room, where Idris was looking at a parchment map of the south with two of the guards. Madoc couldn't read what was written on it but understood the landmarks. He recognised the big Island of Ynys Mon with its hill fort, and the castle at Flint, where he had spent some time as a boy. He was interested to see that the south was at least twice as wide as the north and realised that the castles at Pembroke and Caerphilly were a really long way apart.

Idris noticed his visitor. 'You man, what are you doing in here?'

Madoc looked Idris in the eye as confidently as he could. 'I've been sent by Bishop Emrys to help plan the battle,' he lied. He had never given it thought before, but if the map was right his opportunity had come sooner than expected. 'The land of the Gwyn is not easily defended. We will turn that to our advantage.'

Idris looked at Madoc with renewed interest. He'd risen quickly to the position of captain, not by ability, but by claiming the ideas of others as his own. He knew Bishop Emrys must think highly of this man, to spare him at such a troubled time. 'Glad to have your help,' he said. 'The king has asked us to recommend the best line for our lookouts, what do you think?'

～

Hywel woke with a start and realised he was lying face down in a strange room. It was comfortably warm and lit by large white candles in skilfully engraved gold holders, like those he had seen in the royal apartments.

His back was a mass of burning pain but Queen Rhiannon

was seated next to him, gently soothing his brow with a cold cloth. He decided he must be either dead or dreaming. The last thing he could remember was drifting into unconsciousness as the whipping continued past the point where he could stand it no longer.

'You are awake at last,' she said softly. The queen sounded pleased. 'I made a compress of herbs, comfrey root and a little camomile, to speed the healing and ease the pain a little.' She continued to gently caress his brow as if he were a child.

Hywel enjoyed the sensation, which helped take his mind off the agony of his back, but his mind was racing. Had Rhiannon discovered his feelings for her? He tensed, realising that they would both be in great danger if discovered.

'My queen,' he said, 'You must leave me now.'

'I'm not the queen,' she laughed. 'I am the queen's sister. You needed help and I have knowledge of how to tend these wounds.' Ceinwen moved her chair so that he could see her more clearly.

Hywel realised he had seen her many times but they had never spoken. She was the image of the queen but a little older, with the same long black hair and dark, twinkling eyes, but was about the same age as him. In a sudden insight he understood they shared knowledge of things that had changed them, left them lonely.

'Of course, you must think me stupid.'

'No, but it will take time for you to recover your strength.'

The memory of the brutal whipping came flooding back. He looked away from her in shame. 'I was foolish, to be goaded like that by the Commander.'

'You were defending the queen.' She touched his arm with affection, 'I am grateful that you did.'

The significance of her words was not lost on him. Hywel could smell her light perfume and the warmth of her hand felt good. It had been a long time since any woman had cared about him. He knew that Ceinwen looked after Rhiannon when her parents died and that she was unmarried. He did not know if she was spoken for, or if the affection she had shown was simply the way she was with everyone. These things he had never considered before were suddenly very important to him.

'Thank you, Ceinwen, for tending to me.'

'I will sit with you a while, if you wish?'

'Yes,' he said. 'Would you tell me about yourself?'

She laughed again. 'There isn't much to tell that would be of any interest.' She looked down at him again and he noticed her eyes flick to the raw marks on his exposed back. As if deciding something, she moved her chair a little closer and told him everything.

How happy they had been at the hill fort in Conwy. Her sadness after the loss of both her parents from the cruel plague, and how she decided she had been spared to dedicate her life to her younger sister, Rhiannon. Her eyes lit up when she explained her delight when Rhiannon became queen.

Hywel listened carefully, then asked the question that had been burning in his mind. 'Is there someone to look after you now Ceinwen?'

'No,' she said, shaking her head. 'I think my time for that has passed.'

Hywel lay in silence. They stared deep into each other's eyes and an unspoken bond formed between them.

CHAPTER 5

$\mathcal{E}$lfred looked up at the bright morning sky, relying on his farmer's instincts to read the weather by the clouds. There was a sea mist hanging over the river Cleddau and the air was damp but the signs were good.

Once the mist lifted it would be another fine day. He was with a group of soldiers assembled for training in the grounds of Pembroke Castle. Each of them held a sword and stood next to a large tree trunk set into the ground.

Hayden, assistant to the knight Sir Gwynfor, had been assigned to turn them into fighting men. He drew his sword and held it in the air. 'See how the point of balance sits close to the guard,' he said, demonstrating with several fast and vicious slashes in the air. 'I want to see wide, effective cutting - and get some force behind the swing, your life may depend on it!'

Elfred drew the old sword he had been given by the bishop and chopped hard into the tree trunk. It was the first time he had used it and was pleased to see it bite deep, leaving a wide slash across the new wood.

Hayden nodded approval and reached out to take Elfred's sword. It was old but clearly the work of a true craftsman. He examined the blade and tested the weight in a swing. 'This is a fine weapon.'

'It was a gift, from my master, the Bishop of St Davids.'

Hayden looked surprised. 'This is the sword of a soldier of the Gwyn. It will serve well if we have to fight the northerners.' He handed the sword back to Elfred and seemed to have a new respect for the farmer. Turning his attention to the others, he was pleased with their progress. 'Good, work men,' he said. 'You need to develop powerful arm and elbow cuts. The more power you can get behind the stroke the better for this blade.'

He stood back and watched Neb as he hacked repeatedly at the tree trunk, making up for lack of skill with enthusiasm. Large chunks of wood flew into the air as the sharpened blade sliced through the air and chopped into the timber.

'If this had been a man he would be dead for sure,' said Neb, as he realised that Elfred and Hayden were watching. He was a heavy drinker and a gambler but Elfred liked him. He had helped the farmer adjust to the very different life in Pembroke Castle.

Neb had grown up in Pembroke and one drunken night had confessed he had never travelled outside the parish, so knew little of the world. He listened spellbound to Elfred's accounts of the bishop's palace in St David's, the mysterious Viking raiders and his sea voyage around the coast.

'Now the thrust!' called Hayden. These are no practice swords, I want to see them buried so deep you can't get them out again.' The soldiers changed their stance as they had been trained and charged at their wooden enemy with bloodcurdling yells, enjoying the training and stabbing the points of their short swords as hard as they could. Hayden smiled and hoped they would show the same spirit with an enemy who fought back.

～

Sir Gwynfor had returned to his home at Picton Castle with

mixed feelings. He had enjoyed his time with the king but was impatient with the way events were heading. He decided to visit the garrison at Pembroke to see how the training of the soldiers was progressing. He was hungry after his journey home and had ordered roast venison to be prepared, when a servant told him he had a visitor.

Bishop Cledwin was waiting for him in the great hall. Gwynfor was surprised. Although he often called to see the bishop whenever he ventured to St Davids, he could not recall a time when he had ever entertained him as a guest.

He greeted the bishop warmly. They had, after all, effectively divided the running of the estates in the west between them. Gwynfor was grateful for the old bishop's hand in making sure the Welsh laws were to their advantage. The bishop in turn was glad to have the powerful young knight and his garrison at Pembroke to defend them.

'Sir Gwynfor, it is good to see you looking well.'

'Bishop, what brings you to Picton? He grinned. 'I am sure it is not to enquire about my health!'

He looked at the knight for a moment, as if making a judgement. 'You are shrewd, Gwynfor. I do have a favour to ask of you.'

'Tell me over dinner. I have some fine venison and you must try my red wine. I have a special arrangement with traders from Arbois.'

They sat down at the big banqueting table, which had been hastily set with a second place and plates of fresh bread and olives. In the middle was an unusual silver candlestick holder, in the shape of a mythical Welsh dragon.

Gwynfor noticed the bishop looking at it and explained it was a 'trophy,' taken from the Du by Gwynfor himself in a skirmishing battle. It now held a fat yellow candle that lit the banqueting hall brightly. Gwynfor looked across at his visitor, who was helping himself to the rare Italian olives, and was intrigued. 'You are being mysterious, Bishop Cledwin, tell me about this favour.'

The bishop was about to answer when they were served with the meal, so he waited and watched the servants leave. 'It is a great secret I wish to entrust you with. I have a son, but he does not know I am his father. It was for the best, at the time. He is now at your garrison, being trained as a soldier.'

Gwynfor poured them both a large goblet of the good red wine and watched as Bishop Cledwin tasted it, with obvious approval. 'You want me to release him from the king's service?'

'No,' said the bishop. 'I would be grateful if you can do what you can to see him safely home once we have won the war.'

'What is his name?' asked Gwynfor.

'Elfred,' replied the bishop. 'My son is called Elfred.'

~

Archbishop Renfrew had received no reply to his letter to the bishops of the north. He made a decision and called to his servant. 'Summon Cade, my bondsman, if you will. I need him to deliver an important message.'

The servant hurried off and Archbishop Renfrew went to his study. He prepared a sharp quill and wrote a long letter to the king on fine new parchment, procured at great cost from the English. A perfectionist, he made a second, identical copy for his records and sat for a while, trying to decide which was best.

When he had made his choice, he folded the parchment carefully, pressed his bishop's seal into the hot wax seal and placed the letter in a leather pouch. It would take a while before his messenger arrived, so he went to pray for guidance.

Renfrew felt the cold of the chapel seeping into his bones. He had been kneeling in prayer longer than he had intended when he heard the creak of the door opening. He turned to see Cade waiting for him.

His assistant lived locally and had become a useful travelling companion for the archbishop. As well as acting as a bodyguard, he had a detailed knowledge of the roads and knew the best short cuts. A stocky, well meaning man, Cade had learnt a great deal from working with the archbishop but had not realised that his master had learned much in turn from him.

More than once Archbishop Renfrew had saved him from going hungry and now Cade had ambitions to become a freeman. In time, he may even afford to rent some land, settle down and start a family.

'I have important work for you Cade. A message is to be delivered to the king at Pennard. You are to take my bay gelding and leave as soon as you can.'

'Yes bishop, I should be there before nightfall, God willing,' replied Cade. He was not a religious man but had been around the archbishop for many years and had picked up some of his sayings.

Renfrew handed Cade the leather pouch. 'Guard this with your life. 'It must not fall in to the wrong hands.'

Cade nodded. He had been on many such errands for the archbishop in the past and knew that lives often depended on them.

The archbishop looked at him intently. 'I need you to wait for a reply and bring it to me as quickly as you can,' he said, counting out some small Saxon coins. 'Here is a purse for your troubles.'

True to his word, Cade arrived at the Royal Llysoedd in Pennard in the early evening after a hard ride of fifty miles, having stopped only for some lunch at a farm on the way. He gave the letter to the king's guards, explaining its importance, and took the archbishop's fine horse to the stables.

King Gwayne read the letter carefully. Archbishop Renfrew was his most trusted advisor and was warning of a possibly imminent attack from the north. His counsel was to meet with King Athelstan to seek the support of the English armies.

It was to be done with utmost secrecy to avoid loss of face if the request was refused and to maximise the element of surprise if the Du attacked. Gwayne turned to the waiting servant. 'Ask the queen to join me. As soon as she is able to, we have important matters to discuss.'

~

Sir Gwynfor arrived at the garrison in Pembroke to find it a hive of activity. Everywhere he looked there were men building up the new stone walls or practising with various weapons. He handed his horse to one of the guards who had travelled with him and went to find Hayden.

News of the knight's arrival had spread swiftly, however, and he found his loyal retainer already waiting for him at the tall entrance tower. He was pleased to see his orders had been followed. A new drawbridge had been fashioned to span the defensive ditch, which had been dug deeper and wider.

'My Lord, welcome.'

'I have come to see that you have made progress.'

'You may be surprised, said Hayden. 'The men have worked hard and long. They are ready for a fight and will be glad to see you.'

They entered the castle, which opened out into a wide field, with the barracks and other buildings round the edge. In the grassy central area a small army of men were being taught to fight. Hayden led the knight to steps which gave them access to the castle walls. From the top they could see right down the river, where small boats and trading ships were constantly coming and going with supplies for the town. They turned and looked into the open ground in the middle.

'What news of the Du?' asked Hayden.

'Sir Padrig counsels peace and weakens the king's resolve. I have argued that we should take them by surprise and take the fight to them.'

'And the king?'

'He knows the value of preparation, as do we.'

The two men exchanged a look. Although Hayden was Gwynfor's servant, he could be a freeman at any time if he wished.

'There is a soldier called Elfred training here, what do you make of him?'

'He's a good man. He can read and write and has a natural way with the sword. What of him?'

'You are to see he survives this war,' said Gwynfor. 'If anyone can do that, it is you.'

~

As an experienced guard in the queen's household, Owen was used to the unpredictable comings and goings of royalty. When the queen's personal handmaiden told him to attend a meeting that was not to be spoken of, he was unsurprised. He had admired Bethan since they first met and when he was off duty would sometimes talk with her about the last war with the Du.

She was a good listener and laughed at his stories, but had a slightly mocking way with him, so he suspected she knew that he exaggerated his own part in the battles. He had been very young at the time and could do nothing to save the life of the old king, although he had of course been able to save his own.

He waited at the appointed place, wondering despite himself what all the secrecy was about. He had oiled his leather jerkin as well as he could and carried the short, highly polished sword of the Royal Guard. He drew it now and checked the blade. It had never been used and he wondered if the day would soon come when his life may depend on his skill with it.

The door opened he saw Bethan, looking attractive in a blue dress, with her long dark hair tied back, after the fashion of the queen. He commented on it as she led him down a long corridor, brightly lit with flickering candles. She laughed at the compliment and wished him luck as she showed him into the queen's private apartments.

Owen had never been allowed to the queen's rooms before and was amazed at the lavish furnishings. The scent of an exotic perfume hung lightly in the air and everywhere he looked was gold ornament, any one piece worth more that he could expect to earn in his lifetime.

There in the middle of the room was Queen Elvina, seated in an ornate high backed chair, carved with designs he assumed were Saxon. He had seen her many times before but she looked particularly regal in an emerald silk gown, with a necklace of fine pearls.

'My lady,' said Bethan. 'Do you wish me to remain?'

'Yes of course. I am learning your language and I need you to make sure there is no misunderstanding.' The queen had a way of winning the loyalty of her staff and Owen was no exception. She addressed him directly in perfect Welsh. 'If we are attacked I will need information about the course of the war. I have to know if the English become involved, if we are winning or losing. I need someone in the field, Owen. I have chosen you.'

Owen paused before replying. This could be his chance to profit at last from the long hours spent guarding the Royal Llysoedd. 'I am honoured, my lady. I have been in battle with the Du and there is little chance to keep watch on borders. I will do what I can but will need money for bribes and to pay informers.'

'You will be well rewarded,' said Elvina. 'My messengers will contact you. Your job will be to tell them the truth, so that I may know of it.'

'How am I to know the messengers, my lady?'

She smiled. 'We must have a secret sign.'

~

The news that the archbishop had sent Cade with an urgent message to the king soon reached the rest of the servants at the Royal Llysoedd. As the preparation for battle progressed, the soldiers of the Gwyn became increasingly impatient for action and hungry for any information.

One of them, a tall man called Delwyn, was from the king's household and had been sent for archery training at Caerphilly Castle in the east. The other soldiers naturally looked to him for information.

'What of the king?' asked Afon. A straight talking local man, he was furthest from the Royal Court and keen for news. He had the distinctive accent of the Caerphilly area and was already emerging as a ringleader, demanding better food and pay for risking their lives.

'The king is well,' said Delwyn, pleased with his new importance. 'He is prepared for anything the Du have planned!' He looked at their eager faces and recognised one as a servant of the queen.

'Owen! What are you doing here?'

Owen grinned. 'Same as you!' He produced the vicious looking dagger from his belt and waved it in the air. 'Learning to kill the evil northern hordes!'

'You have a family to care for?'

'Yes, I need the pay of a fighting man to keep them from starving,' grinned Owen. He had sworn to keep secret his real reason.

'We can't have your family going hungry.' said a deep voice behind them. Owen turned. It was Kane, the most skilled archer in the garrison. Kane was Sir Padrig's man and had trained in the Druid religion as a young man, although he never spoke of it. Kane had mystical ways and was heavily tattooed with strange Celtic symbols. He wore his dark hair long for an archer, in the fashion of the tribes and had a measured way of speaking that made some men fear him.

Kane had been asked to make archers from these rough soldiers and held up his longbow for them all to see. It was as tall as he was and they fell silent. 'This bow, well used, can kill a horse at a hundred paces.' He looked round at their now serious faces and held up a long arrow with an unusual point. 'These arrows can pierce chain mail, or pass right through a man. It takes years to master the longbow, yet we have just a few weeks, so it will be hard work and long hours of practice. Are you prepared for that, men of the Gwyn?' His answer was a roar of assent from the group.

Afon was sent to set up a straw target, with a red painted circle at the far side of the courtyard. As well as the longbow, Kane had provided smaller fighting bows and a range of different size practice arrows. Each man chose one and Kane explained how to hold the bow, how to draw the bowstring and even how to breathe before firing.

It was a lot to remember and difficult to control, but Delwyn slowly pulled back the powerful yew longbow and sighted on the distant target. Just as he was about to fire he was distracted by the sharp scream of a pig being slaughtered somewhere in the Castle grounds. He paused, breathed out deeply as he had been told, then let go the string and had the satisfaction of seeing the arrow make its mark.

It was Afon's turn next. He fired three arrows in quick succession. Two found the target and the third went wide, biting deeply into the wooden wall of the garrison barracks with a load thud.

Delwyn slapped him on the back. 'It is fortunate you are on our side Afon! The Du will think we have an army of mad men.'

Kane nodded. 'They would be right,' He didn't smile but there was a twinkle in his eye. 'There is more to any battle than skill with arms. You must find the will to win in your heart.'

Delwyn looked thoughtful. 'I have been wondering about this war with the Du. Should we not look for peace? They have the north and we have the south.'

'We have two kings.' said Kane, 'Both men who find good reason to fight.'

'The Du are murderers,' added Afon. 'They tricked our old king and deserve to be taught a lesson.' He fired another volley of arrows, all of which went wide except for one, which struck the red centre of the target so hard that only half its length was visible.

'Now that is a good shot Afon,' said Kane. 'Mind that each of your arrows is aimed so true.'

~

Hayden sought the opportunity to work for the Sir Gwynfor as he hoped one day to win recognition from the king. He was athletic and hard working, qualities which Gwynfor had liked from the first. The knight had been glad to have a worthy sparring partner and it had started well. Hayden had become skilled with the short sword and learnt the secrets of self defence with the small dagger that was now never far from his left hand, ready to deliver an unexpected death blow to any unprotected area.

It was once they started with the deadly longsword that Hayden began to fear for his safety. As a trained knight, Sir Gwynfor had learnt to cut with precision and force. Once, he had opened up a deep and painful wound in Hayden's arm that was cut through to the bone. There was a long scar where it had been sewn together but it was weeks before they could be sure of it healing.

Another time it was a surprise stab to the chest which penetrated deeply, despite the blunted tip of the sword. That had nearly been the end of Hayden, but he was fit and strong, and recovered in time. It had earned him the right to wear the longsword, however, a special privilege only allowed to the holder of rank of personal attendant to a knight.

Sir Gwynfor summoned him early to the courtyard and had

already taken position, with the rising sun behind him. A small group of serving girls had come out to watch the practice. 'Come at me man,' he said. 'Hard as you like.'

Hayden had learnt not to waste time with a feint or to hold back his blows against the knight and swung the sword suddenly and hard, as Gwynfor stepped slightly off line to his left, engaging Hayden's blade to expertly deflect his thrust.

'See how the power of the blow is used,' said Gwynfor, with a glance at the serving girls. Hayden realised that he was in more danger with this audience. It was his turn next and he narrowly missed another serious injury as the knights longsword flashed at him. Despite himself he parried the blow, feeling the force of it through his whole body as their blades struck in a violent clash.

Gwynfor looked scornful. 'To parry is a sign of weakness, you must know to turn the blow to advantage.'

'I will learn, Sir Gwynfor, I am here to learn.'

'Stand ready, then,' said the knight and once again delivered a deadly blow with the heavy blunted sword. The watching servant girls gasped. He had hoped to take his assistant by surprise with the swiftness of the strike but Hayden was a quick learner. It was far from perfect but he caught the edge of the long blade and swept it to the side, then swiftly brought up his dagger and stopped just short of Gwynfor's exposed throat.

'Now that shows promise, Hayden.' conceded Gwynfor. 'Be ready again!' This time the ferocity of Gwynfor's attack forced Hayden to step back with his left foot to avoid falling backwards. Gwynfor deftly stepped behind Hayden's leg, driving his blade back and throwing him across his leg. It was a powerful throw, done forcefully and quickly.

Hayden fell heavily, hitting the back of his head on the flagstones of the courtyard. Dazed and confused, he felt Gwynfor's sword tip at his throat.

CHAPTER 6

*K*ing Gwayne woke early and went for a bracing walk along the towering sand dunes overlooking the ocean. It was an unusually high tide and he could see breaking crests far out to sea. His white cape flapped in the fresh easterly breeze as he stood watching waves crash into the rocks at the foot of the cliffs.

A piercing screech made him look up, just in time to see a buzzard swoop from the sky to take an unsuspecting rabbit. It was not a hawk but he took it as an omen. His father would never have waited for the Du to surprise his people.

He smiled with the memory of the old king. His father lived on through the stories of his battles, now part of the legends of the Gwyn, but had deserved a better end. Those responsible for his murder had never been found but Gwayne drew strength from his need for justice.

All he knew was that the assassins had struck at night and fled from the scene before the alarm was raised. It was a typical tactic of the Du and he struggled to understand their ways, or their reluctance to accept the inevitable changes taking place in their country.

Gwayne returned to Pennard and sat alone in the great hall considering his options. Archbishop Renfrew's counsel was to bargain for peace while Sir Gwynfor argued that they should take the initiative. Many lives would depend on what he did next.

He looked up at the battered shield on the wall and knew exactly what his father would have done, the old king would deal with the threat from the north before it was too late. It was time for him to act like a king. He sent word for his knights to return to Pennard to discuss what was going to be a long and dangerous battle for them all.

Padrig was the first to arrive on an impressive white stallion. The king was pleased to see his old friend looking fit and well and was impressed. 'Fine horse, Padrig. I've not seen it before?'

Padrig grinned proudly. 'No my lord, I've been training him as a war horse. He is fast so they call him Mellt! He dismounted and handed the reins to a waiting groom. 'How was your meeting with the Saxon?'

'I didn't see him,' replied the king. 'Renfrew set up the meeting but when we arrived Athelstan had gone north, to deal with the Vikings.' Far from being disappointed, however, the king seemed in a good mood. 'If we need the Saxons they will not let us down but I've decided it is time to take matters into our own hands.'

'When you sent for me I guessed as much,' said Padrig. Despite his earlier reluctance to make the first move, he now had parchment maps of the lands they called the 'wilderness' and they went into the king's lodge to spread them out on the table.

Gwayne studied the first map closely. 'The wilderness has good farmland.'

Padrig nodded. 'Yes, but I don't trust the people living there. They help the northerners get closer to our borders.'

Gwayne recognised the careful hand of his archbishop. Their line of defences had been neatly marked in blue ink.

Padrig pointed at the castles marked on the parchment. 'The garrisons at Pembroke and Caerphilly stand ready when needed.'

The king looked closely at the map. 'We don't have much information about Du fortifications?'

Padrig shook his head. 'Apart from Flint there is no sign.'

'Where will we find their king?'

Padrig pointed to where the map showed the coast in the north. 'They move from place to place,' he said. 'You never can be sure with these people. Have a look at this.' He unrolled another map that showed the island of Ynys Mon. It was old and crudely drawn but was marked with numerous dark circles, representing the hill forts of the tribes.

'It's a hard land to attack and easy to defend,' Padrig scowled. 'Gwynfor's man was headed up this way but we've lost touch with him, so we need to hope he can get back soon to tell us of their strength in the west.'

'Keep a look out for him,' ordered Gwayne. 'In the meantime we should send some good men into the wilderness. Let's give the Du something to think about!'

~

King Gethin had been away for several days, making sure their defences were ready for what was to come. Rhiannon missed him but was relieved, as he had been pacing up and down and very restless.

At least he would be happier now he was doing something about the Gwyn. She had Ceinwen for company and help with the baby, which was still waking her in the night. She had teased her older sister by teasing about the guard Hywel. 'I think this soldier has you under a spell,' she laughed.

'He is a good man and very loyal to you!'

'Is he recovering well?'

'The scars will be there always but he is strong.' She looked at Rhiannon as if she wanted to say something else but was holding back.

'What is it?' Rhiannon knew her sister well and wanted no secrets between them.

'If there is a war, I fear that Commander Idris will not treat him kindly. He bears a grudge against him. If it were not for the king....'

'I will speak again to Gethin. We will need someone to guard us if the Gwyn come north and there would be nobody better to do it.'

'Thank you.' Ceinwen looked relieved. 'It would mean a lot to me.' She looked into the crib where the baby Prince Evan was sleeping soundly. 'I'm scared of what the war could bring for us,' she said, almost to herself. 'I wish we could just live in peace with the Gwyn.'

'Yes,' agreed Rhiannon. 'There was a time when I believed we could, but we cannot live the rest of our lives with the threat of war.'

'Are you not afraid of what a war could bring?'

'Not for myself, but I worry about Gethin and of course the baby changes things.'

~

Sir Gwynfor rode as fast as he could when he received the message from the king, but was forced to stay overnight at a farm due to the heavy rain. The downpour turned the lanes to slippery mud which was dangerous for his horse and the going had been hard.

Soaked to the skin, he was glad to see a good fire blazing in the hearth. The farmer welcomed the knight before scurrying off to clear a room for his guest. His wife prepared a hot stew and took his wet clothes to wash and dry by the morning.

Gwynfor had an unexpectedly good night, sleeping on a bed of straw and dreaming of the Lady Elvina. He had known many women but the queen had a special fascination for him. He woke early, and called to the farmer for his horse to be made ready. He ate a good breakfast prepared by his wife, before rewarding them with a Saxon coin and galloping off to Pennard.

He recognised the groom who took his horse to the stable. 'Is Sir Padrig here?'

'He left yesterday, my lord.'

Gwynfor was irritated by the knowledge he'd arrived long after Padrig had departed and swore at his bad luck with the weather. After waiting impatiently for his meeting with the king, Gwynfor was a last shown into the lodge of the Royal Llysoedd, where the king was studying several parchment maps.

'Sir Gwynfor, good to see you.'

Gwynfor wondered if there was a note of criticism in the king's voice. 'My lord. I came as soon as I could.'

'I have been thinking about your plans, Gwynfor. You are right, we can't just wait for the Du to come knocking at our door.'

'Good,' said Gwynfor, 'We have prepared well and my men are ready for your orders.'

We need to send scouts to the wilderness, men we can rely on.'

'My own squire Hayden is training the garrison in Pembroke. There are some good men there.'

The king nodded. 'Have them leave as soon as they can.' He looked at Gwynfor. The knight seemed reassuringly confident. 'What of Cadell, the mercenary?'

'He is in the Du lands now. I sent him to Ynys Mon, as we know little of their strength there. I don't expect him back until he has useful information.'

'He needs to get back quickly. The trouble with the tribes is that we never know where to find them. Their king is the same, he moves all the time.

'You should do the same, my lord. We don't want to make it easy for them to find you either.'

'Yes, you are right Sir Gwynfor. It is time for me to go to Caerphilly. I will leave the protection of Pennard in your hands.'

'It will be an honour, my lord.' Gwynfor was pleased that the king was at last taking his advice. Events had moved more slowly than he had wished but his plan was falling into place.

After discussing tactics for a little longer with the king he made his excuses and went in search of Bethan, the queen's handmaiden. He had important unfinished business with her mistress and was in the mood to do something about it.

~

St Fagans Castle bustled with excitement as the staff prepared for a journey. Sir Padrig had finally received orders from the king. He told the servants to pack for a long absence and had selected those who would travel with him. He took one last look at his home before urging his war horse into a brisk trot.

He was proud of how well he had trained the white stallion, as it had a frisky temperament. Despite his relief at finally seeing some action, it was with mixed feelings he led his small group out through the gates and into the bright autumn sunshine.

Padrig looked impressive with a white cloak over a specially made 'coat of plates', burnished armour fastened with small leather straps, that would deflect all but a direct hit from a Du arrow or lance. His long greying hair was tied back, in the old style of the Welsh knights, and he looked fit and strong, much younger than his fifty years.

They rode on through the small village of St Fagans, where the local people had turned out to see them off. Padrig was a popular master and had seen to it that none of his bondsmen or their families went hungry during the last hard winter. He was pleased with the support and threw a handful of small Saxon coins to the children, who started fighting and scrabbling excitedly for them.

As the countryside became more wooded Padrig noted that the trees were beginning to take on an autumnal gold. He loved his lands but had managed the income from them poorly. Drinking and gambling in the past meant he was in debt to many of the merchants and traders his people relied on.

Sir Gwynfor was a very rich man, but had inherited his wealth and position, so Padrig started thinking about how he could benefit from his new role as guardian to the queen. The behaviour of Sir Gwynfor would need to be dealt with soon, before it damaged the reputation of the royal family.

Lord Vorath rode with his men into the early mist. His black war horse was named Ddraig, which meant 'Dragon' and it snorted loudly as they rode, its breath visible in the cold air. Ddraig was a powerful animal, with a broad back, strong loins and the long legs of his breed.

Impressive in his 'barding' armour made from leather and steel, his head was decorated with a sharp spike horn, making him look like a black unicorn. Ddraig was feared by Vorath's servants and had been trained to bite and kick on Vorath's command and to trample the bodies of fallen enemies. They had been through a lot and together.

Vorath still made a striking figure, with a long black cape flowing behind him as they galloped, the horse's hooves thundering on the narrow track south. He was enjoying himself and heavily armed, with one sword at his waist and a second slung across his back. In the tradition of the mounted warriors of the tribes he had no shield, keeping his left hand free for his dagger, which he could throw with deadly accuracy.

Vorath was ready for a battle with his old enemy the Gwyn. He had selected some of the finest and most experienced riders, many of whom he had fought with in the past. Some were looking for glory, others hoping for the spoils of war.

By Du standards the Gwyn were wealthy and there could be rich pickings, with plenty of livestock and land for the taking. He looked back to see that his men were keeping up and remembered his meeting with the king.

'The way is clear for you to take your warriors south, Gethin had said. 'We will not sit by our hearth waiting for the Gwyn, we will take the fight to them!'

Vorath smiled darkly to himself as he rode. His men were battle hardened raiders, with little concern for the conventions of war. The Gwyn knights were not to be underestimated, but the Du warriors would strike when least expected. The Gwyn had a surprise coming and he had a personal score to settle with their king.

~

Hayden stood alone on the windswept ramparts of Pembroke Castle, looking down at the boats plying their trade on the river below. He heard laughter echoing through the chill evening air and turned to see what was going on. Some of the men were making their way noisily across the wooden drawbridge to the town.

He smiled to himself. They deserved it, as they had worked hard and the time for drinking was nearly over. Sir Gwynfor had been pleased with the progress he had made training the men and now wanted them to scout the border with the north. He noticed Elfred watching the others leave and went down to the castle gatehouse to join him.

Elfred saw him approaching and grinned. He had done well in the practice sword fights and had nearly beaten Hayden several times. His teacher had taken it well, however, and they were now good friends. 'I hope they don't come back worse for wear...'

'I'll hold you responsible if they do!' He looked at Elfred, remembering for a moment the young farmer who had first come to him, not sure if he wanted any part in the war. He had become not just a good swordsman but a confident leader of men, with a reputation for being fair and just. Hayden had noticed how the other men looked to Elfred for guidance and was pleased.

'They've promised to be back by midnight.'

Hayden pretended to look surprised. 'It would be the first time ever.'

Elfred laughed. 'They're good men.'

'They are as ready as they will ever be,' agreed Hayden. He looked around to see if they could be overheard, then turned to Elfred and spoke quietly. 'I have to select a man to warn us if the Du move south. I was going to ask you to stay behind and help train the next group of men, but I'd like to hear what you have to say.'

'I'm from St Davids so have a good knowledge of the area north of there.' Elfred looked north, towards his home. 'The bishop wants me to extend our grazing land, so I've travelled a day's ride into the wilderness. I once saw riders that may have been Du warriors, but they were far off and I stayed out of sight. The wilderness is mostly deserted, just a few crofters trying to scrape a living from the land.'

Hayden looked serious. 'It will be dangerous. You would ride ahead of the men and learn the enemy position. We need to know where they are and in what strength.' He put his hand on Elfred's shoulder. 'The main weapon of the Du is surprise, they will be on the lookout for you and would spare you no mercy if you were captured.'

'I'd be glad to see the farm again, even for a short while.' Elfred looked to the horizon. The sun was now set and he could make out the stars. He had surprised himself at how much he had enjoyed life in the castle but he missed his home. 'I have no quarrel with the Du but if they come to take our lands we must be ready for them.'

Hayden was happy with his decision. He had been put in charge of the men and Sir Gwynfor was back at Picton Castle. 'You are to leave at first light and get back safely soon as you sight the enemy. I will tell the stables to have a good horse saddled and ready.'

'You can rely on me,' replied Elfred, grinning, and went to pack his few possessions for the journey.

Hayden watched him go, with mixed feelings. He had considered taking on the mission himself but knew he had to continue training the remaining men as best he could. He had never fought the Du but knew their reputation for savagery and wondered if he had really prepared the farmer for what he may face in the wilderness. Elfred had become skilled with his sword and picked up a few scars from combat training but was untested in a real battle situation.

Elfred set off at first light on one of the garrison horses, a lively white mare with a comfortable saddle. He carried only his sword and enough food for a few days. It felt good to be back in the country again and he'd missed the freedom of the outdoor life.

As well as staying out of sight he would live off the land once his supplies ran out. If he could give early warning of any action by the people of the Du he could be saving lives, and it was this thought that kept him going as night fell. Eventually Elfred reached a clear stream, where he re-filled his leather water bottle and found shelter in an old wooden barn where he could get some sleep.

He woke to find the rain lashing down on him through holes in the poorly maintained roof. He'd brought a broad brimmed hat, so put it on and continued until he saw familiar landmarks.

In the wilderness there would always be the risk of danger. Elfred ate some of the bread and cheese he carried and took a swig of water before saddling his horse and setting off down the track.

He was a long way from the lands of the people of the Du, but all manner of bandits and raiders had been known to settle in the lawless 'no man's land' between the kingdoms.

It was good to be heading toward home again and his mind turned to the farm at St Davids. This was the first time he had ever missed the harvest and wondered if they had managed to gather the crops before the rains came. He decided that he should stay a day or so before continuing with his mission.

He was, after all, Bishop Cledwin's man, not Sir Gwynfor's, and he wanted to hear more from the bishop about the original owner of the sword he now carried. His hand fell to the handle and he drew the heavy sword in a single flowing motion, slicing down on one imaginary attacker to the left then sweeping the blade swiftly over to the right. If he did have to fight, he was ready.

CHAPTER 7

*T*ristran grew tired of the confines of the fort at Flint. More men of the tribes arrived every day, bringing horses, cattle and supplies, so they were rapidly outgrowing the limited space of the old fortress and it would soon need to be expanded or even rebuilt completely.

The location was ideal, on raised ground at the mouth of the safe harbour on the Dee estuary. The salty sea air refreshed Tristran's lungs as he looked out to sea. Another supply barge would soon be joining the two tied up at the quay, which was busy with men loading heavy sacks onto wagons. The air was filled with shouts and curses and there was a buzz of anticipation as they made ready for the war with the Gwyn.

He wished he'd persuaded Lord Vorath to take him on the raid. Before he left, Lord Vorath placed his hand on Tristan's shoulder and looked at him intently. The boy had grown into a man.

He had taken to wearing a black tunic that made his hair look even blonder and he stood out clearly among the dark haired warriors of the tribes. At his waist was a fine Du sword, a special gift at his coming of age ceremony and he carried a new black shield, decorated with a snarling red dragon.

Vorath smiled. It was a break with Du tradition but Tristan had grown into a strong and capable warrior and was his favourite. Tristan's Viking ancestry meant he'd had to work hard to earn the respect of the men, who now looked up to him without question.

'I am leaving you in charge,' Vorath had said, his deep voice loud enough for everyone in the vicinity to hear. 'Make these tribesmen into warriors.'

It was a clear sign that Vorath accepted him as a successor and Tristan was pleased and surprised that he felt quite emotional. The old warrior had been hard on him all his life but was the closest he had to a father. 'It will be my honour, my lord.'

He knew he had done well but the men were from different tribes and there was always a tension. Arguments quickly flared up into fights and more than once he had to make an example by having trouble makers flogged. This has made him enemies within the garrison and he knew he would always have to watch his back.

'Be ready for the king. I expect he may be here before long.'

Tristan saw a flicker of regret in the old warrior's eyes at his mention of the king and remembered the stories of their great battles together. Without waiting for a reply the Warlord mounted Ddraig and shouted for his men to follow. It was an impressive sight, as the black war horses thundered into the dawn mist.

The finest warriors of the Du were finally going to battle. As he watched them go he wondered when he would see them again, as Vorath had told him their plan was to ride deep into the Gwyn homelands. He knew Vorath and his men could look after themselves but the Gwyn were well armed and strongly defended.

Now Vorath and his men were gone, Tristan looked out over the green fields that surrounded the castle. All the trees within sight had been felled to reduce cover for any attackers and provide firewood for the garrison.

A scatter of crofts had been built as closely as the garrison had permitted but most of the area around Flint Castle was pasture, grazed by sheep and goats. A section of straight road, made by Roman invaders, led in the direction of Chester, but Tristan was looking at a different path, towards the lands of the Gwyn.

An idea occurred to him. The men were under his command and did not have to remain in the castle. It would be good for them to gain some experience in the field. He found Dafydd, who he had appointed the Master of the Guard and told him to have the men assembled in the courtyard.

He knew Dafydd was his main rival to one day become warlord, but he would lead the best men south and prove to Lord Vorath that he was a true warrior.

By the afternoon of the same day he placed Dafydd in temporary charge of the fort and marched on foot at the head of a band of warriors, all dressed in black and hand picked for their loyalty to him. In his excitement he had already forgotten his promise to be ready for the king.

~

Hayden was confused by Sir Gwynfor's reaction to the news he'd chosen Elfred to warn of the Du advance. 'You said to send a good man, my lord.'

'I did. I also asked you to look after young Elfred but you've put him in danger.' He gave Hayden a withering look.

Hayden recalled their conversation. 'May I know what is so special about the farmer?'

'I made a promise to his family, that's all.' Gwynfor brightened as an idea occurred to him. 'The king has agreed that we can take the fight to the Du. Have my outriders here by morning and instruct the servants to prepare provisions and supplies for a journey north.'

'Yes my lord. I will put the men on standby ready for your command. They still have some rough edges but looking forward to some action now.' Hywel left to make the arrangements, relieved to have got off so lightly for his error.

The messengers travelled fast, as Gwynfor's outriders soon arrived and added to the clamour and sense of excitement by practice-fighting in the courtyard. Word of this spread and by dusk Picton was filled with local villagers and soldiers of the king's army.

Some brought weapons, under the impression the war had already started. Others had seen the chance to sell provisions to the departing men and were busily setting up stalls in an improvised market at the entrance to the castle. Burning torches had been lit and although it was turning dark early it was a dry and warm evening.

A small group of musicians began playing for the crowd. Their instruments were crudely made and although their skill did not match their enthusiasm, before long the old songs of the Gwyn were drifting raucously through the night air.

Gwynfor heard the singing and went to the window overlooking the central courtyard. He was pleased to see so many supporters in such good spirits. He told his servants to invite them into the great hall and provide jugs of ale. His estate was running low on funds but the war would soon make him a rich man again.

As well as extending his lands to the north, he planned to get his hands on the legendary Du gold. Most importantly, he would remind anyone who mattered that he was the right man to lead the people of the Gwyn, if anything were to befall the king.

At the thought of the king he had a powerful memory of Elvina, not of their moment of passion but of the sadness he had seen in her eyes as he left. He'd known since they first met that she would change his life but never expected she would become his lover.

Although he was one of the most powerful men in the land, he was the king's champion and she was the queen of the Gwyn, the king's wife. The one woman he could never have. He wished he could see her one last time before leaving for the north, but the risk was too great.

As he watched the merry-making of the villagers through the window an idea occurred to him. Taking a sharp knife he cut a fresh nib on a quill and wrote a note to Queen Elvina. It was in Latin, for secrecy and deliberately obscure, but he was certain she would understand its meaning. He sealed the small parchment with wax then summoned one of his most trusted servants.

'You are to take my fastest horse and deliver this with all speed to the queen's handmaiden at Pennard. Her name is Bethan and you are to tell her it is a private matter for the queen.'

'I understand, my lord.'

'I hope you do, for your life depends on it.'

The seriousness of the threat was not lost on the servant, who immediately left for Pennard.

Sir Gwynfor watched him go and smiled. One day, if he were to become king, he would establish a new tradition. He would marry the old king's widow. Feeling a little happier, he went to join the revellers. They had good cause to celebrate. The greatest battle ever fought by the Gwyn was about to start.

Sir Gwynfor and his riders left for the north early the next day, with a surprisingly large crowd gathered at Picton to see them off. The knight was wearing his best armour, covered with a blindingly white tabard.

He held up a gloved hand to signal the cheering crowd to silence. 'People of the Gwyn,' he paused to have their full attention. 'We ride on the orders of the king, to keep our lands safe for all time.' Another loud cheer came from the crowd and someone shouted 'Good luck to you Sir Gwynfor!'

The mounted men laughed and turned their horses north. They trotted at a leisurely pace as they had a long ride ahead. As they rode, the light autumn breeze tugged at flowing white pennants carried by two of the outriders on silver lances. Gwynfor knew they could be seen from far off by any Du invaders but cared little. His riders were more than a match for the men of the tribes.

∾

Bishop Deniol had a secret. He had chosen a life in the Church not through a devout Christian faith but as an escape from the world of the Du. As well as gaining a better education than he could ever have hoped for, he had risen quickly to the position of bishop to King Gethin.

He had never felt at ease in the tribes and had grown more apart from them as each year passed. He knew that even the simple farmers who regularly attended his services clung on to the old ways, covering their bets for the afterlife.

He made several attempts to reply to Archbishop Renfrew's letter as directed by the King, but each time he had failed and thrown the draft letter into the hearth. Watching deep in thought as the flickering flames turned the last draft letter to ash, he realised his dilemma.

Putting the king's rejection of peace with the Gwyn in writing made it seem more real, yet Deniol was clever enough to know that great care had to be taken with any letter to their enemy. Anything he wrote could prove damaging in the future, whatever the outcome of any war but particularly if it did not turn out well for King Gethin.

He decided to the best solution was to meet with Archbishop Renfrew in person. The thought occurred to him that he had more in common with the bishops of the Gwyn than he did with his fellow Bishop Emrys, who he suspected of being a Druid.

If anyone could work for peace it should be the Church and, as the only true representative of the Church in the north, it would have to be him. As he made preparations for the journey he wondered how he would explain his absence to the king.

He had his servants load his sturdy farm cart with supplies and was driven by his bondsman Rhys, who now had additional pay as a bodyguard to the bishop. Rhys was grateful for the work and had been practising with his home made crossbow, hoping he would get the chance to show the bishop what it could do. As it was no longer a secret, the crossbow was now slung over his back on a leather strap, alongside a quiver he had made to hold the bolts. The bishop was as usual unarmed.

The weather was fine when they left but Deniol was soon glad of the cover they had over the cart, as it started raining hard and they were both able to keep fairly dry. The track was another matter, as the wheels of the cart were cutting deep ruts into the mud. Deniol was a poor traveller and clung grimly to the side of the cart, muttering the occasional prayer when the track was particularly rough.

They were making good progress when Rhys pulled hard at the reins, bringing them to a halt. A fallen tree lay across the track ahead of them, its roots reaching into the air. There was no room for the cart to pass.

'We can't go on, bishop.'

'I must. Many lives could depend on the work I have to do. Sort out supplies for a few days. I will have to continue my journey on foot.'

'Do you wish me to come with you?'

'I would be glad of your company, Rhys, but we cannot leave the cart here.'

Rhys jumped down from the cart and put some food in a bag for the bishop, together with one of the blankets they carried to keep out the cold at night. He was unhappy to be leaving the bishop to carry on alone, as he'd been looking forward to the journey south.

He handed the bag and a leather water bottle to Bishop Deniol, who watched as he managed to turn the cart round.

'Have a safe journey, my lord!'

'God go with you Rhys.' Deniol watched until the cart disappeared from view then climbed past the fallen tree, with some difficulty, and began his long trek south, towards the border with the Gwyn. As he walked, he wondered if he would ever see his home again.

~

Owen finished his training with the garrison at Caerphilly castle and made the long journey home to Pennard with mixed feelings. There would have been a good chance that as a member of the Royal Guard, he could have quietly waited out the war safely protected within the palisade of the Royal Llysoedd.

This was not to be now that he was the queen's chosen man in the field, so Owen volunteered for training as an archer. He liked the idea of being as far as possible from the enemy, as fighting at a distance was far more preferable to him than hacking at close quarters with a sword.

He had seen the injuries sustained by swordsmen. It was hard to look heroic if you were missing an ear or worse, your nose. He wasn't even certain he could kill another man face to face. He was no coward, but had a wife and family to look after, which brought responsibilities.

His wife, Myfanwy, had actually grown very capable of looking after the family on her own, cooking for the royal household. He teased her about her name, which meant 'little one' as she was no longer very 'little'.

He had married a lithe and attractive servant girl, but the woman now welcoming him home had put on weight over the years. She had also developed a fondness for 'bara lawr', as the area around Pennard was one of the only known places where the edible seaweed, known as 'lawr', could be found.

Myfanwy would make the seaweed into heavy dough, mix it with oatmeal then cook it in bacon fat. Her body had also paid the price of having four children in quick succession, as well as many years of hard work in the kitchens of the king's residences.

Myfanwy was glad to see Owen safely home and had put on a clean apron and washed her unruly brown hair to look her best. Although many soldiers had been seriously injured or even killed in training, she was sure he would have avoided placing himself in any real danger. She knew he could easily have taken the opportunity to desert over the border and take his chances in England, rather than risk his life fighting in a war with the Du.

Owen hugged his wife. 'I've really missed…. a decent hot dinner!' he joked, 'The food in Caerphilly Castle isn't fit for pigs to eat.'

'Well you don't look as if you've starved. I bet you were out in the taverns every night!'

'Chance would be a fine thing,' replied Owen.

'You know what I think of your drinking,' She wagged an accusing finger at him. 'You're not to go wasting your pay in those ale houses.'

Owen decided not to tell her about the drinking that passed the evenings while he was away, or that he had lost most of his pay and won it back again gambling with the other soldiers. 'I have orders to go north,' he said.

'But you've only just got here?'

'I have to make an early start, first thing tomorrow.'

Myfanwy looked at him, concern in her eyes. 'You'll take care now Owen. I'll cook you fried oatmeal patties, with eggs, bacon and cockles. That should make you think again about rushing off in the morning!'

He gave her another hug, then after the best meal he'd eaten for a month, washed down with a whole jug of ale, Owen told Myfanwy he had to report to his Captain. He went to look for Bethan, the queen's handmaiden and found her in the queen's outer hall, repairing a tapestry by the light of a candle.

As he approached he thought she looked more like a noble lady than a servant, with an expensive dress and a richly woven shawl over her shoulders. Her long dark hair was tied back with a white silk ribbon and she was concentrating hard on her sewing, making small stitches with a silver needle and fine thread.

Bethan looked up at the sound of his boots on the polished wooden floor and smiled as she recognised him.

'Owen, I am so glad to see you made it back safely.'

'Good evening to you, Bethan. I was hoping to find you here. Did you miss me?'

'Of course,' she smiled. It was only a little lie. 'How was your time in Caerphilly?'

'It wasn't so hard for me,' he couldn't help bragging to her. 'You remember I've experience of battle, so the others looked to me as a something of a leader.'

'And now you are ready to do your duty?'

'I am. I turned out to be a natural archer and have learnt to use the longbow. It's a powerful weapon, more than enough to keep me safe from the Du.' Owen looked around to see if they could be overheard. 'What of your mistress, the queen? Is there any message before I go, Bethan?'

She looked serious for a moment. 'The queen wishes you to keep safe, Owen. You are to watch over the area north of here.'

'What do I do if I sight the enemy?'

'You must find a way to get word back to the queen, as soon as you can. There are messengers we can trust, so you must look out for them. '

He looked at her expectantly, hoping for more, but she smiled at him and went back to her sewing as a sign he was dismissed.

'I will leave in the morning.' He sounded awkward and unsure of himself.

Bethan surprised him by laying down her tapestry and giving him a hug. 'Come back safe Owen,' she said softly.

He was to remember that meeting as he headed further and further away from the safety of Pennard.

CHAPTER 8

*K*ing Gethin urged his black horse to a gallop, not because he was in a hurry but with the sheer exhilaration of the ride. He looked behind to see his warriors were falling back and slowed a little, enjoying the fresh breeze from the sea.

The long track along the northern shore had been a favourite ride since he was a boy. He knew it well and as his horse cantered easily on the sandy road he remembered the excitement of the first time he made the journey alone.

He'd been about fifteen years old and a proud Du warrior. He was also the heir to the throne of the Du, so it was risky to be out alone, as foreign raiders and pirates often attacked the coastal villages, taking whatever they could find.

A prince would be a great prize, worth a king's ransom, yet he remembered hoping they would try. He was ready to use the fighting skills he had practiced since he could first hold a sword.

He felt that same sense of excitement now, as he made his way to the outpost at Flint. All his life he'd lived under the threat of another war with the Gwyn and at last he was going to bring that to an end.

He had listened to the stories of the old warriors by the fire, tales of battles lost and won, kings and queens triumphant or deposed. The last war had resulted in a country divided, with the Du forced to retreat to the northernmost part of the country. Their rich farmland was quickly turned back into the 'diffeithwch', a dangerous and lawless place where people simply disappeared.

For the first time ever, Gethin allowed himself to picture his life after victory over the people of the Gwyn. His name would become a legend, stories of the battles passed from one generation to the next for all time.

His people would be free to roam where they wished and the Saxons would stay the other side of the huge defensive dyke they had built to keep the Welshmen out of England. He could not bear to think of the Gwyn invading the Du lands.

If they did he would want a warrior's death rather than the humiliation of watching his people enslaved and subjugated. He spurred his horse on with renewed urgency, his life depended on it.

When at last the fort came into view King Gethin could see no guards or activity, just a wisp of smoke coming from one of the chimneys and a few stray goats grazing on the grass at the entrance.

His first thought was that he'd arrived too late. The Gwyn had somehow reached the north already and his warriors gone. It was impossible that they could have moved so quickly and without raising the alarm. A shout from a high lookout reassured him.

'Turn out the guard, the King is here!' There was a sudden commotion and men started appearing at the entrance to greet him. Gethin recognised Dafydd, who seemed to be in charge.

The king had known his father, a good man who had ridden with him before he was cruelly struck down with a fever. Dafydd appeared unshaven and was wearing a jerkin that had seen better days. He was looking curiously at the king and his warriors, who were all dressed in black and clearly ready for a fight despite their long ride.

'Welcome, my lord, we were not expecting you so soon.'

'It seems you were not.' The king shook his head and dismounted. 'Who is in charge here?'

'I am, lord, but only until the commander returns.'

'Who is the commander and where has he gone?'

'His name is Tristan, my lord. He has taken a party of warriors to the border.'

'I know this Tristan, he is one of Lord Vorath's men.'

'Yes, my lord, he made no mention of when he would return.'

The king looked at Dafydd. He had won a reputation as a swordsman and would be useful to him now that he had sent Vorath south. 'Tell the men to assemble, I will speak to them.'

It took longer than it should have for the men to gather and while he was waiting a movement caught his eye. He looked up at the top of the castle's single tower and saw they had raised a large black flag, which now fluttered proudly in the breeze.

Gethin smiled, Vorath may be on his way to the southern border but his hand was evident in this. The tribes of the Du could never agree on a single battle standard, but Vorath had suggested that they would unite under a black flag, which would be a clear challenge to the white pennants of the Gwyn. He looked at the sea of faces and could tell they were glad to see him.

'Warriors of the Du,' his voice was deep and carried well. 'We must make ready for the greatest challenge ever to face out people. The Gwyn are building an alliance with the Saxons. A sister of King Athelstan sits alongside their king and it is only a matter of time before they plot to enslave our people and take our lands.' He looked around to see they understood. 'I shall take command of this castle and you are to all be known as 'rhyfelwyr y brenin', warriors of the king, my personal guard.'

A loud cheer rang out and those who carried swords and spears raised them high in a salute to the king. Gethin smiled, there was a lot of work to do but it was a start and he felt a surge of pride. The people of the tribes would remember this day.

~

Flies buzzed around the head of Bishop Cledwin's horse as he carefully picked his way along the stony track. Soon after he left the comfort of his home he had nearly turned back, fearing for his life and unsure of the wisdom of his dangerous plan. It had come to him while he was enjoying a hot bath, thinking of the implications of the war.

One of the advantages of his position was that he had the protection of the Church, so it made sense to take advantage of the situation. He did not expect the uncivilised Du would be any match for the well trained soldiers of the Gwyn, yet they had little to lose and could do great harm to the property of the Church if they wished. Instead of sending men to help him defend St Davids from attack, the king had taken his best men to reinforce the south.

He had been resigned to this unsatisfactory arrangement, partly out of loyalty to the King and also because he did not feel he had any choice in the matter. His view changed when his housekeeper Anwen announced that Elfred was waiting to see him. There had been no word from his son since he left for training at Pembroke Castle, so the bishop was surprised and happy to know he was safely home once more.

'Elfred, you look well.' He looked at his son more closely, as his eyesight was not as it should be, and realised what was different about him. '...and that beard has gone,' he laughed.

'Thank you, Bishop, it's good to be back.' Elfred thought the bishop seemed older since their last meeting.

'There is much to do, as usual,' Cledwin gestured for Elfred to sit and had to admit he looked a true soldier now, with a new confidence that reminded the bishop of himself in his younger days.

'How was the harvest? I called at the farm but the men were out in the fields, so I came straight here.'

Cledwin shook his head. 'It has been hard with the farm so short handed. As well as yourself, I had to send five of my best workers for the service of the King.' He smiled at Elfred. 'At least you have returned.'

'I can't stay for long, Bishop. I've been sent on a mission to the north and was glad of the chance to see my home again.'

Cledwin was astounded. He had travelled all the way to Picton to ask the favour of Sir Gwynfor, yet it seemed he had broken his promise at the first opportunity. Although Elfred was quick witted and now had some military training, he would be easy prey for battle hardened Du warriors.

Elfred was surprised at bishop Cledwin's reaction to the news. 'I will do what I can to help before I go...'

'I understand that soldiers have to fight,' interrupted Cledwin, his mind racing as the full implications sunk in. 'It's just that I don't see the need to take unnecessary risks.'

'We need to bring an early end to this war,' said Elfred. 'Then I can return and we will be even safer than before.'

'I can see your mind is made up. Take care in the wilderness, it has hidden dangers.' Bishop Cledwin felt a surge of annoyance at Gwynfor of Picton, who would be held to account if anything were to happen to Elfred.

'You know the wilderness, Bishop?'

'Yes, I have travelled through Du territory on the business of the Church. The men of the tribes have long memories and bear a grudge against us. You are not to trust them. They have no honour and would strike you down without mercy.'

'I am not looking for a fight with them. My work is just to warn if they come too far south.'

The bishop took an engraved silver crucifix from around his neck and handed it to Elfred.

'I'd like you to have this, Elfred. It will show the Du that you fight with God on your side.'

'Thank you, Bishop, I will wear it always.'

'We will pray for your safe return.'

Those fateful words came back to Cledwin as he rode deep into the wilderness. His plan had been to track down Elfred and order him home, which he was within his right to do. Despite Elfred's head start, it should have been easy, as he had left his horse in the bishop's stables and continued on foot.

There was no sign of his son. Cledwin realised he had ridden too far to return before darkness fell, so decided to press on, hoping to find somewhere to shelter for the night. As he rode, Cledwin formed a new plan. He knew of a chapel, built in the middle of the wilderness by a Du priest who was charged with saving the lost souls who lived there. There was no certainty over the outcome of the war, so it would be well to make his peace with the influential bishops of the Du.

~

Commander Idris was a proud man and had been affronted by the king's decision to over-rule his dismissal of the insubordinate Hywel. Not long after receiving the message he issued an order that Hywel was to be sent into the field immediately.

He respected the king's wishes in returning Hywel to duty but was perfectly within his rights as Commander of the Guard to assign him to other duties. Idris also knew that the king was away reviewing the outposts, so by the time he found out it would be too late.

Hywel was still recovering from his beating and keen to not cross the Commander again, so when he received the order he had no choice other than to follow it. Before leaving he called secretly at the royal apartments to see Ceinwen, so that he could explain it was his duty as a soldier of the king.

Ceinwen looked at him in disbelief. 'You can't go! Your *duty* is to protect the queen!'

Hywel took both her hands in his and looked into her eyes. 'I am a soldier and we are going to be at war. I promise to be careful and come back safely to you, as soon as I can.'

She pulled him close to her and he felt the warmth of her body. 'Stay with me tonight.'

He nearly resisted but instead kissed her slowly and passionately. Ceinwen locked the doors to make sure they would not be disturbed and led him to her bed. She looked down at him and slowly undressed them both.

Hywel stroked her naked body, admiring her soft perfect curves, lit by the flickering light of a single candle. 'I have been dreaming of this,' he said softly. 'You are so beautiful…'

Ceinwen smiled. 'I've longed for you.' She grabbed his strong arms and held him close.

She caressed the dark hairs on his chest. She kissed him softly at first, then harder and longer. He was surprised at how wonderful it felt to make love with a woman who loved him in return. Their bodies were as one and nothing else mattered.

He woke to find her still in his arms, her long black hair cascading over his chest and her dark eyes shining. 'I love you.' He whispered to her in the dark.

Hywel thought of that moment over and over again as he made the long trek to the south. He smiled to himself. Life was good.

～

Queen Elvina lay awake in the dark, unable to sleep, her mind racing with thoughts and memories. She remembered the first time she had seen the king. Her brother Athelstan had kept the reason for the journey from her but she had always known.

She was a Saxon princess of marriageable age, an asset her brother could hardly ignore. Elvina had taken care with her education, so was one of the best educated women in the land, fluent in Latin and making good progress with conversing in Welsh.

She had been married as a 'fricwebba,' a 'peace-weaver,' as her brother Athelstan, the Saxon King, considered it an ideal role for her to work for peace between the Saxons and the Welsh.

Elvina decided it was time to take control of her destiny after her handmaiden, Bethan, brought her a message sealed with wax. The queen had read it many times in the last few hours. It was written in a Latin script known to few in Wales and she recognised a line from the Roman poet Virgilius: *'et nos cedamus amori'.*

Although he did not mention either of their names she knew it could only have been from Gwynfor. He suggested that she travel to visit him in secret in the country, close to the town of St Davids. There was no clue to why he was there or for how long and it had been a daring risk to send the note, yet she understood, as she had been longing to hear from him.

She rang a small bell to summon Bethan, who arrived to see the queen putting the flame of a candle to the parchment. 'We are going on a journey, Bethan. I would like to see more of this country before the war makes it impossible.' She looked at Bethan, watching her reaction to the news.

Bethan seemed unconcerned. 'Will we be away for long, my lady?'

'A week, if this good weather holds.'

Bethan watched as Elvina threw the burning note into the stone hearth and watched as it quickly turned to ash. 'You don't think we should wait until the fighting is over?'

Elvina smiled. 'My place is with my people. One day I will be queen of the whole country, and then my brother will have to take notice.'

Bethan picked up a hairbrush from the table and began to softly comb the queen's long hair. 'It will not be an easy war. The people of the north will fight to the last.'

Elvina looked at Bethan. Something about her was different. She seemed to have gained in confidence and was wearing a white dress that looked well on her. Around her neck was a silver chain with a Celtic pendant that twinkled in the candlelight with the rhythmic movement her gentle brushing.

'What do you know of the Du?'

Bethan stopped combing as she remembered. 'I imagine they make a dangerous enemy.' She hesitated. 'I think they just want to live in peace, if we will let them.'

The queen turned and put her hand on Bethan's arm. 'They murdered Gwayne's father. He can never forgive them.'

'Has the king ever told you how his father died?'

Elvina shook her head. 'Not really. He doesn't talk of it.' She knew Bethan well as they spent a lot of time in each other's company and she could sense that she was holding something back. 'Tell me. Tell me what you know?'

'His father was fighting the Du when he died. He wanted to wipe them out. Kill every last one.'

'You sound bitter. Were your family caught up in the fighting?'

Bethan looked at the queen. 'My family are Du, my lady. I come from the north.'

Elvina put her hand on Bethan's arm and looked into her eyes. She had been easily persuaded by the king that the northerners were illiterate tribes but now she realised there was a way to learn something of their enemy. Bethan had never mentioned her background, although she had stood out from the other servants, which was why Elvina had chosen her as a handmaiden.

The king had tried to dissuade her from the journey but

agreed it would be good for her to see more of the country. There was no question of him travelling with her, but he insisted on an escort of soldiers from his personal bodyguard. The men were pleased, as it was easy work and they were under strict orders from the king to stay within the safety of the Gwyn territory.

Before she left, the king handed her a small ornate dagger in a white leather scabbard. The silver handle was decorated with Celtic symbols.

'What would I do with this?' She turned it slowly and the sharp blade glinted in the light.

'Hide it somewhere you can reach it quickly.'

'I don't know how to use a knife to fight! I would be better just running away if the Du ever get this close?'

'We must be ready to defend ourselves, Elvina. It could be much worse for us if we don't.'

～

The queen and her handmaiden talked as they rode inland together towards the mountains. Elvina was enjoying the ride and glad of a change of scenery from the Royal Llysoedd at Pennard. She was a skilled rider, having grown up around horses since she was a young girl, and was riding her favourite white mare, a gift from her husband. Bethan was also a very capable rider and was alongside her on one of the royal horses.

Autumn was turning into winter and they wrapped up well against the chill breeze. 'This beautiful mare is called Ceffyl Blaen. That means forward horse?'

Bethan laughed. 'It is a Welsh saying, it means someone who is always making things happen...'

She turned to Bethan. 'That's a good name for my horse! The king thinks I should wait in my rooms until this war is won. I will not. I am going to make things happen and you, Bethan, are going to help me.'

'What do you have in mind?'

Elvina did have a plan but was not sure the time was right to share it with her handmaiden. 'You must tell me about the Du, Bethan. I need to understand your people.'

Bethan looked at her, trying to make a judgement.

Elvina smiled to put her at ease. 'You haven't told me about your parents, are they still alive and well?'

'My father disappeared over the English border when I was young, but my mother is well.'

'Does she live in the north?'

'No, my lady, she lives not far from Pennard, I see her as often as I can.'

'How did you end up in the king's household?'

'My mother found me a position there, we came south as many others have in search of work.'

'I need to understand more about the people of the north. I want to know about their queen, what do you know of her?'

'There is a new queen since I was in the lands of the Du. All I know is her name.' Elvina looked at Bethan but it was impossible to tell if she was telling the truth. 'What is her name?'

'Rhiannon. Her name is Queen Rhiannon.'

CHAPTER 9

*H*ywel was lost. An ominously swirling mist was looming over the hills and he realised that the path he had been following had become so overgrown it could not possibly lead to the outpost at the southern border.

He took shelter under a gnarled old oak tree from the biting wind and checked his supplies. He had some rough bread and cheese, enough drinking water for another day and some oat cakes. These were a parting gift from Ceinwen. She had wrapped them in a clean cotton cloth and handed them to him as he left. She was trying to look happy for him but her eyes betrayed her.

He'd been saving the oat cakes but now uncovered them and ate one slowly. They had unexpected exotic flavour of cinnamon, a rare and precious spice he had only tasted once before in mulled wine. Cinnamon was traded from far off lands by Venetian merchants and was far too expensive to use except on very special occasions.

The taste reminded him of Christmas and he savoured the memory of their night together. For the first time he realised Ceinwen must be wealthy. It had never occurred to him before but he realised that when he married her he would become a member of the royal family, rather than just their bodyguard.

The chill was beginning to seep into his bones, despite his thick black woollen cloak, which doubled as a blanket to keep him warm at nights. Hywel decided he had no option but to take a track which rose steeply into wooded mountains, so he could use the height to find his bearings.

The sun was barely able to penetrate the leaden clouds but he could see that it was setting to his right, which meant he was still heading south. He kept walking until the failing light made it difficult to see the way ahead.

There was nowhere to shelter but he found some comfort in soft grass in the lee of a rocky outcrop. Hywel had a troubled night, as he needed to stay alert and there were many strange noises in the darkness to keep him from sleeping, despite his exhausting walk.

The next day was brighter and after a breakfast on another of Ceinwen's oat cakes, he climbed to the highest point he could find to see the lay of the land. The only sign of habitation was a distant wisp of grey smoke rising lazily into the morning sky, so he decided it would be better to head for it than to try to retrace his steps.

He moved warily now, looking for cover wherever he could find it. Hywel had no idea how far he was from the northern boundary of the Gwyn and had been warned of ambush from marauding bandits.

The smoke was further off than it had seemed at the top of the mountain, so he took bearings using natural landmarks to make sure he was still heading the right way if it stopped. After several miles of hard walking he came across a sunlit clearing in the trees, where he found the fire he'd been looking for.

It had been made by someone who knew what they were doing. A good sized rabbit was roasting nicely on a cleverly improvised wooden spit and the aroma reminded Hywel of his hunger.

He looked around but there was no sign of anyone, so he decided to wait as they couldn't be very far away. He was right. A soldier of the Gwyn appeared as if from nowhere, carrying a water bottle, which he promptly dropped to the ground and drew his sword in a flowing motion that told Hywel he was dealing with a trained sword fighter.

'Surrender, Du!' the soldier shouted.

Hywel was an experienced man of the queen's guard and without hesitating drew his own sword and closed the distance between them with a powerful lunge. He knew that a fight with swords often ended with first cut and swung his blade in a deadly arc at the head of his enemy.

The man surprised Hywel by quickly side stepping to avoid the blow rather than attempting to parry the attack. In a flash the Gwyn soldier retaliated with a well aimed slash of his sword that clanged dangerously against Hywel's parry as it struck. Hywel pushed the soldier's sword back with his own and thrust as hard as he could at the man's chest, only to be swiftly parried once again. He noted how the man kept his arms and sword outstretched, rather than bent close to his body, so pretended to be forced back then lunged again, this time cutting deep into the artery of the man's unprotected neck.

The Gwyn soldier was mortally wounded and dropped his sword to the ground, then fell to his knees. Hywel felt a rush of remorse. The soldier had been well trained but was young and inexperienced.

Hywel had acted instinctively but was alarmed at the sight of the red blood spurting from the man's neck. He searched through the leather bag that was still over his shoulder and found Ceinwen's white cotton square. Throwing out the remaining oat cakes, Hywel made a desperate attempt to stem the bleeding. It was no use and he watched as the life faded from his enemy.

'You fought bravely,' said Hywel, his voice heavy with emotion. The soldier tried to say something but more blood flowed from the wound in his neck and with a final gasp he died. Hywel began digging a grave at the edge of the peaceful clearing where they had fought so savagely.

As he was working, he noticed the sword of the Gwyn soldier had fallen in the undergrowth and picked it up. It was a fine old weapon, so he used it to mark the finished grave. After saying a silent prayer Hywel continued on his way. A gentle breeze made something dangling from the handle of the sword flash in the autumn sunlight. It was a small silver crucifix the man had been wearing.

~

Queen Elvina had a difficult decision to make. She was longing to meet Sir Gwynfor but it would be impossible to see him in secret without Bethan's collaboration. Her dilemma was that she was not certain how far her handmaiden could be trusted.

The news that Bethan was from the Du raised a question about where her loyalty would be, if it were tested. It crossed Elvina's mind that Bethan was an enemy spy, placed deep within the royal household to gather information for her people.

She dismissed the idea just as quickly, as it would have been a simple matter for Bethan to remain silent about her past. She had chosen to be quite open about it, even though she must know that the queen could have had her arrested immediately.

They stopped overnight at one of the king's farms after a full day of riding. There was no bath and only stubs of old beeswax candles for light, yet Elvina was delighted to experience the simple way her people lived.

She had to share a low ceilinged room with Bethan but the bed had clean linen and they both slept comfortably. Elvina woke to the relaxing sound of the farmer taking his cattle out to pasture.

Elvina lay for a while, listening to the dawn chorus until the shrill call of a cockerel reminded her it was time to prepare for the busy day ahead. She breathed deeply of the fresh morning air, which raised the invisible golden hairs on the skin of her arms. Bethan must have woken early and opened the ancient wooden shutters covering the window.

She rose from her bed and looked out to the mist covered blue hills that marked the edge of the Gwyn territory. These were her lands now, for as far as the eye could see, and she was not going to let any invaders take them easily.

Elvina unrolled the small but detailed parchment map the king had given her and traced their route from Pennard with her finger. She heard a gentle knock at her door. It was Bethan, carrying an earthenware bowl of hot water and clean clothes.

'Are you ready to dress, my lady?'

'Thank you, Bethan. It looks to be a fine morning so I would like to leave early.'

'There is a rider waiting to see you, he asked me to tell you he has a message for you.'

'Quickly, help me dress so I can hear what he has to say.' Her heart was beating fast, she could not believe that Sir Gwynfor would take such a risk.

The rider waited in the kitchen of the farmhouse. He was a tall man and made the low ceilinged and cluttered room look even smaller. He put down the mug of hot broth he was drinking and bowed when he recognised the queen.

'I have to speak with this man about a private matter,' said Elvina to Bethan and the farmer's wife, who were waiting to hear what had brought the rider at such an early hour. After they had gone and closed the door, she turned to him.

'Keep your voice low, if you will.'

The rider nodded. 'My lady, I have a message from your man Owen. He says to tell you he has news of the Du advancing.'

In her hurry to see Sir Gwynfor, Elvina had forgotten Owen and the mission she had sent him on. 'Where is Owen? Did he say where he saw them?'

'He is waiting there for your orders, close to our border north of here, my lady.'

Elvina knew she should return to Pennard but decided that the message from Owen offered a solution to her problem. Rather than travel directly to the place suggested by Sir Gwynfor, they should continue to the north for a short way to meet with Owen.

She would pretend to chance upon the knight on the return journey. There was no need to give anyone reason to suspect the true purpose of her visit to the countryside. She gave the rider a Saxon coin for his trouble and told him to find Owen and have him meet them at the next farm, some ten miles north. After he had gone she could see that Bethan was curious.

'The message is from Owen. It seems you chose him well, Bethan, he already has news of the Du.'

Bethan looked worried. 'They are attacking?'

'Not yet, but I have asked him to meet us north of here, so we must leave soon.'

They had a hurried breakfast, watched from a respectful distance by the farmer's wife, before setting out on the trail again. Several of the king's guard rode ahead of them and the rest followed behind with the pack mules carrying their supplies. The land was more densely wooded and Elvina was enjoying the ride in the unexpectedly sunny November morning.

'I love the colours of the leaves in autumn,' said Bethan.

'It is good to see more of the country. I am learning from this journey. The king gave me the impression that the wilderness is a wasteland but it has a wild beauty, I like it.'

They rode on until they reached the farmstead where they

were to meet Owen. He had not arrived, so they waited to rest the horses and two of the guards went to refill the water bottles.

It wasn't long before Owen appeared. He'd been riding hard but was pleased to have found them. He explained he'd seen the Du a short way to the north. It was only one warrior, who Owen guessed was probably a scout, sent ahead to test their defences.

Elvina felt a sudden surge of excitement as she realised how close they were to danger. Ideas and possibilities flashed though her mind. 'We could capture him! Quickly, before he goes to cover.'

Owen looked uncertain. 'Du warriors fight to the death rather than be taken, my lady. He is heading this way, we must take you to a place of safety.'

Elvina hesitated. 'No! I have my guards and you said he seems to be alone. Take us to where you saw him.'

Owen could see the queen was determined, so led them back the way he had come until they reached the top of a ridge that gave them a view into the far distance. The land was uninhabited for as far as they could see.

For a while they waited on the ridge, then a distant movement caught Elvina's attention. At first she thought it was one of the black Welsh cattle she had noticed on the way there, then she realised it was a man, crossing the open ground between two small wooded areas and heading in their direction. She beckoned Owen.

'See that,' she pointed. 'Is that him?'

Owen squinted into the distance then saw the man as well. 'It's hard to be sure but I think it is,' he said.

'Quick, Owen, we must take him before he goes out of sight,' She dismounted and handed the reins of her white mare to one of the guards. 'Wait for us with my handmaiden.'

Bethan looked as if she was going to object but could see that Elvina had made her mind up. She nodded. 'Take care, my lady.'

Elvina followed Owen and the other guards as they

descended the steep hillside on foot, heading towards the man but taking care to remain concealed within the cover of the trees. They took some time to reach the path being taken by the Du warrior but he was clearly not aware of them.

They came to a rocky outcrop that offered a safe vantage point for seeing anyone heading up the narrow track and waited. Her guards were armed with bows as well as swords and two of them silently sighted arrows on the dark figure in the distance.

She'd never expected to see the Du so soon yet now she held a man's life in her hands. It was a heavy responsibility but she felt excited as she watched him approach. To capture a Du warrior would really show the power she had as queen of the Gwyn and, if he could be taken alive, he would have information useful to the king.

The arrow struck home in the blink of an eye.

The warrior of the Du felt an instant searing pain and the frightening realisation that he was going to die. He looked down and saw the feathered flight of a thick arrow sticking out of his chest.

The blood poured from the wound and he felt his body going numb with shock. He'd not even seen where the arrow had come from. This was not how it was supposed to end. A single word came from his lips as he fell dead. 'Ceinwen.'

Bishop Emrys was alarmed to learn that his servant Madoc was advising the Commander of the Guard. He felt some guilt when he pointed out the mistake, but would have been more concerned if he had known Idris would act so swiftly by sending Madoc straight to the front line.

Even for an experienced warrior, the advance guard would have been a high risk but for Madoc it was bad news and he knew it. He left quickly, however, aware that he had only escaped a severe flogging because of the impending battle.

The punishment for desertion was execution but although the idea of making his name as a warrior appealed to him, Madoc knew he would not last long in a real battle. The only way he could see to survive was to find one of the isolated crofts that dotted the hillsides and lay low until the war was won, or lost by the Du.

Before he left he'd been equipped with old black cloak, which kept out the cold, and enough food for his journey. Madoc had never been so far south, so the country was strange to him and he would have to learn to live off the land.

Eventually he came to a croft that was far enough off the track to avoid unwanted attention. It was well built of local stone and had a sound roof of slate. There was a small vegetable garden, where Madoc could see leeks and potatoes growing.

He knocked at the door. The crofter was a wiry man who had managed to scrape a living by tending a small flock of sheep on the hills. He opened the door and stood looking at Madoc in silence.

'I have been assigned by Commander Idris of the king's guard to protect the area,' explained Madoc. 'There is to be a war against the Gwyn, so in return for food and lodging I will ensure your safety.'

'You'll work for your food?' asked the crofter.

'I am well used to hard work,' lied Madoc. He was not, but after his long walk was prepared to agree to anything.

He spent the night sleeping on a straw bed and the next day rounding up sheep and fetching water from the spring. He soon started enjoying his new life, safely isolated from whatever terrors the war would bring to the people of the north.

The longbow was awkward to carry but Delwyn had spent the last few weeks practising with it until he could hit the targets almost as well as Kane, his mentor. Kane was not a man who was easily impressed but had described Delwyn as a 'natural archer' and presented him with one of the best longbows in the castle for his own personal use.

It was with mixed feelings that Delwyn set out on his mission for the king, however. He'd enjoyed the longbow training and could not have had a better teacher than Kane, but had never killed a man and wasn't sure if he was able to, even at a distance.

The ground was marshy and he could feel his feet getting wet. They were his only pair of boots, so he worried about how long they would last and wished he had insisted on new ones before he left. Delwyn had decided that he should go ahead and the other men would follow out of sight behind.

It was a long walk and with every step he was closer to danger, so he slowed down and wondered how far away Owen was. Owen had left a few days earlier and knew the way better than him, so it would be good to meet up.

To pass the time on the long journey Delwyn remembered Kane's teaching about the deadly longbow. He had been surprised to learn that it was invented by his people and was only used by the English after they saw how successfully it was being used against them.

Every bow was made to measure, usually from the sacred yew tree, although Kane had bows made from ash, hazel and even elm trees. Delwyn had learned to protect the wood from the rain with a rub of fine tallow and to soak the hemp string of the Longbow in glue made from bones as further protection against the damp Welsh air.

Kane trained him for hours until he could fire ten arrows in a minute, by letting his mind focus on the target. He'd practiced at targets including old metal plates he could pierce at over two hundred paces, and he could imagine Kane's crisp instructions in his ear now, as if he were standing next to him.

The surprising power of the longbow meant that at first Delwyn was almost unable to draw it back quickly enough, but with practice it became a mechanical act he did without thinking, and he could hold it there for the long moment before the command 'Loose!' and the arrow would strike its mark in the blink of an eye.

Delwyn was tired and wet, so was glad to see some soldiers of the Gwyn in the distance. They were building a camp and happy for him to join them.

'Watch out for the Du,' warned one of the soldiers. 'They're not far away.'

Delwyn looked around. They had a good fire going and he had to camp somewhere for the night. 'I need a meal and a good night's sleep.'

'You are welcome,' said one of the soldiers, 'We could use a good bowman and you can take your turn on lookout duty.'

He was given a wooden bowl of thick mutton soup that was hot and tasty, and he gratefully made a bed and fell quickly to sleep. Delwyn woke with a start, wondering where he was for a moment as he looked around. His boots had dried out by the fire over night and he felt much better than he had for some days.

CHAPTER 10

*L*ord Llewelyn was recovering well from the fever that had nearly taken his life. The fresh sea air of Ynys Mon had been good for him and although he still needed his fighting staff for support and was often short of breath, he could feel his strength returning.

Under his command the hill fort had been strengthened with fighting men from all over the north west of the country. Some were little more than boys, looking for adventure but others were battle hardened warriors. The old warlord had shaped them into a formidable army, well trained and loyal. They were ready to defend their land, to the last man.

The narrow and treacherous stretch of dark blue water that separated the island from the rest of Wales also isolated them from news of the war. This meant that Llewelyn had to rely on messengers and knew that rumours spread quickly through the men of the tribes.

One such rumour had come to his hearing from his servant and retainer, Bryn, that the Gwyn were already advancing towards them, not as an army but using Saxon assassins to murder and kill. He dismissed Bryn's gossip as nonsense but was aware of the unsettling effect such talk would have on the super-stitious waiting men.

Llewelyn was alone in his cramped rooms at the hill fort, considering his next move, when there was a confident knock at the door. He had sent for Cadell, a good man and one of the many foreign mercenaries that now swelled their ranks. He went to the heavily studded oak door and opened it.

'Lord Llewelyn?'

'Cadell, come in,' said Llewelyn, closing the door behind him, 'I need to talk with you, in private.'

Cadell wore a black cloak and it suited him well. Mercenaries were not usually allowed to wear the black of a warrior but Llewelyn spotted the man's potential when he first arrived and granted his personal consent. Cadell's eyes were alert and quickly took in the sparse furnishings of the room, noting that the parchment on the table bore the royal seal.

Lord Llewelyn saw his glance and nodded. 'I have received word from the king. He has taken command of the castle at Flint to protect the eastern border with the Saxons, but mentions nothing of the threat from the Gwyn.'

'Are the Gwyn and the Saxons not one and the same?'

He looked at the mercenary. There was something about his manner that Llewelyn liked.

'Experienced fighting men like you are always welcome here, Cadell.'

'Thank you, my lord.'

'You have shown spirit, but the reason I wanted to see you was for your knowledge of the people of the south.'

'I've travelled through their lands, my lord, but cannot claim to know a great deal about the Gwyn.'

'You've heard that the warlord Vorath has gone after the Gwyn king?'

Cadell nodded. 'The men are full of talk of Lord Vorath. They say he will cut off the Gwyn from their border with the Saxons.'

'I know him well, Cadell, he will succeed.'

'The men also say that the Gwyn castle in the east has a thousand archers, trained with the longbow. Lord Vorath will not have an easy victory.'

'The men exaggerate. Vorath will take them by surprise, you mark my words, Cadell.'

Cadell watched with growing curiosity as Llewelyn folded the letter from the king then took a valuable parchment and spread it on the table. He sharpened a goose feather quill with his knife before producing a pot of black ink and began to draw an outline. At first Cadell was at a loss to understand the shape, then recognised it as Wales and nodded with appreciation. Lord Llewelyn was making a map.

'Here is the fort at Ynys Mon,' said Llewelyn, carefully drawing a circle within the outline of the island. 'The castle at Flint is close to here.' He drew a square on the north eastern coast. 'Now, Cadell, I need you to help me mark the places of the Gwyn, as best as you can recall?'

Cadell placed his finger to the outline of the south western point of the coast. 'There is a garrison at the castle here, at the town of Pembroke,' he suggested. He knew the garrison well, having lived and worked there, but remembered his allegiance to Sir Gwynfor. It would not do to be too helpful to the enemies of the Gwyn but he needed to earn Lord Llewelyn's confidence.

Llewelyn marked the castle with another square and drew a dashed line across the map at where he thought the southern boundary of the Du would be.

'There is another castle at a place called Caerphilly, here,' said Cadell.

'Where is the king's residence?'

'I have no idea,' lied Cadell, noting that the map omitted the finger of land that formed the peninsula where he had visited Pennard.

Llewelyn did not challenge him and they worked on the map

for another hour or so, adding landmarks, hills and tracks where they could until the warlord seemed satisfied.

'I am grateful for your help,' he said. 'I plan to use this map when I leave for the south.'

'When are you going, my lord?'

'Right away. I have someone close to the Gwyn queen who will help me find her. When I do, this war will be quickly over. I feel it will be soon.'

Cadell looked at the elderly warlord and made a mental note not to underestimate him. He also had to find a way to send the information had had gained to Sir Gwynfor, before it was too late. Even as he thought about returning to the south he knew he never would. He had won the respect of the people of the Du. Sir Gwynfor paid him well but treated him like a servant. Cadell had become a warrior of the Du.

Llewelyn's servant Bryn was disappointed he would not be accompanying the warlord on his journey to the south but was reconciled with the knowledge that his time would come. He whistled an old Du song tunelessly as he packed his master's few possessions.

Bryn was fond of the old man and would be glad to see him safely back. Without telling Llewelyn, he carefully removed the old warlord's sacrifice knife, used in secret Druid rituals, from its hiding place and placed it in his master's pack, for good luck.

Llewelyn had selected a band of trusted warriors to travel with him and left on the first boat to the mainland early the next morning. Before heading south, they rode to visit Queen Rhiannon. Llewelyn had been close to Rhiannon's father in his youth and felt a close bond to her after his untimely death.

Rhiannon was pleased to see him. 'Come, Llewelyn, I want you to see Prince Evan.'

The baby prince was by the fireside with Rhiannon's sister Ceinwen. He smiled at the sight of the man dressed in black.

'The child has your eyes, Rhiannon, and reminds me a little of your father.'

'He has the ways of the king, Lord Llewelyn,' said Ceinwen. She too remembered the old warlord and would always be grateful for his protection when they were young girls.

'I've heard from the king,' said Llewelyn, 'He has asked me to protect the west.'

Rhiannon was not surprised, Gethin had told her of his plans before leaving for Flint. 'Will you stay and be our guest for the night?'

'I must see my men and horses are looked after, then I would be honoured, Rhiannon.

After he had left Ceinwen looked at her sister. 'Do you think it would be right to ask Llewelyn to look out for Hywel?

'Of course, though you need not worry so much Ceinwen, I'm sure Hywel can look after himself.

❧

The garrison army of Pembroke received orders from the king to march to the port of Abertawe. As well as being able to directly support the king, from this central base they could march quickly in any direction and better protect the border with the north.

The castle was busy with activity as men were divided between those who would stay to defend the west and the men who had been chosen to make the sixty mile march. A long caravan of wagons and carts were loaded with supplies and the men assembled in straggling rows outside the castle, their breath misting in the frosty morning air.

Some had made the mistake of celebrating their departure in the town's taverns and looked worse for it, but their commander was more concerned to see that none had deserted, rather than face the war. This was no easy task, as the sheer number of new men brought to the castle for training meant that the records were unreliable.

Once he was satisfied they were all present and correct, the commander give the order to march. The long procession made its way out of the town, towards the open countryside. The men at the front struck up an old Gwyn marching song, which helped them keep up their spirits. Some girls from the village called good luck to them and small children ran alongside until they had passed the town boundary.

The long column of men arrived at the town of Carmarthen after thirty miles of marching, tired and hungry. As one of the main training towns of the area since Roman times, Carmarthen had many merchants, so some who could afford it were able to supplement the very basic rations or pay for a room.

Others made the mistake of spending the little pay they had in the town's taverns and had to sleep in a barn or even in the open. In the morning they were greeted by thunderous skies and a stiff wind, and the commander had trouble again ensuring that all the men resumed their march to Abertawe.

～

Lord Llewelyn said farewell to the queen and her sister and led his men towards the mountains, heading directly south. He'd wondered if he would ever ride with the warriors again and thanked his gods for answering his prayers. His old bones would suffer on the long ride ahead but if he had to die before he saw his lands again, he would make sure it was a warrior's death.

Unlike Lord Vorath's men, who rode the mighty black fighting horses, Lord Llewelyn preferred the Welsh Cob. The legacy of Roman occupation of their land long ago was that the invader's Arabian horses bred with the native mountain ponies, producing a hardy horse, with spirit. His own black stallion was a good jumper, able to carry a substantial weight on his back for many hours.

Llewelyn knew his men thought the horse too old for battle but they had been through a lot together. Although he would not discuss the matter, some of his favourite stories were about how the old horse had saved his life on more than one occasion.

Once he had been alerted to an impending ambush by the stallion's ears, which twitched at the unusual sounds, just in time for Lord Llewelyn and his men, who pounced instead on the would be ambushers.

Llewelyn's stallion had also fathered many fine black horses, and the warlord had spent years improving the breed for the harsh land, training the Cobs to haul heavy loads on the upland farms and timber to the top of the hill fort.

His tough black horses could cover great distances, matching Vorath's heavy war horse's stride for stride at the trot. They also had the advantage of being trained to drink well when water was available and, if necessary, press on when it was not. The Cob was also content to graze the rough pasture they were riding through, so there was no need to find food for them on the long journey.

The mountains on the skyline broadly followed the dotted line on the map he had drawn, and as he looked across the open ground to them he recalled the adventures of his youth. He had told the stories many times, of fighting off invaders who came by sea and over those mountains, sometimes following rumours of Du gold and silver.

The tribes of the Du had seen off the foreigners, each time becoming more skilled at their own form of warfare, using their knowledge of the land. In his heart Lord Llewelyn knew that the Gwyn were not so different from him. They had more men, with better weapons and powerful allies. He would never admit it to anyone but as he rode ever further south he prayed to the ancient secret gods.

~

Elvina was shocked at the sudden death of the Du warrior. She looked into his face and saw a handsome man, with kind eyes. She watched as the guards buried the man where he had fallen. It was hard work as the ground was stony and they had no proper tools to dig with.

The grave was shallow, so Elvina ordered them to make a cairn of stones over it to protect the body from scavenging animals. It was the least they could do. She had never intended him to be killed, as any knowledge he may have had of the positions or the battle plans of the Du had died with him.

Elvina wondered about the death of the man she had never known, if he had a family, a wife, or children, when one of her guards interrupted her thoughts.

'We must go, my lady. There will be more where he came from.'

Elvina was torn between wanting to head back to meet with Sir Gwynfor and the tantalising prospect of seeing the mysterious lands in the north. They were so close to the border and the idea that the king could forbid her to go there simply strengthened her resolve to do it. She was the sister of the king of all England and was used to getting her way but there was another reason.

Elvina loved her brother and shared a terrible secret with him that created a bond between them. When their father King Edward died Athelstan was not the first in line to succeed, as they had an elder brother, Aelfweard. She was the only person other than Athelstan to know that Aelfweard's sudden death before he could be crowned was not an accident.

She could have sent a message to her brother to help her become the queen of all Wales but she wanted to succeed without his help. The key to this would be to learn more about the strengths and weaknesses of the people called the Du, but most of all she was intrigued by their queen.

All Bethan had been able to tell her was her name, Rhiannon, and that she live on the far north coast, not in a palace or a castle but in a simple house.

'I wish to travel to within sight of the lands of the Du,' she said to the guard, 'Please bring the others.'

The guard looked concerned. 'We have orders from the king to ensure your safety.'

'Now you have new orders,' the Du are coming and this may be the only chance we have to see this place that men are prepared to die for.

Against the advice of their guards, Elvina and Bethan followed the path the warrior of the Du had taken. The ground became hilly and more densely wooded. Bethan was becoming nervous. 'I think we should turn back, my lady, there could be an ambush.'

'Yes, I wanted to see the country on the other side of these woods but they seem to go on forever.'

'I have asked Owen to wait behind. If we do not return before sunset he is to raise the alarm and organise a search.'

One of the guards had been sent to scout ahead and was the first to find the sunlit clearing in the woods with the marked grave. He could see it had been freshly made, and took the sword out of the ground to examine it.

As he did so, he saw the silver crucifix. It looked valuable and he considered taking it but he was a superstitious man and it seemed wrong to take it from a grave. Instead he went back along the trail and explained to the queen about the grave and showed her the crucifix.

'I know this, she said quietly, I have seen it around the neck of Bishop Cledwin.'

~

Bishop Emrys lived at the church close to Rhos Point, a finger of land jutting out into the Irish Sea. The old chapel was founded by a 6th Century Saint, St Trillo, but Emrys knew the altar was built over a pre-Christian well and it had originally been King Maelgwn's church, visited as a place of Christian pilgrimage for the holy water.

He had commissioned a comfortable lodge to be built next to the church and it was here that he was relaxing with a large goblet of his best wine and reflecting on his recent visit to Queen Rhiannon.

Bishop Emrys had looked at Rhiannon's writing and complimented her on her progress.

'Thank you Emrys,' she had said, 'I am grateful for your teaching. It is important for a queen to be able to read and write the language of her people.'

He had been waiting for such a moment and chose his words carefully.

'I fear our knowledge will be lost if it is not written soon.' His words had the desired effect, as he noticed her eyes went to the old oak chest where he knew she kept her secret writing. She had smiled and took the key, opening the compartment where she hid her papers. Pulling the first page from the growing pile of parchment, she handed it to him.

'I have been doing my best to write the history of our people.'

Emrys remembered reading her vivid and passionately written account of the earliest days of the tribes. She had looked at him with a new fondness. His patience teaching her to read and write had been repaid many times over, as the queen now looked forward to his visits to feed her own hunger for learning. Emrys smiled to himself. If he had not been a bishop the king would never have let them spend so much time together.

His peace was disturbed by a knock on the door. He opened it and recognised one of his young priests. A pale man with darting eyes and a shaved head, he was leading a pack mule and looked relieved to see the bishop.

'You are a hard man to find, Bishop Emrys!'

'In the Lord's name, it is a surprise to see you at this hour.' Emrys helped him to take the mule to the rear of the lodge, where there was a small stable. 'You travel alone? It is a dangerous time for such a long journey. Did you know there is a war starting?'

'That is why I am here, Bishop Emrys. I found Bishop Cledwin of St Davids, who had lost his way and have given him sanctuary in my chapel.' He looked grim. 'I fear he cannot stay there much longer but he asked me to see if you would meet him on neutral ground, to talk about how the position of the Church in regard to the war.'

Emrys nodded. He had no liking for Bishop Cledwin, but he was a wealthy man of some influence in the south and it could be useful to have a closer alliance with him if the tide of the war turned in the favour of the Gwyn. 'You are welcome to my modest home. I have no servants here but can make some mutton broth to warm you.'

'Thank you Bishop Emrys, may the lord be with you.'

In the morning they set out together, taking the drover's road to save time. It was a long journey so they were tired when they arrived at the little stone chapel, to find Bishop Cledwin of the Gwyn kneeling at his prayers. He looked up when he saw them.

'Bishop Emrys, it has been a long time. You look well.'

'So do you, Bishop Cledwin, so do you.' Emrys made a sign to the priest, who made his excuses and left them.

Cledwin looked at the Du bishop. 'Thank you for travelling so far to see me, Emrys. I will come straight to the point. We both know this war is going to change everything.'

'You are right, Cledwin, so what do you propose?'

'When the Gwyn secure a victory over your king I will see to it that you and your priests are treated well.'

'You seem sure of the outcome of this war, Cledwin?'

Cledwin looked at him, making a judgement. 'Privately, I am not,' he confided. 'Bishop Renfrew has worked for an alliance with the Saxons, yet so far I see little outcome from his efforts.'

'You have a Saxon queen?'

'One woman is not going to shift the balance of power in this country.'

'I know you well enough, Cledwin, to be sure there is a price for your offer?'

'You are right, Bishop Emrys. I need you to help me meet in secret with your king.'

Bishop Emrys was surprised to hear Cledwin's request. 'With what purpose?'

'If the war is won by the Du, I need to be certain that my lands at St David's are safe. I know, Emrys, that if your warriors reach St Davids you could do nothing to stop them. It has to be the king, he is the only one they would listen to.'

'Why do you think the king of the Du would bargain with a bishop of the Gwyn?'

'I have information, Emrys. Vir sapiens et fortis est et vir doctus robustus et validus!'

'Proverbs from your Vulgate bible? A wise man is strong, yet a man of knowledge increases strength.'

'Exactly. My knowledge is my greatest asset.'

'You would side with the Du?'

'The Church does not take sides, Emrys, we respect any king who rules Wales.'

'It will not be easy for you to see the king. He is organising the men in the east and may not return for some weeks.'

Cledwin looked at him with shrewd eyes. 'The queen then?'

'I think the queen could be persuaded to see you, Cledwin.'

They shook hands on the deal, unaware that their actions would soon have the country in turmoil.

CHAPTER 11

*B*ishop Cledwin decided to stay at the isolated chapel for a few days, as he could not resist the opportunity to find out more about the plans of the Du. He had been grateful to the pale young priest for his hospitality and for arranging the meeting with Bishop Emrys.

As well as finding a way to do what he could to secure the safety of his lands at St Davids, the bishop learned much that would be of value to his neighbour, Sir Gwynfor of Picton.

With a little careful prompting, the priest told Cledwin he had heard King Gethin was rallying a great army of warriors to the east, at the castle in Flint. Cledwin confided in return that there was a plan for the Saxon allies of the Gwyn to invade the north.

It was not entirely true but he knew the priest travelled widely and hoped that word would spread. If it reached the Du king there was just a chance he would be forced to keep enough of his warriors back to defend their eastern border.

He had also found out from the priest that there was a Du encampment near a natural spring not far from the little chapel. The men of the tribes would stop there for water and to rest their horses, so although it was within Du territory, Bishop Cledwin hoped he would be able to visit without drawing attention to himself.

He could not take his own white horse, as there was a risk it would mark him as a man of the Gwyn. Instead he borrowed a heavy black woollen cloak from the priest to keep out the chill of the wind and proceeded on foot. Cledwin removed the valuable gold rings he always wore and remained unshaven.

It also helped that he looked too old and out of condition to be a fighting man, so when he arrived at the encampment the men were indifferent to him. No one asked where he had come from or what he was doing there, and he knew better than to volunteer the information.

The nomadic Du had few permanent towns or villages, preferring instead to build temporary shelters that could be easily transported. This meant much of the land was common grazing and farmers would simply move to the best areas with the seasons.

As Cledwin explored the camp, smoke from the many fires caused the bishop to cough and made his eyes water. Worst of all was the unpleasant smell reaching his nose, which he realised must be caused by the lack of proper drainage.

Cledwin was a fastidious man and had personally overseen the refinements to his home at St Davids. The farms had all been surrounded with fences or hedges and gates to keep the livestock safe. Nearly all the original wooden buildings had been replaced with local stone with roofs of slate.

He was fortunate in that Roman invaders had long ago shown the benefits of the irrigation and drainage systems he had built to serve his lands. He was particularly proud of his bath, which had been made for him by the town blacksmith. As he explored the Du encampment he realised that the Gwyn now lived a very different life in the south.

He was disappointed to find that most of the men in the camp knew or cared little of the war. Cledwin considered returning home but realised that it would only be a matter of time before he found out something of value, so he paid a silver coin for the use of one of the empty huts.

It contained little more than a rickety bed and it was here he waited for news of the Du, passing the time by eavesdropping on the people coming and going through the camp and slowly building a picture of their lives.

Cledwin's patience was rewarded when a noisy group of young warriors arrived and soon began drinking in what passed for a tavern in the camp. He bought a mug of rough beer and sat listening to their bragging, quickly learning that the blond haired man at the centre of the group was their leader, called Tristan.

It was easy to overhear that they were from the castle at Flint as they argued about the merits of returning back or joining a warlord. Cledwin was stunned to hear that the warlord was already on his way, with the best of the Du warriors, to find and kill King Gwayne.

~

As Lord Llewelyn and his men approached the boundary with the lands of the Gwyn he said silent thanks to the gods that his illness had not returned. When he first became ill those around him had readily accepted his explanation that he suffered from a fever, secretly Llewelyn feared it was something much worse.

He'd been in constant pain and the combination of poor appetite and loss of sleep weakened him. He had taken potions made from willow bark and boiled valerian roots which eased the pain a little, but at one time he could barely walk without the aid of a stick.

His solution had been to carry a heavy wooden fighting staff to support him during his recovery. Llewelyn found that exercises with the staff helped his muscles regain their strength and he quickly became skilled at swinging the heavy staff in the complicated figure of eight that could be both defensive and an attacking technique. At nearly eight feet long Llewelyn's fighting staff it was a formidable weapon, allowing him to stay well out of range of any sword thrust.

His servant Bryn doubled as the blacksmith at the hill fort and had fashioned a savagely sharp metal point, that was now fixed to one end, so that when on horseback the warlord could use the staff underarm, like a lance. He carried this staff with him now, in preference to a sword or spear, as in practice he had found that the point could easily pierce all but the best chain mail armour.

Lord Llewelyn and his men travelled under the cover of dusk and through the night, finding good hiding places to sleep during the daylight hours. This was becoming increasingly difficult as they moved deeper into the land of the Gwyn.

Llewelyn wanted to have the advantage of surprise but was sure that word of their presence would travel quickly through the countryside if they were seen. He knew there was a sizeable garrison in the west, so stealth was an essential part of his plan to establish a safe base from which his men could make their raids.

They had been living off the land for days. The warriors knew how to find water from the clear springs in the hills but although they had seen plenty of the wild rabbits which were a legacy of the Roman occupation, they had been unlucky with the snares they set.

Their hunger overcame their caution when they discovered a fat sheep, which they slaughtered and roasted over a blazing fire. Llewelyn knew this was a risk but his men had to eat and they had long since exhausted the supplies they carried from the north.

King Gethin had only given Lord Llewelyn and his men general orders, leaving the moment of attack to the judgement of his warlords, but they knew what was expected of them. The soldiers of the Gwyn were to be prevented from crossing the wilderness at any cost. When the moment was right he would unleash the army waiting at the hill fort. He was to do whatever it took.

~

Queen Elvina returned to Aberteifi, a quiet fishing village on the banks of the River Teifi by the western coast, where she was hoping to meet Sir Gwynfor. She was disappointed to find he was not there and there was no message for her. As she had no way to contact him, all Elvina could do was take Bethan into her confidence and explain the reason for them staying.

Bethan understood and soon found them rooms in a slate-roofed farmhouse overlooking the sea. The guards kept constant watch over the queen, as there were rumoured sightings of Du warriors in the hills. There was also a risk of invaders from the sea, so guards were posted to keep a lookout from the high cliffs overlooking the shoreline.

They were close to St Davids, so Elvina sent one of her guards to summon Bishop Cledwin to see her. She was curious to know if the silver crucifix was the same one she'd seen being worn by the bishop, and if so, how the warrior had come by it.

The guard was an intelligent man and greatly admired the queen. He easily found the bishop's well appointed home and knocked on the door, which was answered by Anwen, the bishop's housekeeper.

'I am on a mission for Queen Elvina,' explained the guard. 'I have an important message for Bishop Cledwin.'

Anwen looked at the guard, her welcoming smile turning to a look of concern. 'I am afraid he has been away for nearly a week now. I don't know when he will return.'

The guard was disappointed, as he did not want to fail the queen at this simple task. 'Where will I find him, please?'

'He was going to check the northern boundary of the property.' She was curious now. 'Can you tell me why the queen wants to see him? I am the bishop's housekeeper so I may be able to help you.'

The guard hesitated, then took the silver crucifix from his pocket. 'Do you know if this belongs to the bishop?'

Anwen took the crucifix and recognised the distinctive Celtic engraving immediately. 'It does, how did you come by it?' There was a sudden sadness in her voice.

'I had best come in,' said the guard. 'This is a private matter of concern to the queen.'

Anwen showed him to the Bishop's study, her mind running through the possibilities, none of which were good.

'I regret to tell you this was found on a newly dug grave, close to our border with the north.'

Anwen tried her best to remain composed but tears formed in her eyes. 'I tried to persuade him to stay here, that it was too dangerous to travel in the wilderness alone at his age. Do you think he was robbed and killed?'

The guard felt pity for the woman. She had clearly been fond of the bishop. 'The grave was marked by an old sword. One of the other guards said it was the sword of a warrior of the Gwyn.'

Anwen gasped. 'Elfred!'

The guard looked confused.

'Bishop Cledwin gave an old Gwyn sword to a soldier from our farm who was on his way to watch for the Du.' She looked again at the silver crucifix held tightly in her hand. 'I can't be sure but he may have given this to him, it was the sort of thing the bishop would do.'

'His name was Elfred?'

'He was a good man,' Anwen felt relief that the bishop was probably alive but great sadness at the death of the young farmer. She had known him all his life.

Anwen looked at him with sad brown eyes. 'You said you are on a mission for the queen. What interest does the queen have in this?

'We were escorting the queen when we found the man who killed this Elfred. It was a warrior of the Du.'

'I need your help to find Bishop Cledwin, he has to be told.'

~

Sir Gwynfor was angry to be roused from his sleep but decided to check the condition of the horses for himself. Gwynfor had grown up around horses and knew that colic could be fatal.

He had lost some of his best horses to colic in the past and although walking them was known to help relieve the pain, he didn't want to risk them. He realised he would have to delay his meeting with the queen while the horses recovered, and consoled himself with the knowledge that she would wait for him, if it was possible for her to do so.

Several of his best white horses had been showing the signs of colic, pawing the ground and kicking, so Gwynfor suspected the problem was with their feed or water. At the back of his mind he worried that he had overdone their training.

Colic was a fact of life but could be brought on by over-working horses too quickly. He carefully picked his way through the tents of his sleeping men in the darkness, following the groom who had woken him. Something was wrong with the horses but not what he expected. They were restless and excited, something had spooked them.

Gwynfor called for two men to follow him and sent another to fetch his sword. They began a cautious patrol of the perimeter of the camp. It was a cold and moonless night and even once his eyes became accustomed to the dark, Sir Gwynfor strained to see into the trees that encircled the clearing they had chosen for the camp.

The threat of ambush by the Du had been on all of their minds as they had pressed closer to the wilderness and many of the men had seen what the Du were capable of. They took no prisoners.

He was just cursing himself for being as jumpy as his horses when the Du attacked. The man next to him yelled as a spear hit him square in the chest. Several burning arrows flashed into the camp, setting fire to the makeshift cotton tents where men were sleeping.

One of Sir Gwynfor's most trusted riders screamed in sudden agony as another well aimed spear plunged into his back. There was no clue to where the Du were firing from, as the arrows and spears seemed to be coming from all around them.

Sir Gwynfor shouted for the man he had sent to retrieve his longsword but the whole camp was in panic, all the hours of training forgotten in an instant. He dashed to his tent and grabbed his sword, throwing the scabbard to one side. Gwynfor hesitated for a moment, not sure what to do, how to fight an enemy they couldn't see.

The Du had yet to even show themselves but had managed to create chaos amongst his men. Someone shouted for help and he realised that one of the burning arrows had set fire to the hay and straw for the horses that were now violently thrashing at their tethers to escape the flames.

He ran to them and slashed through the leather straps with the sharp blade of his sword. One of the horses reared up in alarm and kicked him hard in the head before bolting into the trees.

As he watched them go he saw sinister dark shapes lit momentarily by the flames. Du warriors, on horses as black as the night, using the cover of darkness to kill and maim as they pleased.

A sudden memory came to him. As a boy he had nightmares, terrified by Archbishop Renfrew's description of purgatory. The peaceful night had turned into a living hell. Warm blood began flowing down his face from the wound where he had been kicked by the horse and he felt a surge of anger at the raiders. This was his land.

'To me!' Gwynfor shouted at the top of his voice. Heads turned in his direction and the men looked alarmed to see him wounded but glad of his leadership. 'Find whatever weapons you can and form a circle,' he yelled, 'We need to hold our ground.'

Men began joining him in the clearing, standing with swords and bows ready. Smoke from the fires drifted across the camp and stung their eyes, making it even harder to see the charge when it came.

Du warriors appeared out of the night, throwing more deadly spears as they galloped. Another of Gwynfor's men went down with a loud yell, the force of the spear throw knocking him from his feet. For a moment it looked as if the warriors would ride right over the soldiers of the Gwyn, then they turned at the last moment and slashed down with viciously sharp swords.

Sir Gwynfor swung his longsword in a practised arc and cut the right arm from the closest of the riders, then turned and slashed the neck of another's black horse, which collapsed to the ground, trapping its rider by his leg. Gwynfor didn't hesitate and sliced the helpless fallen rider's head from his body.

Even his own men were shocked for a moment by the knight's brutality, then they began to show the Du what the months of training had achieved. Gwynfor's archers now had targets they could see and wasted no time, launching a salvo of deadly arrows that brought down another two riders.

The swordsmen hacked and sliced at their enemy, slowly turning the tide of the battle and Gwynfor realised that he had been lucky. This was a small raiding party but many men had been left dead or dying. He had allowed them to be caught unprepared and made a mental note to make sure it would not happen again.

Lord Llewelyn held back from the first wave of the attack but now urged his old horse into a gallop and lowered his wooden staff with its deadly sharpened iron tip into position. He charged the Gwyn soldiers, ignoring the arrows that zipped past as he chose his target, the knight wearing the white cape, spattered with the blood of warriors of the Du. Their eyes met and there was a silent understanding that cut through the noise and chaos of the fighting. One of them was about to die.

Sir Gwynfor felt unexpected admiration for the bravery of the old Du warrior charging towards him. The man was dressed entirely in black and seemed to emerge from the darkness of the trees like an apparition.

His eyes had a look of steely determination that showed he was feared nothing and was prepared to die fighting. As if in slow motion, Gwynfor's powerful two handed swing of the longsword sliced through the air and smashed into the warrior's lance, cutting cleanly through the wooden shaft.

Llewelyn felt himself falling. He had been lifted from the saddle with the force of the blow, feeling at least one of his ribs crack as he crashed heavily to the ground. The knight was distracted for a moment as he parried the sword another of the riders.

This was the chance Llewelyn needed. What was left of his heavy wooden fighting staff was still within reach and he grabbed for it. With one hand at the butt and the other a shoulder width above, Llewelyn raise the heavy staff above his head, wincing with the sharp pain from his ribs, then brought it down as hard as he could on the back of the Gwyn knight.

Sir Gwynfor saw the blow approaching out of the corner of his eye and moved just in time to avoid most of its force but still painfully winded as it thumped into his unprotected side.

Instinctively he swung his sword at the warrior's head but the old Du was ready for him and deftly deflected the attack, then reversed the swing and knocked the sword from his hands. The knight did not even see the next blow coming. He was reaching for the fallen sword when the heavy fighting staff broke his back.

Lord Llewelyn looked down at his enemy. He seemed unable to move his arms or legs, or even speak, but his eyes were fixed on the warlord with a look which Llewelyn mistook for a plea for him to stop the pain. He reached inside his black tunic, found the small sacrificial knife his servant Bryn had thoughtfully packed and quickly ended the life of the champion of the Gwyn.

CHAPTER 12

*H*ayden questioned a survivor of the Du attack and couldn't believe that his master Sir Gwynfor, the champion of the Gwyn, was dead. The man was confused about the details but had a terrified look in his eyes as he described the events of the night. He thought he had escaped the murderous warriors only because he had been knocked unconscious and left for dead.

One of Sir Gwynfor's most trusted outriders, he had suffered serious sword wounds that the apothecary had stitched up as best he could. Hayden was hopeful that the man would live. He'd lost a lot of blood but they were fortunate he was strong enough to find his way home and warn of the attack.

As Sir Gwynfor's assistant, Hayden had always needed to plan and prepare for the knight but now he felt the true weight of his responsibility. He had hoped one day to become a knight himself but never expected to command the west so soon, or without Sir Gwynfor to guide him.

He sent a fast rider to inform the king of the loss of his champion and called for the captain of the guard to help him consider his options. The captain looked stressed and tired, as none of them had slept since the news of the Du attack. A burly, short tempered man with a reputation for strictly enforcing discipline, he probably thought Hayden too young to be in command.

'I need your help,' said Hayden when the captain arrived. 'You have experience of fighting the Du?'

'I have, but I did not expect them to take Sir Gwynfor so soon.'

'None of us did,' agreed Hayden. 'We need to be more prepared.'

'The castle guards are on full alert,' said the captain. 'We can hold Pembroke safe but I need the garrison to return as soon as they can.'

Hayden nodded. The main garrison force from Pembroke had left to support the king and could not return in time to help deal with the Du raiders. 'Good, there is no telling how long we have.'

'What do you plan to do?' asked the captain. 'We have mostly untrained men, with no experience of fighting.'

Hayden had an idea forming in his mind but it was high risk. He looked at the Captain. 'Sir Gwynfor and his men would have put up a good fight against the raiders.'

The captain agreed. 'The Du will have also suffered losses and injuries, they won't have gone far.'

'I need your help. I will take a group of our best men and see if we can find them.'

'Yes, I will come myself,
I know which men we should bring with us.'

'Thank you captain but I need you to stay here in command.'

'I understand,' replied the captain. He looked at Hywel with a new respect. 'You need to move quickly, they may have sent for reinforcements.'

'We'll leave in one hour,' said Hayden. 'Take care to keep this plan secret, we need to have the advantage of surprise. He watched the man go, wondering if he was right to leave him behind.

True to his word, the captain had found half a dozen battle hardened swordsmen, dangerous looking soldiers all keen for some action. Hywel grinned at the sight of them and ordered they should have the pick of the horses and arm themselves well, as they had a hard ride and a tough battle lay ahead.

He personally chose to wear the longsword Sir Gwynfor spent so many hours training him to use, and led the men towards the border, retracing the steps of the lone survivor of the fight with the Du. The wounded soldier had given them as much information as he could remember but it was still difficult to be sure they were on the right track.

When they thought they were close, Hayden ordered the men to wait while he sent two of them to scout for their enemy from the top of the highest ridge. There was no sign of the Du but Hayden had a feeling that they would not be far away, so they rode on, staying to open ground where they could, aware of the danger of ambush from behind any cover.

They reached the wooded area near the scene of the battle and stopped, listening for any noise. Hayden was struck by the eerie silence of the woods. Even the birds seemed to have stopped singing. He held his finger over his mouth as a sign to the men to remain silent and they continued, riding as quietly as they could until the narrow path through the trees divided into two.

Hayden held up his hand for them to stop. They were waiting for him to decide what to do when the silence was broken by the distant whinny of a horse. Their own horses pricked up their ears and the men tensed, aware that the noise could be their enemy approaching.

The sound seemed to come from direction of the woods closest to the right hand path, so Hayden made his decision. There was no way of knowing how many Du warriors they could face so he was reluctant to split his men, yet if they took the wrong path they could lose valuable time.

More noises could be heard as they rode closer to the hiding place of the Du and each time Hayden held up his hand for them to stop, while he strained to listen. Voices, deep and hushed but clearly audible, drifted through the dense trees and he knew they could only be the warriors they were searching for.

As far as he could tell it sounded as if the enemy were not far away from them, heading north. He was relieved they had not taken the wrong path but felt secretly anxious about what they were about to do. It had seemed a good, if risky plan but now he wondered how he could possibly succeed where Sir Gwynfor, with all his skill and experience, had failed.

Hayden and his men rounded a bend in the track and suddenly had a clear view of the track through the woods ahead. There were riders in the distance, dressed in black. They seemed to be completely unaware of his men approaching and there was something odd about the way they were riding.

Several of the black horses were carrying two men and some were hunched awkwardly. Hayden suddenly realised why. They were far from unscathed from their fight with Sir Gwynfor. Normally he would have hesitated to order an attack on men wounded or injured but he needed every advantage he could and ordered his men to charge.

The silence of the forest was shattered with the staccato drum beat of thudding hooves and the blood curdling war cries of the charging men. The Du riders span round, realising they were under attack and turned to face them, some quickly dismounting and dashing for the cover of the trees.

Hayden unsheathed his longsword and urged his men forward, a shaft of sunlight flashing from the long blade as he lifted it high above his head with his right hand. He focussed on his target, as Sir Gwynfor had told him to do so many times. It was the leader of the warriors, an older man on a fine black horse, who was shouting urgently to his men, making sure they stood their ground, spears and bows at the ready, waiting for Hayden and his men to get in range.

As the two sides closed one of Hayden's men dropped from his saddle, an arrow in his chest from Du archers in the trees. Another was hit in the shoulder and yelled with alarm with the pain.

Hayden's fear of the Du was replaced in an instant with a surge of anger. He had been trained to use the longsword on horseback against riders wearing armour and slashed down with all his might. The blow cut deep through the black wool cape and tunic into unprotected flesh and bone, violently ending the life of the legendary warlord of the Du in a single deadly stroke.

~

Lord Vorath loved the wilderness, even when the mist swirled around the mountains and the rain seemed relentless, as it did now. He had ridden since early morning with his men to the heart of the country and was looking forward to something good to eat.

They were like brothers to him, every one chosen for his bravery, prowess in battle and loyalty to the people of the Du. Ddraig, his black warhorse, seemed as fresh now as when they had set out on the long ride and their spirits were high and they would be rewarded well once they had driven the Gwyn out of the south.

Delwyn had been soaked to the skin by the heavy rain and sought shelter in a small wood. He was hungry and tired and beginning to wonder what he was doing there, alone. Feeling thirsty, Delwyn immersed his leather water bottle in the creek that ran through the wood and drank deeply of the clear fresh water.

It tasted good and reminded him of his hunger. He had been looking for a croft or farmstead where he could find food and dry his clothes but the area seemed uninhabited, so for now he decided to rest and wait for the others to catch up. It had been a mistake to allow them to fall so far behind.

He grinned at the realisation that he had managed to lose an army. With only the sun and stars to rely on for direction, the wilderness was so vast it was easy to become disorientated. He had been counting the days and knew it was over a week since he set out, but had no idea how far away the rest of them could be.

He was just wondering if they had also decided to stop for the night when he heard the unmistakeable sound of horses approaching. With great relief Delwyn gathered up his few possessions and started back down the path he had been following, glad to have company again.

He had been too quick to volunteer for scouting duties and would ask to be replaced. He missed the company of the others and had seen how dangerous and unpredictable the Du could be. He heard a shout and was just about to shout back when he realised that the sound had come from behind him.

For a moment he wondered if the army had somehow gone past him when he was resting, but he knew it was impossible. He was not going to be caught in open ground, so raced back to the woods where he had been a moment before.

Diving for cover, he brushed against nettles that stung his arms and hands painfully but served to help him focus on his situation. The sound of hooves was closer now, the voices of the riders still too far away to make out the words but he had been lucky to have any warning.

Delwyn counted eight arrows remaining in his quiver and wished he had more. He carefully moved to have a better view of the enemy and realised his choice of the wooded area had been a good one, as anyone approaching would have to cross open ground while he could easily remain hidden.

The Du warriors suddenly emerged into the clearing and Delwyn was surprised by their appearance. He had been expecting them to look like the men of the tribes he had sometimes seen in the south, but these were clearly fighting men, armed with swords and spears and dressed in black tunics which gave them a sinister look.

Delwyn froze where he was, hoping that they would simply pass his hiding place, but the man at the front was heading directly for him. Too late Delwyn realised that they could be looking for the creek to replenish their supply of fresh water, just as he had.

Delwyn had to stand to use his longbow, so he chose a giant oak and quickly moved behind it, keeping his bow in line with the trunk and reaching into his quiver for an arrow. Four horsemen of the Du were now crossing the clearing towards him and he could see more behind them.

For a moment he considered surrender but he had heard gruesome tales of what the Du did with prisoners. Delwyn stealthily brought the Longbow round to the firing position. Again he could hear in his head the familiar words of command from Kane.

'Ready the bow!' He brought it to full height, bracing his body against the trunk of the tree that was shielding him from the enemy.

'Nock!' Delwyn quickly fitted a long arrow into the taut hemp string.

'Mark!' He sighted carefully on the target, allowing for the gentle crosswind and distance as best he was able to.

'Draw!' He pulled the bowstring back effortlessly as he had been trained.

'Loose!'

Drawing back the powerful bowstring in a fluid motion he sighted and loosed the arrow. It thudded into the belly of the closest Du warrior, causing him to call out in alarm and fall heavily from his horse.

He lay unmoving on the ground but his companions acted

quickly, two dismounting and dragging the wounded man back to cover. The remaining riders charged towards the trees, crouching low in the saddle and making rapid changes of direction to provide the hardest possible target.

They remained silent for a moment then the woods echoed to shouts between the Du warriors. It was something that Delwyn couldn't make out, the language of the tribes, the old Welsh tongue. Someone called out a reply and there was another cry of pain.

Delwyn guessed that they must have pulled out the barbed arrow. Delwyn thought he could see a dark shape approaching his position from the left. He considered waiting until he was sure of his mark, unwilling to risk wasting an arrow with only seven left, then fired and instantly regretted the sight of the arrow plunging into the trees.

Delwyn looked over his own shoulder. There were more trees not far away but it would mean crossing another clearing, so he decided to move to the furthest tree of his cover. From his new vantage point he could see more Du warriors starting to encircle him from the right.

He took careful aim and fired at the closest. It was a good shot as the man fell to the ground without a sound and others froze where they were. Six arrows left. He looked down at his sword and wondered how well he would be able to use it in hand to hand fighting. He gripped his bow, taking comfort from its familiar strength and power and said a silent prayer. It was just a matter of time before the others caught up, so his best hope was to wait and see what the Du did next.

The answer terrified him. A dozen black clad warriors charged the woods at once, some armed with swords and others with long spears tipped with sharp iron points. It seemed they thought the woods were full of Gwyn soldiers, as they looked ready for a fight.

Delwyn fired three arrows as quickly as he could. Kane's

lessons had been well learned, as the first hit a man square in the chest, throwing him onto his back. The second went clean through a warrior's leg, causing him to drop his weapon and fall to his knees. The charge faltered then a roar went up, the battle cry of the Du, covering the ground at a run.

He had three arrows left. Beginning to panic, he failed to aim with enough care. One went right over the heads of the charging men, with the next falling short, thudding to the ground in front of them. With just one arrow remaining Delwyn dropped his bow and drew his sword. He had chosen to become a bowman because he had no stomach for close combat.

Surrounded by Du warriors, he could not expect to kill them all so surrender was his only option. He put his hands in the air and waited. The end was swift. Warlord Vorath's sword pinned him to the tree and he felt searing pain quickly followed by relief. His dying thought was to notice how raindrops had settled on the leaves, glistening in the autumn sunlight like tiny jewels.

Bishop Cledwin had more than enough information about the Du and decided to return to the south to warn King Gwayne. When he arrived at the small chapel the young priest was pleased to see him safely back.

'Welcome, Bishop Cledwin, I was concerned for you.'

Cledwin smiled, 'They can be a little boisterous but I have the protection of the church and travel with God.'

'A messenger was looking for you, Bishop.'

'My meeting with Queen Rhiannon?'

'No, it was a message from your housekeeper.'

'I don't understand how she knew I was here,' said Cledwin, confused. 'What was the message?'

'You had best come in and sit down, Bishop, I fear it is not good news.'

Bishop Cledwin felt a sense of foreboding. Anwen would not have found it easy to find him at the remote chapel.

'The messenger asked me to give you this,' said the priest, handing Cledwin the silver crucifix. 'He said to tell you that Elfred has been killed in a fight against the Du.'

Cledwin looked at the crucifix in despair. There was no mistake, as he knew it was the one he had given to his son and something deep inside him changed at that moment. He had tried to be a good man, living a pious life as a man of God, yet in his heart he was a warrior, as his father had been. He felt overwhelmed with regret that he had not openly acknowledged his son. Now it was too late.

'Was there any information about how he died?'

The priest recounted as much as he could remember of what the messenger had told him, including the involvement of Queen Elvina and her wish to see the Bishop when he returned.

'This soldier of the Du,' said Cledwin, 'Did they know what he was doing alone in the wilderness?'

'There is a curious detail,' recalled the priest. 'The messenger told me the warrior had a badge on his tunic, but they did not know the meaning of it.'

'Did he describe the badge?' asked Cledwin. It was a slender chance of identifying the killer of his son.

'He did, and what is more I recognised it as the mark of the queen's household. He may have been a member of Queen Rhiannon's personal guard, although I have no idea what he was doing on the northern border of the Gwyn.'

Cledwin thanked the young priest for his help and hospitality, explaining that he had much to do. He did not leave for the south as planned, but instead chose the path north.

As he rode through the lands of the Du he could feel the need for vengeance flowing through his veins. He held the rank of Bishop of the Gwyn and would make such use of that as he could but his heart was that of a warrior.

Cledwin swore an oath to find those responsible for the death of his son and make them pay. He had been prepared to make a deal with the queen of the Du but now she was his sworn enemy.

It was late evening by the time he reached the barracks of the guards and found just two men on duty. Cledwin knew better than to try questioning the guards about the man who killed his son but was able to learn that the captain of the royal bodyguard was a man called Idris. They had no idea where he could be found so late but suggested that Cledwin could do worse than try the local tavern.

Captain Idris was easy to find and happy to accept a drink from a stranger. Cledwin quickly had Idris talking about the importance of his position as captain of the guards.

'Tell, me, captain, is it true your men are picked from the very best of the Du?'

'Of course,' agreed Idris. 'King Gethin has personally entrusted me with the safety of the queen and his heir, the young prince.'

'You must be proud of them,' said Cledwin, refilling the captain's pewter tankard from a jug of strong dark ale. 'I've heard stories of their bravery, that they even take on the Gwyn single handed?'

Idris was enjoying the evening and saw no reason to hide the truth. 'Only recently Queen Rhiannon asked me to send Hywel, her personal guard, to find out what the Gwyn are up to.'

'Hywel is a favourite of the queen?'

'I trained him myself. The Gwyn are no match for the men of the queen's guard.'

'You serve your queen well, Idris,' said Cledwin as he deftly refilled the captain's tankard with the rest of the jug of dark ale and called to the landlord for another.

Idris was proud of his ability to hold his drink but as the night wore on he failed to notice that the generous stranger had hardly touched the second now empty jug. He felt dizzy, and was grateful for help from the stranger to return to his private rooms near the barracks. With some difficulty, Cledwin managed to remove the captain's black leather boots and get him to his bed.

'He was a good man,' said Cledwin. 'We will truly miss him.'

Idris was drunk and confused. 'Who are you talking of?'

'My son. His name was Elfred.'

Idris tried to clear his head but he had drunk more than his share of the jug of ale. 'I don't know what you are talking about.'

'You sent this man Hywel to the border with the Gwyn?'

'Yes. It was on the queen's orders.' Idris looked at the stranger more closely, he had never said who he was.

'You killed him.' Cledwin's voice was dark and threatening.

Idris was starting to become alarmed. He was feeling very drunk and disorientated. Even if he called for help, his quarters were too far from the guard house for them to hear and the rest of the men would probably be sleeping at such a late hour. 'You are a spy from the Gwyn?'

Cledwin didn't answer. He took the soft cotton pillow of fine feathers from under the head of Captain Idris and held it down firmly over the man's puzzled face. Idris struggled and made muffled noises that may have been a call for help, but he was right in thinking no one would hear. Cledwin felt no remorse. That would come later.

No questions were asked when Idris was found dead in his bed the next morning. He was not a popular man and, if anything, the men of the royal bodyguard were glad to see the back of their captain. Bishop Cledwin was nowhere to be seen. He had long since left to find Queen Rhiannon and her infant son.

CHAPTER 13

*Q*ueen Rhiannon nursed her baby and stared deep into his dark eyes. She sang to Evan softly, a sad and haunting song of the people of the Du. He eventually went to sleep, so she carefully laid him in his bed and unlocked the heavy oak chest.

Inside, hidden under her best clothes and dresses were her painstakingly written scrolls that told the story of the tribes. She took them out one by one and carefully read them, as she had done so many times since King Gethin had left to defend the east. As she read, a plan began to form in her mind that could help secure the future of her people.

She decided to share her thinking with her sister Ceinwen, as she had since they were children. Rhiannon would willingly give her life for her husband, for her son, for her people, to see an end to the feuding with the Gwyn. She did not want to say this to Ceinwen though. Not yet, not until she was sure.

The next morning was bright and warm, with just a trace of a pleasant autumnal breeze pulling the first brown leaves from the trees. Queen Rhiannon chose to make the short journey to the coast for some sea air and rode in a royal procession.

Two of the king's guards were in the lead, then the queen on a beautiful black horse with her sister Ceinwen alongside. Behind the queen was the special carriage carrying her sleeping son, followed by four more armed guards on black horses. News of their arrival travelled quickly, so when they went through a village people lined each side of the track to see the queen, hoping for their first glimpse of Prince Evan.

Rhiannon was happy to be out meeting her people after her long confinement with the baby. She was quickly recovering her slim figure and, unlike Gethin, who preferred to not be recognised as the king, the queen was proudly wearing a royal tiara and dressed in expensive flowing black silk robes.

The rare black silk was a gift from her husband the king, traded for the precious Welsh gold with merchants who travelled from the other side of the world. Rhiannon and Ceinwen had to ride side saddle because of their long dresses, but they were well used to it and the journey was a short one. Their procession joined the coastal track and the queen's long black cloak billowed out in a gentle sea breeze. She laughed as she held it down.

They looked out to the sparkling sea. A skylark sang musically overhead and when they licked their lips they could taste the faintest trace of sea salt in the air. Fishermen in small boats hauled in their nets and she could see the silvery fish struggling to escape.

'I love this place so much.'

Ceinwen looked back at her sister. 'I know how hard it is for you, Rhiannon. King Gethin will be back as soon as he can.'

'Did you not see how excited he was to go? He has been waiting for this all his life. I don't think we will see him here until this war is over.'

'I saw how much he loves you, Rhiannon. We must stay here. It is as safe as anywhere.'

'I was remembering the story of the warrior queen Boudicca, wife of the king of the Icenii,' said Rhiannon. 'Bishop Emrys told me when the king died and the Romans claimed all her lands, she raised a Celtic army and burned the Roman settlements.'

'So you are going to raise your own army?' Ceinwen had a good sense of humour and often teased her sister. 'Didn't the Roman's kill Boudicca?'

Rhiannon frowned in pretend disapproval. 'Emrys was unsure how her life ended but he said there were rumours she took her own life rather than be taken prisoner by the Romans.'

'I pray every night that Gethin will rid us of the threat of the Gwyn.'

Ceinwen continued to watch the fishermen as she rode. 'He will,' she said softly and turned to her sister. There was a hard look in her eyes Rhiannon had not seen since their parents died. 'We could set a trap for the Gwyn. Catch them like the fish in that net.'

Rhiannon could see her sister was serious. She had always listened to her and realised she was right. The quickest way to defeat the Gwyn would not be through the long battles with spears and swords so loved by the warlords and his warriors. If she could lure their leaders onto her territory, it would be possible to deal with them once and for all. 'What do you suggest?'

'Archbishop Renfrew was hoping that you could be persuaded to talk,' said Ceinwen.

Rhiannon nodded. 'We could somehow get a message out that I may.'

'It could be risky. If the Gwyn took you as a hostage...'

'I will have to make sure that they don't.'

They rode in silence together as the sky clouded over, hiding the sun and making the sea breeze feel suddenly cold.

Rhiannon looked at her sister. 'I can't put Evan at risk, will you keep him safe for me?'

'Of course, but where will you go?'

'West. I will have Bishop Emrys and Lord Llewelyn's men to protect me.'

When they got back Rhiannon quickly packed and made ready to leave.

Ceinwen watched her preparations sadly. 'How long?'

'I don't know,' admitted Rhiannon. She hugged her sister tight. 'Look after my baby, Ceinwen, I don't want this, but as queen I must put my people first.'

Rhiannon rode west with a handful of guards and few possessions before she could be talked out of it or change her mind. She felt in her heart it was what she should do.

Archbishop Renfrew of the Gwyn was deeply troubled. The king had blamed him for their wasted journey to see Athelstan and now, instead of brokering peace, he had inadvertently triggered a war against the people of the north.

Word of the Du attack and the loss of Sir Gwynfor had quickly travelled through the south and even though those responsible had paid for their actions, this was small consolation to the archbishop. He woke in the middle of the night and resolved to do something about it.

He considered making the long journey to see King Athelstan again, but there was no guarantee he would agree to a meeting or could intervene in what he could see as a civil war. The only realistic alternative was to make the even more dangerous trip to see the bishops of the north personally.

Renfrew knew Bishop Deniol had already failed to persuade King Gethin to discuss peace, so he would have to see Bishop Emrys. He didn't know Emrys and had only met him once before, but he was an advisor to the mysterious Queen of the Du, so there was hope.

As he packed to leave his comfortable rooms at Llandaff,

Archbishop Renfrew wondered when he would ever see them again. He considered hiding his priceless Bible, the Vetus Latina, but worried about it being stolen by looters if he was away for a long time.

Feeling it would be safer if it travelled with him, he decided to take a pack mule, as well as his best horse, a reliable white mare, so that he could carry the heavy Bible as well as plenty of supplies. A cart of any kind was out of the question as he would have to travel diagonally across the wilderness and the tracks through the wilderness would be poor or non-existent.

Renfrew was glad it was a bright sunny morning. The sun had risen in the east. He looked up at it and made sure he kept it to his right. Once it set in the west he could rely on his good knowledge of the stars but he was worried about travelling at night.

He finally reached the small church in mid Wales he had been looking for and decided to stay for a few days, to recover from his long journey. His horse was tired and his pack mule seemed grateful to have its burden removed. He tried the heavy oak door and was greeted by an elderly priest, the first person he had spoken to since leaving Llandaff.

The old priest looked at Renfrew, taking in the quality of his bishop's robes and noting his gold crucifix with the precious ruby in the centre. When he spoke it was in the old language, with the accent of the north and Renfrew realised he was close to the territory of the Du.

'Come in, come in,' said the priest. 'You are welcome to our church.'

'I am Archbishop Renfrew. I have had a long journey. Can I trouble you for a bed and a hot meal?'

The priest looked doubtful but Renfrew pressed a silver coin into his hand and was ushered into the thatched roofed wooden building next to the church. It was simply furnished but clean and tidy. 'It's not so grand but there is a small stable at the back where you can keep your horse and mule.' He pointed to an old well on the other side of the road. 'That's our only water. I'll fetch you a bucket if you want to have a wash after your journey?'

Renfrew nodded appreciatively. 'Thank you. That would be very good of you.'

After the archbishop had eaten an unexpectedly tasty lamb stew, washed down with some of the locally made wine, he explained to the elderly priest that he was hoping to meet with Bishop Emrys. He was surprised to learn that Emrys had not yet returned from a meeting with Bishop Cledwin of St Davids. Renfrew had learnt to trust in his intuition and he felt an inexplicable sense of foreboding. He hoped that this time he was wrong.

～

Unlike Llewelyn's men, who travelled stealthily at night, Lord Vorath was unconcerned about staying out of sight and was half hoping that the king of the Gwyn would hear of his arrival in the south. His fearsome reputation had been hard earned and proved useful, as *even* the mention of his name could strike fear into the ranks of his enemy.

King Gwayne would also be alarmed if he had known how many of his people openly welcomed the Du warriors. It could be they heard what happened to those who tried to run away or refused to give Lord Vorath food and water, but many had a secret longing for the old ways and resented the Gwyn laws and taxes.

It was from these supporters that Vorath and his men heard of the battles in the west. Vorath had great respect for Lord Llewelyn and was angry to hear of his death. They had never been friends, coming from different tribes and very different backgrounds, but they were both warlords of the Du.

Lord Vorath rarely visited the hill fort at Yns Mon, yet he had been able to appreciate the savage beauty of the place. He admired the achievement of his fellow warrior in slaying the champion of the Gwyn and called for Llewelyn's life to be remembered with a feast and drinking, in the way of the tribes. Whole trees were felled to build a huge bonfire and they gathered round it.

'For Llewelyn!' roared Vorath, throwing a burning torch into the dry timber of the bonfire. He held up a metal cup of the strong beer, 'He had an honourable death, a true warrior!'

Flames leapt high from the crackling fire and the men cheered noisily. Before long the beer was flowing freely and old Du drinking songs were ringing out into the gathering dusk. Unlike a Gwyn funeral, this was a celebration.

Many of the people of the north followed the Druid belief that after death the soul of a warrior was reborn into the afterlife. A good death, which brought honour to the tribes, was to be rejoiced, not mourned. They knew it was what Lord Llewelyn would have wanted.

Vorath approved of the celebrations but his regret was that Llewelyn's body was in a shallow grave somewhere, not on a warrior's funeral pyre. He sent for the local man who had brought the news of the battle and questioned him further.

Not only did the man know where Lord Llewelyn had been killed, he knew the Gwyn soldiers were still in the area and told Vorath he could guide them to his camp. Still angry and fired up with the beer, Vorath shouted to his men and called for his warhorse Ddraig to be saddled. Their mission to find the king of the Gwyn forgotten for now, the warriors charged off into the night, out for revenge.

～

Hayden had mixed feelings about his first encounter with the Du. He was suddenly a hero, being talked of as the next champion of the Gwyn, yet four men had lost their lives in the charge and the vicious hand to hand fighting afterwards.

These were good men, with families, who could still have been alive. The king personally sent a message of congratulations to Hayden and his men, ordering them to remain in position, so they made camp on a good area of high ground surrounded by open meadows.

He posted lookouts around their camp and made sure all the men kept their weapons ready. They took turns to rest and sleep, so a surprise attack on them would be impossible, even at night. Hayden even considered banning cooking fires, which could give away their position, but the nights were cold and the men needed to eat. As a compromise, he ordered the men to only burn dry wood from oak trees, which was plentiful in the wilderness and reduced the amount of tell-tale smoke.

Finding food in the wilderness was a different matter. There were a few scrawny goats grazing in the meadows and they were some way from the nearest farm, so he assumed they were either wild or would not be missed.

Hayden sent some of the men to catch one. The goats ran off bleating loudly as they approached but undeterred, they gave chase and eventually managed to bring one down, slashing its throat with a knife. In no time they were enjoying a good pot of stew and had cut up and dried as much of the remaining stringy meat as they could.

Hayden slept well and was washing his face in a bowl of cold rain water when he heard one of the lookouts shout that riders were approaching. Men grabbed swords and rushed over to see. A band of dark clothed men were brazenly riding towards them, making no attempt to avoid being seen.

Hayden's first thought was that they must be something other than Du warriors, possibly of the many bands of mercenaries coming to Wales to work for whoever would pay. As they continued to approach he could see they were on black warhorses and carrying spears as well as swords. A chilling realisation came to him. The riders were definitely warriors of the Du and they didn't care about being seen.

Hayden called to his men. 'We can stand and fight, or leave now,' he told them, trying to hide the nervousness in his voice.

The men looked at their young leader. He was waiting for their answer. Sir Gwynfor would never have asked for their opinion, but instead of seeing it as a sign of weakness, the men could sense he really cared about them. One of them drew his sword.

'We have beaten the Du warriors once, we can do it again!'

The others agreed and Hayden quickly weighed up the odds. The approaching Du riders would be getting tired, while his men were fresh. He had the benefit of having chosen the high ground and his enemy would have to climb a long steep slope to reach them.

He looked again at his men. They had been a rough and ill-disciplined bunch when they first set out but had bonded well after the success of the battle and he had earned their respect. Hayden realised they had never really had a choice. He took the flowing white cape he carried in his saddlebag and put it on over his silver chain mail, no longer concerned about being seen by the enemy.

'Soldiers of the Gwyn,' he shouted, 'mount your horses!'

Hayden and his men lined up on the ridge overlooking the meadow, holding position on the high ground as the Du riders steadily closed the gap between them. A slowly building roar of noise came from the warriors and Hayden realised it was their famous battle cry.

His horse started in alarm and pulled at the rein but he held it back. The men on each side of him stared straight ahead, eyes fixed on the approaching warriors. Hayden noticed that there was early morning dew on the grass at his feet and looked up at the clouds. There was a patch of clear blue autumnal sky but he could also see clouds with the look of rain about them. The day could go either way, in more ways than one.

The Du didn't hesitate when they reached the bottom of the slope, continuing their relentless charge towards the row of men on the ridge. Hayden could see them clearly now. The leader of the Du held his sword high and yelled something in a booming voice to his warriors.

He was a powerful figure of a man with a dark beard and bare muscular arms, covered with tattoos. The riders with him were different from any Hayden had seen before and he suddenly remembered tales of a legendary warlord. This could only be Lord Vorath.

Hayden drew his longsword and pointed it at the advancing Du. 'For King Gwayne and the people of the Gwyn!'

They swept down the hill towards the warriors. The clash was violent and brutal. Hayden sliced the longsword viciously at the closest warrior, feeling satisfaction as it cut deep then panicked as his blade stuck fast. The sword was dragged from his hand as the man collapsed from his horse and Hayden instinctively reached for the dagger he wore on a belt at his waist.

He looked down at the weapon in his hand and smiled at the absurdity of it, despite the seriousness of his situation. He was taking on the finest warriors of the Du kingdom with a knife he had used to peel apples.

Lord Vorath saw what had happened and charged at Hayden, ramming his sword into the young man's chest. The chain mail vest Hayden was wearing saved his life but he was winded and bent double with the sheer force of the blow.

All around him the tranquillity of the autumn morning had been shattered by men hacking and chopping at each other, the sound of horses snorting and stamping mixed with cries of pain and shouts of anger.

Hayden remembered how Sir Gwynfor trained him to breathe deeply and focus. He pictured himself being knighted by

King Gwayne, with his men cheering loudly as he was appointed the new champion.

He saw the beautiful Saxon Queen Elvina smile at him admiringly, as he had seen her smile at Sir Gwynfor, with an attractive twinkle in her eye that won men's hearts. He imagined inheriting Picton and the vast estates of farms and forest that came with his new knighthood and decided he would treat his people fairly, as he would wish to be treated himself.

All these thoughts went through Hayden's mind before he even looked up at his savage enemy. Vorath quickly drew back his sword and roared loudly as he thrust at Hayden's unprotected neck. It was a quick end. Hayden felt nothing when he died with all his men and the wilderness was claimed in the name of King Gethin by Vorath, warlord of the Du.

CHAPTER 14

*C*einwen welcomed the stranger in the dark wool cloak when he explained he had called on behalf of Bishop Emrys. She was also intrigued about why he was so keen for an audience with Queen Rhiannon.

'I was told by the guard that the queen is not here and may not return for some time?'

'That's right,' said Ceinwen. 'I am the sister of the queen. I am sorry you have had a wasted journey. There was something familiar about him. At first she thought it was a slight resemblance to her father, then she realised he had the same assured confidence as Bishop Emrys. 'Come in and warm by the fire. Would you like some hot mulled wine?' He had a kindly face and she was glad to have company. She had been lonely since her sister left and was missing Hywel.

'I am grateful for your kindness, my lady, it is a cold night.'

Ceinwen sent a servant for the mulled wine and looked more closely at her visitor. He was unshaven and dressed like a traveller, but seemed polite and well educated. She sensed a trace of the man's sadness and loss, but there was something about him that made her feel at ease.

'My sister left yesterday, you have just missed her. I wished to go with her but she asked me to stay here and look after the Prince Evan.'

'She was right,' said the stranger. 'There is no telling what the Gwyn are capable of, the prince is safer here with you.'

Ceinwen nodded. 'He is quite a handful but I love looking after him.'

The servant brought two elegant silver goblets and a jug of mulled wine. She filled a goblet for them both and the stranger sipped his appreciatively. It was rich and spicy although Ceinwen found she drank it a little quickly, glad for its comforting warmth.

She smiled at the stranger. 'What were you hoping to see the queen about?'

The stranger stared into the crackling fire. 'Bishop Emrys offered to arrange for me to see her about how I could help.'

Ceinwen leaned forward, her curiosity aroused. 'Help? In what way?'

The stranger poured more mulled wine for them both and looked to see that the servant was out of earshot before he answered. 'I have information about the Gwyn that Bishop Emrys thought would be useful to the queen.'

'She may still see you. I know where she has gone.'

'You are so kind to me,' said the stranger,

Ceinwen was thinking that helping her visitor may even bring Hywel home to her sooner and gave directions to the lodge where the queen planned to stay. She was touched by the stranger's gratitude. There seemed no harm in telling him why Rhiannon had left so soon.

It may have been the richly spiced wine but she felt comfortable sharing the plan to divert the Gwyn from King Gethin. Only after he had left did she realise that she didn't know his name or even what he did. Fortunately Ceinwen considered herself a good judge of character, and she was hardly ever wrong.

~

Cledwin was no longer a man of God. He had committed a mortal sin. As a bishop he knew better than most, as he had studied the Latin bible and preached the words of St. Paul. 'To sin wilfully, after having knowledge of the truth, there is now no sacrifice for sins'.

As he walked south to find the queen, like St Paul on the road to Damascus, he had time to reflect on how he had not murdered the captain of the guard by accident. There would be no miraculous conversion for Cledwin, but he did know that one journey had ended and another begun. His action was premeditated, truly a rejection of the law of God.

The small deception of the queen's sister came easily, as he no longer thought of himself as a bishop of the Gwyn. He was the son of a warrior of the Gwyn and the hunger for vengeance flowed through his veins. Around his neck he wore the silver crucifix, no longer as a sign of his faith, but as a memento mori, to remind him how life is short and how shortly it will end.

He was the father of a soldier of the Gwyn, killed by the people of the Du. From Ceinwen he had learned how Queen Rhiannon of the Du planned to lure the Gwyn into a trap. That could not be allowed to happen. Once he would have thought that God had shown him where the queen was to be found, but now he knew that God had no part in this war.

~

The men of the Flint garrison sang lustily as they marched west along the coast road, following the black flag of King Gethin. Differences forgotten, the men of the tribes were proud to be the king's warriors.

They knew that at any time they could receive orders from the king to march all the way to the south, so it was important to be ready to defend their way of life from Gwyn, Saxons, Vikings or whoever else tried to invade their country.

Travellers brought word to the castle at Flint that Lord Vorath had seized huge tracts of land from the Gwyn. Although they knew that the old warlord Llewelyn was now dead, they had cheered when they heard he had died a warrior's death in a victory against the Gwyn. Their spirits were high, and King Gethin made sure they were well paid and well fed.

King Gethin dressed simply, as a warrior of the tribes and would not have easily been recognised as king, were it not for his dark, penetrating eyes, which seemed to know so much. The king ordered Dafydd to ride with him to check the border with the east, as he was concerned about the threat to his lands from the Saxons.

Gethin slowed his fine black horse to a trot, as the track narrowed and became more overgrown, and looked across as his old friend matched his speed. 'The men showed good spirit!'

'Yes,' grinned Dafydd. 'They are ready for the Gwyn.'

The king reined his horse in and looked to the skyline. They had reached their destination, the line of the old King Offa's Dyke. The Saxons had dug out the ditch to the height of a man and restored the high ramparts with wooden palisades. Gethin knew what this meant and had passed a new law. He had decreed that to go beyond the dyke was to go into exile.

'We need to watch these Saxons,' he said, as much to himself as to Dafydd.

Dafydd halted his own horse next to the king. 'They are worthy warriors. It is good they have retreated.' The Saxons had made many border skirmishes over the years and the Du had learnt to respect them as fighting men. More than once it had been too close for comfort.

The king nodded in agreement. 'We will ride the line of the dyke and see what they are building down there.' He pointed to a tall shadow on the highest point of the dyke. When they got closer they could see it was a watchtower, built from freshly cut timber and facing out over their lands. At the top they saw movement but were too far away to tell who it was.

Dafydd pointed. 'They're keeping an eye on us!'

Gethin laughed. 'It's good news. The dyke is intended to keep us out. They wouldn't go to all this trouble if they were planning to attack us.' He turned to Dafydd. 'The way is clear for the men to head south. We will not sit by our hearth waiting for the Gwyn, we will take the fight to them!'

~

The heavy white cape gave King Gwayne some protection from the chill autumn breeze and he was glad of it as the grey skies signalled rain before long. It was a long journey to Caerphilly Castle but the waiting at Pennard had been frustrating so he was pleased to finally be seeing some action.

His powerful white horse led the Royal Guard, followed by servants driving carts laden with supplies. Their procession attracted an audience of villagers to either side of the road, as well as opportunists who tagged on to the end, hoping for a change in fortune.

A cheer went up as they approached and Gwayne raised a hand to halt the procession. He waited a moment until the cheering had subsided then looked around the crowds, recognising some with a nod. 'My people,' he said, his voice carrying well in the crisp autumn air. 'Your loyalty warms my heart!'

Another rousing cheer came from the growing crowd and the commander of the guard drew his sword and held it high, 'Victory to the king!' he shouted, a cry which was echoed by hundreds of voices in the procession. The king signalled for them to proceed and they could hear the cheering until Pennard was well behind them.

The good road from Pennard eventually turned into a track

and they had to slow the pace to let the carts catch up. The king rode in silence, wondering what fate held for the cheering villagers. There was a reason he had agreed for his queen to visit the country, as there was for him to travel far to the castle at Caerphilly.

The Du warriors were raiders and used cowardly hit and run tactics. They would know of his home at Pennard and he had two choices, to defend it more strongly or move to a place that was better fortified. His plan had been to create a new garrison but events had moved too fast and his decision was now made. He said a prayer to the old Gods that his people would remain safe but even as he did so, he heard a crow cawing nearby, a bad omen.

Gwayne's thoughts were interrupted by the thudding of hooves drawing close and the commander appeared alongside him. He had risen quickly to the position and Gwayne had already noted him as a potential future knight of the Gwyn. He was quick to learn and had worked hard, selling his inherited lands to buy a fine horse and sword in keeping with his position.

'Are we to follow the route through Sir Padrig's lands, my Lord?'

'Yes, although he will not be there to greet us, more's the pity.' The king turned in the saddle to look at the commander. He carried the royal standard in a leather support on his saddle and the breeze extended the flowing white pennant to its full length. The man would have been handsome but his face was marred by a scar that had been poorly tended, leaving a jagged line across his cheek which made him look dangerous.

'Sir Padrig is a legend,' said the commander. He had heard many tales but this was his first chance to hear the king speak of it.

'I owe my life to him,' agreed the king. He smiled as he remembered that fateful day. 'We chanced upon a group of Du warriors, they were on foot and should have been no match for our riders.' Gwayne shook his head with the recollection. 'The Du scattered like a disorganised rabble, but it was a trick.' He remembered the sudden blast from a horn as if it was yesterday. It had been the sign for them to suddenly turn and attack.

The commander realised he too would soon be facing the Du and was keen to learn as much as he could of their ways. 'What did you do?'

'I cut down several of the closest man and thought it would be an easy victory, but another of the black warriors put his spear into the chest of my horse. The poor beast collapsed onto my leg, breaking it in two places...' He paused, lost in the memory of the moment. 'It hurt like hell but although I managed to keep hold my sword, I was in no position to use it.'

'I heard that Sir Padrig fought well and killed many Du that day?'

'It's true,' said the king. 'I thought I'd had it when Padrig appeared from nowhere and set about them. The Du fought bravely but Padrig was like a man possessed! Even though he was wounded he somehow managed to lift me on to his own horse, then went back into the fray and didn't stop until the last of the Du was dead.'

'We must not underestimate the Du.'

The king grinned. 'You are right, Commander. That was not the first time the Du took us by surprise and it will not be the last.'

～

Bishop Emrys was starting to regret agreeing so readily to Bishop Cledwin's request to see the queen. It was already too late for the church to do anything to stop the war, if the accounts he had heard about the recent battles were true.

He decided that although he'd already given his word, he would have to visit the queen himself and advise her of caution.

Whatever information Cledwin may have, Emrys worried that the price could somehow compromise the position of the queen.

He was right to be concerned. Cledwin was already close to where Ceinwen had told him the queen planned to stay. He had made good time on his journey by travelling since the first light of dawn, which also meant that he avoided unwanted attention.

His Du black cloak had served its purpose well but Cledwin now visited the market place and replaced it with a Carthusian monk's habit of coarse greyish-brown undyed wool. As well as a tunic, the habit had a long wide piece of woollen cloth worn over his shoulders with an opening for the head, and a cowl completed his disguise.

Cledwin also purchased a length of good strong cord, which he wound around his waist and covered with a cloth belt. He carried a leather water bottle and used a stout walking stick, which meant he looked older and more infirm than he actually was.

Even his own servants would struggle to recognise him now and he could easily be mistaken for a monk or one of the pilgrims who travelled throughout Wales, visiting the relics of the saints.

He was clear in his mind about exactly what he would say to the queen when he arrived at the lodge. Bishop Cledwin had spent all his life building up his reputation and nurturing his career in the church but none of that seemed important to him now. He no longer cared about making any deals regarding his lands at St Davids, which seemed so far away now, but was determined to make certain that her plan would fail.

Rhiannon was also wondering about her plan. It was essential that she did not allow herself to become the prisoner of the Gwyn, as they could use her to force Gethin to surrender his throne. It was important that her presence in the area was known, if she was to successfully divert the Gwyn resources.

The queen had never visited the lodge before and was pleased to find it was an attractive building with a slate roof, in a remote and beautiful valley not far from the border with the Gwyn. A clear spring provided water and vast forests of old oak trees had ensured that the kings of the Du enjoyed good hunting grounds for generations.

She had chosen this place as her destination because it was close enough to the border to be within the reach of her enemy but as far as it could be from King Gethin and the garrison at Flint.

Cledwin waited in the shadows, watching the hunting lodge from a safe distance. There was no sign of the queen but she was clearly in residence, as he could see the queen's guard were already in place. He counted four men in total, smartly dressed and well disciplined in immaculate black tunics. Cledwin smiled wryly to himself at their inefficiency.

None of them seemed to even look in the direction of his hiding place and he remembered the ease with which he had gained the confidence of their unfortunate Captain Idris. A black cloud momentarily obscured the sun when he remembered what he had done and he looked up at it, nearly giving in to the nagging regret in his mind, then cursed himself for being superstitions and went back to his study of the lodge.

Queen Rhiannon took a fresh quill and parchment and wrote a long and difficult letter to her sister Ceinwen and another to her husband, the king. She knew neither of them could read or write as well as her, but Gethin had the services of Bishop Deniol and Ceinwen could ask Emrys for help.

Her writing was interrupted by one of the guards, who reported sighting a stranger. As ordered by the queen, they had not apprehended him and he seemed to be noting the activity at the lodge. Rhiannon thanked him and went back to her writing. The success of her plan depended on spies reporting her presence there back to the Gwyn.

Cledwin had been able to rely on the protection of the church but felt less confident that the queen's guard would welcome a wandering pilgrim to the hunting lodge. He continued watching as dusk fell and noticed that two of the guards were saddling their horses.

They were possibly going to the nearby village for more supplies or to find a tavern where they could pass the evening. That still left two of the queen's guards on duty. Cledwin realised he would need to find some way past them if he was going to carry out his plan. He would just have to wait.

Rhiannon finished her two letters and read them through carefully while the black ink dried. She wiped a tear from her eye as she made sure there was nothing that would compromise her position if they fell into the wrong hands.

The letter to Ceinwen asked her to do all in her power to ensure the safely and good upbringing of the young prince if she did not return. She thanked her sister for all her kindness, love and dedication throughout her life, particularly following the death of their parents.

Her last requests to Ceinwen were to send the second sealed letter to the king only if she was certain she would not return. She was also to make sure Evan learned to read the stories of the tribes, hidden in the old oak chest, for him to better understand the reason for his mother's sacrifice.

Folding both parchments, she lit a small piece of sealing wax from her candle and sealed them with her mark, using her gold signet ring. Rhiannon called for one of the guards and told him to deliver the letters to her sister right away.

Cledwin couldn't believe his luck when he saw the third man ride off. His patience had been rewarded and out of habit he nearly said a prayer of thanks to God but stopped himself just in time.

The remaining guard was grooming his black horse with a brush and seemed unconcerned about any threat to the queen, so Cledwin decided it was worth the risk to approach him directly.

He shuffled down the path towards the lodge, his cowl over his head, and called to the guard as he approached.

'Good day, sir, can you help a poor pilgrim?'

The guard looked up and recognised him as the figure they had seen watching the lodge for some hours. He did not understand why the queen wanted them to take no action. He put down his brush and looked at the stranger. He seemed harmless enough.

Cledwin smiled at the guard, trying to put him at ease. 'All I ask is some water and a little food if you can spare it?'

'Where have you travelled from?'

'The north, I have been meeting with Bishop Emrys of the Du,' replied Cledwin. It was the truth and seemed to do the trick, as the guard obviously recognised the name and relaxed.

'There is a spring where you can fill your bottle, pilgrim, not far from here. I'll show you.'

He led Cledwin to a clearing at the rear of the lodge where there was a wooden water pump at the edge of a tranquil lake, fed from the spring. It was a serene and peaceful spot and Cledwin was suddenly reminded of home. The guard cupped his hands and took a refreshing drink of the cool water.

As he did so, Cledwin swung his heavy wooden stick at the man's head as hard as he could. He had never used a stick in this way before and meant to knock him unconscious. The helpful young guard was completely unprepared for the blow. He fell forward into the water with a splash and lay face down in the cold water, a trickle of blood staining the area around his head.

Rhiannon thought she heard the splash and stopped singing to herself for a moment, listening. There was only silence so she continued singing. It was one of the old songs of the Du she had learnt from her mother and made her feel sad.

Although she was glad to be doing something to hasten the end of the war with the Gwyn, she was missing her baby, her sister, her husband. The lodge had a large open hall in the centre with heavy oak beams on the ceiling. The guards had lit a fire in the hearth to warm her, but the windows were small and it was turning to dusk outside, so she took a wooden taper and lit the yellowing beeswax candles to light up the room.

He watched the queen through one of the side windows as she moved from candle to candle. Cledwin had never seen her before but immediately knew he was looking at the queen of the Du. Her raven black hair shone in the flickering candle light and reminded him of her sister, Ceinwen.

He'd heard she lived a simple, nomadic life, travelling with the seasons, yet her gown was made of fine black silk, worth more than most people of the Du would afford in a whole lifetime, and flashes of gold and rings on her fingers spoke of wealth and luxury.

She sensed that she was being watched. Rhiannon had grown up with the knowledge that she was looked at wherever she went, even before she became queen but this was different. Somehow sinister. She called for the guards. The door burst open but instead of the young guards, she saw a large old man wearing a brown cowl, half covering his face.

Rhiannon ran out into the kitchen of the lodge only to find she was trapped. The only exit had been barred and locked by the guards for her own security. She looked quickly around the room for something she could use as a weapon and chose a meat cleaver that had a satisfying weight in her hand as she waited to see what the stranger would do.

Cledwin entered the kitchen and reacted quickly, seeing the queen holding the cleaver and fairly sure she would hesitate to attack an unarmed man. He crossed the room and grabbed her wrist, twisting the weapon from her hand.

'Guards!' The queen was surprised they couldn't hear her. 'Guards!'

Cledwin ignored her shouts. She was stronger than he expected and nearly escaped his grip but he had thought long and hard about what to do next. He took the length of cord he'd been carrying around his waist and tied both of her hands tightly behind her back.

As he held her close he felt an unfamiliar stirring. She was wearing a delicate perfume and her body was well toned and attractive. For a moment he was tempted by her, then he shook such thoughts from his head and made double sure she could not escape before he led her back into the main hall.

She looked at him angrily. 'What do you want?'

'You are my prisoner now, Queen Rhiannon of the Du.' he answered quietly.

Rhiannon suddenly struggled to break free but the cord was tied tightly. It was her worst fear. The stranger would be richly rewarded for handing her over to the Gwyn, who could then use her to force Gethin to surrender.

'Who are you?' she asked, a note of desperation in her voice. He was dressed like a poor man but his voice was rich and educated. She had at first thought him old yet he was quick and strong. There was something about him that scared her yet was familiar. He looked kindly but had shown he was dangerous. She had hoped to divert the attention of the Gwyn but the stranger had ruined her plan.

Cledwin looked around the hall then saw what he was searching for. A long black cloak the queen would have worn when she arrived. He put it round her shoulders and fastened the silver clasp at her neck.

Although her hands were tied behind her back it should avoid drawing attention to her, if only he could think of a way to stop her shouting. He looked intently into her dark eyes, making a judgement. She could yell as much as she liked, the only guard still at the lodge would be of little help to her.

'If you run, you won't be able to go far and when I catch you… I will make sure you can't run again.'

'Where are you taking me?' She already knew the answer.

'Across the border into Gwyn territory. It is not far.'

~

Rhiannon looked around for the guards but there was no sign of them. The stranger was right, it would be hard to run far with her hands behind her back. She would have to play for time and pretend to have given in to the old man. It was getting dark as he pushed her through the doorway into the cold air of the valley and carefully closed the door of the lodge behind them.

She realised her mistake in sending one of the guards with her letters, as the others must have gone to the village. Even when they returned she knew they would think she had simply gone to sleep. She wouldn't be missed until the morning.

Cledwin took the queen by the arm and led her out of the valley, keeping a watch for the guards. He needn't have worried, as they saw nobody before they reached the cover of the old oak trees. The woods were dense and dark, so they had to walk slowly to avoid the brambles and twisted branches reaching out across the rarely used path.

He couldn't believe he'd captured one of the most important women in the land single handed. He would never be able to return to his old life, but King Gwayne would be grateful and his wealth would enable him to live out his days in comfort.

Rhiannon was becoming increasingly desperate. Once over the border, she would be lost. She stopped on the path and turned to the stranger.

'The king will pay you, in gold, whatever you ask for my safe return.'

'I don't want your Du gold.'

'Why then?' She needed to find his weakness.

'For my son. I am taking you back so that my son did not die in vain.'

Rhiannon saw the sadness in his eyes. 'I have a son, his name is Evan and he needs a mother.' She felt a flicker of hope as he looked at her impassively.

'Keep quiet or I will have to gag you.' His voice was grim.

They walked in silence through the dark woods until they reached a clearing.

'The cord is cutting into my hands,' said Rhiannon. 'Please can you loosen it?'

'You know what will happen if you run?'

Rhiannon nodded and he took off her cloak and untied her hands, watching her closely as she massaged her wrists.

'Please can I have a drink of water?'

Cledwin could see no harm in her request and reached for the leather bottle slung over his back. He was not expecting her to reach inside her gown and remove something from a hidden pocket. She put it in her mouth and swallowed.

Rhiannon saw the stranger looking at her in confusion and felt her sight become blurred. It was as if the man had a bright blue halo around his head.

'What was that? Cledwin asked. 'What have you done?'

'A quick death,' she said sadly.

'What is it? He did not want to hear the answer.

'Digitalis. A potion from the leaves of the Foxglove. One of the herbs our people use.' Rhiannon began to feel deep pain in her stomach and sank to her knees. Cledwin held her closely. There was nothing he could do.

'Gethin... Is that you?' She was beginning to hallucinate and imagined that the king had come just in time to rescue her. Cledwin prayed for forgiveness while she gave in to the pain. Her fight was over.

*a*n important part of the work of Bishop Emrys was to visit each of the small chapels in his diocese, offering support and encouragement, as well as checking on the welfare of his priests. It was also a good way to collect and send messages, and now they were at war with the Gwyn, to learn of the latest developments.

On the way home from meeting with Bishop Cledwin he was doing exactly this when he was astounded by the news that the queen had left for the south. The young priest who told him had no details, other than she had asked for Emrys before she left. He couldn't help wondering if he had seen her instead of meeting Bishop Cledwin, he may have been able to persuade her to stay in the relative safety of the royal household.

He was also surprised to receive a message that Archbishop Renfrew of the south had now asked to see him. The prospect of meeting Renfrew again interested Emrys, as he liked the archbishop, who had fascinating knowledge of the church politics and the world outside of Wales and connections at the Saxon court.

Emrys decided it made sense to meet with the archbishop, as

he was already closer to the suggested meeting place than he was to home. It was a long ride and the roads were poor, so he was tired when he arrived and found the archbishop talking to the elderly priest in the thatched house next to the church.

The archbishop greeted him warmly. Emrys thought Renfrew had turned greyer since they had last met, but still had the engaging manner that had led to his rapid progress through the church.

'Thank you so much for coming, Bishop Emrys,' said Renfrew. 'I am grateful that you have saved me having to make the trip all the way north.'

'Your visit is timely, your grace,' replied Emrys, 'These are challenging times for the church.' Noticing that Renfrew was wearing a gold crucifix with a large ruby, he remembered that the role of the church was very different in the south.

'Indeed, Bishop Emrys. Come in, come in.' Renfrew turned to the priest. 'Will you take the Bishop's horse, please?'

'Of course, your grace, and I will prepare a bed for the Bishop in the back room of the house,' said the priest.

Their talks went on through the evening and well into the night. By the time Renfrew went to bed he was feeling tired but content that he had done what he could. It had been a difficult discussion, as Bishop Emrys had strongly held views about the need to keep the north free from Saxon influence.

He had seemed to think Queen Elvina was changing the whole of the south into an English territory, so was a little reassured when Renfrew explained that she was now fluent in the Welsh language and keen to understand their laws and traditions.

As he suspected, Emrys advised there would be no persuading King Gethin to reconsider. He did agree that, as advisor to Queen Rhiannon, he had some influence and would be meeting with her as soon as he could to discuss any chance at this late stage of some compromise or truce.

Emrys woke suddenly, coughing violently as his lungs filled

with acrid smoke. The heat of the fire scorched his face as he realised what must have happened. The old priest had given him a tall church candle for light when he went to bed, but he was so tired he had neglected to blow it out.

That small flame was now growing into a serious blaze, setting fire to the simple furnishings in the room. He looked around desperately and saw the earthenware pitcher of water he had used to wash. He reached for it and threw it at the flames, which died down with a loud hiss, then returned almost immediately as they found new wood to burn. 'Renfrew!' he shouted as loudly as he could. 'Fire!'

Renfrew appeared and grabbed him by the arm. 'We must get out!' They both rushed through the billowing smoke and flames and out into the cold night air. He turned to Emrys, his dark eyes wide with shock. 'Are you hurt?'

Emrys had a coughing fit and found it hard to answer, as the smoke had made it hard for him to breathe. 'I am so sorry, your grace… It must have been the candle?'

Renfrew watched as smoke streamed into the night from the small windows of the wooden house. 'At least we are safe,' he said. 'We must get water from the well and make sure none of the embers land on that thatched roof.' He had turned towards the well when he suddenly remembered. 'The Vetus Latina! The Bible is on the table by my bed!'

Before Emrys could stop him, Renfrew dashed back into the house. It was so unexpected that Emrys stood for a moment, wondering what to do, then followed the archbishop through the door into the billowing smoke.

It was impossible to see anything at first but then Emrys could make out the figure of the archbishop through the smoke. He called to Renfrew to get out and thought he saw the figure stoop to pick something up when the thatched roof suddenly ignited with a roar of flames. A huge gust of fresh air swept into the room and fanned the flames out of control.

Renfrew watched in horror as his precious Bible, the life's work of many men and symbol of his faith, started burning in his hands. Flames began licking at the edges of the beautifully embossed cover, then leapt from the pages of the irreplaceable book.

He sank to his knees in prayer as he felt his hair and clothes catch fire, then sudden searing pain as he realised his flesh was also burning. His prayers were answered by a heavy oak beam that smashed down from the roof and ended his suffering in an instant.

Bishop Emrys lay on his back in the cool grass looking at the terrifying flames engulfing the old wooden house. He was overcome by the heat and struggled to draw breath from his smoke damaged lungs.

His mind was still trying to comprehend what had happened when he heard a heart rending, inhuman scream. His first thought was that it was Archbishop Renfrew, but just before he lost consciousness he remembered the horses, in the wooden stable at the back of the house.

~

The arrival of King Gwayne at Caerphilly castle was marked by a fanfare of trumpets and rousing cheers from the huge garrison now based there. White pennant flew from the high towers and the people of the town had turned out in large numbers to welcome the king.

The men had been training hard for weeks and were more than ready for battle, yet the king had chosen to keep them in reserve, favouring the garrison at Pembroke as the main defenders of the Royal Llysoedd.

Now he had decided to make the castle his base for the duration of the war. This meant chances of promotion for the more ambitious men of the garrison and prosperity for the town's merchants and traders. His main reason was the proximity of his Saxon allies, although he had no intention of escape over the English border.

As soon as he had settled in his new rooms at Caerphilly the king sent for Sir Padrig's man Kane. As well as being a skilled master of the longbow, his old friend Padrig had told him that Kane seemed to understand the people of the Du.

Padrig also confided to the king that there were some who suspected Kane of being a Du spy, but anyone who had witnessed him in battle was left in no doubt of his allegiance. Gwayne had also heard allegations that Kane was a Druid, although no evidence of his involvement in the banned belief was ever put forward.

Kane arrived quietly and observed the king at work while he waited to be introduced. King Gwayne was questioning the officers about the readiness of the men, the latest reports from the east and the whereabouts of the Du.

It was obvious to Kane that the king was skilled at winning the confidence of men. He was impressed by the way Gwayne managed to find the truth, rather than letting people tell him what they thought he wanted to hear. The king finally turned to Kane and immediately recognised him by his Celtic tattoos and long dark hair.

'You must be Kane,' said the king. 'Sir Padrig speaks very highly of you.'

'I have been... fortunate in having Sir Padrig's guidance, my lord.'

'What do you know of the Du they call Vorath?'

'I know... that Vorath is a dangerous enemy, my lord. If we can defeat him this war is won.'

'How do we defeat him? What are his weaknesses?'

Kane thought carefully before answering. 'We need to fight him on our own terms, my lord. He has to be brought in range of my longbow men.'

Gwayne nodded. 'You are right, Kane. We should not be drawn into chasing this Vorath through the woods, where he has advantage. What do you suggest?'

'A trap must be set, my lord.'

The king looked into Kane's unfathomable eyes. 'And what do we use to bait this trap?'

'You, my lord. You already draw him to us.'

Unaware of Kane's words, Lord Vorath and his men were already camped in the mountains of Brychan, to the north east of Caerphilly, waiting for word from the scouts. Vorath cursed the relentless rain that had turned their camp to mud while they waited for news from scouts, sent under cover of night to meet with Du sympathisers. He cursed again when they returned, as the news was not good. It seemed that the king of the Gwyn had taken himself to the strongly defended castle at Caerphilly.

Vorath was afraid of no one and his band of warriors had fought bravely but they had suffered losses in the fight with Hayden and his men. Several of his best men had died from their wounds and others would need time to recover to full fighting condition. He sent the worst of the wounded men back to the castle at Flint with a message for King Gethin. It was time for the warriors at the castle to begin the long march south.

If Vorath had been any other leader he would have waited for the main army to arrive, but that was not his way. They left early in the morning, taking advantage of a break in the weather. An attack on the castle at Caerphilly was out of the question until their reinforcements arrived, but luck had been on their side.

The men who rode with him were the strongest and bravest fighters he had ever known and Vorath knew how to sap the spirit of his enemy. He would show the people of the south that they should side with the Du or face the consequences.

Vorath and his men had been riding for less than an hour when a sudden flash of flame on the hillside caught his eye. He held up his hand as a sign for them to stop and rode up the steep hill to investigate. It was a brazier, burning brightly on the highest point.

He could not see who had started the fire but its purpose was clear, as high on the next hill far in the distance a second flame burst into life. The Gwyn had set up a chain of warning beacons. He smiled at their ingenuity. He wanted them to fear his arrival.

~

The lighting of the beacon triggered a frenzy of events at Caerphilly castle, as it was the warning sign for an invasion. The lookout who spotted the closest beacon flame started ringing a heavy bronze bell in the high wooden tower of the castle.

The bell was new and had only been rung once before, when it was installed, so most of the men assumed the loud clanging was a test and continued with their work until the trumpeters sounded the signal for stand to arms.

King Gwayne watched unimpressed as soldiers swarmed from everywhere, some hastily putting on armour and others grabbing whatever weapons they could find. Although they had practised stand to arms every day, it had never before been called at noon and caught many of them unawares. He waited until they were all assembled then addressed them, his deep voice booming across the courtyard.

'Soldiers of the Gwyn, we have received warning of an attack.' He looked at the men, noting that some of them grinned and others looked alarmed. It may be a false alarm,' he continued, 'If it is I am glad you have seen the need to be ready!'

Gwayne looked around for the archer, Kane, and spotted him standing alone at the back. 'I am appointing Kane as acting commander while I find out who or what has caused the beacons to be lit. I will take twenty of the best archers, longbow men. The rest of you are to man the battlements and be vigilant. We will not be taken by surprise!'

A cry of 'Long live the king!' was echoed by the men, who hastily began preparations for battle. Kane had no difficulty selecting the longbow men and asked permission to lead them on the reconnaissance instead of the king, but Gwayne refused. He wanted to lead by example, and if this was an attack by the Du, his place was at the front, not hiding in the castle.

Gwayne chose a hill top overlooking a wide green valley where he would be able to see anyone approaching. He told the archers to position themselves at intervals in the sheltered ground across the entire hill top, each man close enough to clearly pass a message to the next.

The valley was peaceful, with only a few sheep dotted around and after they had been waiting an hour he started to wonder if the beacon had, in fact, been a false alarm. He was grateful that it was a dry afternoon and looked at the clouds. His father had taught him to read the skies when he was a boy, and he wondered what his father would say if he knew that they still had to defend his lands from the northerners.

One of the archers called out and pointed at the horizon. 'Riders!'

King Gwayne knew at once that this was not the main force of the Du army, although they may not be far behind. It looked like a small group of a dozen or so warriors, dressed in black and riding hard along the old road that ran down the middle of the valley. He signalled for the archers. 'Take cover and only fire on my command.'

Lord Vorath had been thinking about the beacon. Someone must have been keeping lookout, waiting and ready to light the fire. His local supporters should have told him about the warning signals, so that he could have stopped them being lit. It was a lesson for him to remember next time.

He had never been concerned before about relying on the element of surprise but if the Gwyn were so well organised it was time to change his tactics. Vorath looked round at his men and one held up a sword in acknowledgement. They were like brothers, the best men he had ever ridden with.

The first arrow flashed into the ground just ahead of him, causing Ddraig to snort and falter from a fast canter to a trot. In an instant Vorath knew it was a ranging shot. He was within the range of the deadly Gwyn longbows. Even as he shouted a warning to his men the sky was thick with the deadly arrows.

One struck the rider to his right with such force that it lifted him from the saddle, another flashed past his ear so close he ducked, a near miss. Two more of the fine black war horses fell noisily, arrows sticking from their flanks, throwing their riders onto the rocky path. Vorath wheeled Ddraig angrily and ordered a retreat. It was against all his principles to run from the Gwyn but this time they had out manoeuvred him. There was no honour in death from an archer he could not even see.

A rousing cheer went up from the archers as they saw the warriors of the Du fleeing, with several men and horses lying dead and dying. King Gwayne felt a surge of pride in his men. It had been an easy ambush and he was surprised how quickly it was all over.

For many of the archers it was their first experience of action and he would make sure they were well rewarded. Word of this victory would spread quickly throughout the land, no doubt exaggerated with each retelling.

It was exactly what he needed to restore the confidence in his army after the tragic loss of Sir Gwynfor. He had no way of knowing that the leader of the riders was Lord Vorath, or that the warlord had now vowed to do whatever it took to avenge the death of his warriors.

～

Owen was pleased with the way the war against the Du was turning out for him. He had a privileged position as a guard from Queen Elvina's household and was under personal orders from her to observe and report any enemy sightings. Since the incident with the lone Du warrior, he had not seen anyone at all.

This suited him well, as although he had been trained as an archer, he had never been very good at it. His guard's sword had never been drawn in action but he had a good store of tales to tell in taverns, and after the war was over he would be able to give a good account of his secret work in service to the queen.

One drawback of his position was the food. His wife had spoiled him and he missed her fine cooking. He had also grown tired of sleeping rough, with only an old woollen blanket for shelter, and needed to dry his clothes.

There were sheep grazing in the hills, so he realised there must be a shepherd somewhere who could help him. Owen was more interested in some hot mutton stew than the risk the owner of the sheep may be a supporter of the Du, so he watched and waited.

The shepherd was tall and wiry, with alert eyes and the practical ways of someone who scratched a living from the hills. Owen could see the man was wary of him, but didn't look afraid, just unsure what to make of a lone soldier of the Gwyn.

'I've been waiting for you,' said Owen. 'I need food and shelter.'

The shepherd nodded. 'My home is not far from here, but you will need to pay.'

Own reached into his pocket. He produced a coin which he held in the air for the shepherd to see. 'Here's a Saxon silver penny for a bed and some good roast lamb.'

The shepherd seemed satisfied and led him down a twisting path through the hills to a stone built smallholding with a roof made of slate. Several scrawny chickens pecked in the garden and a mountain spring fed a muddy pond. Owen followed the shepherd into the house. It was dark and smelt of sheep. A blackened iron cooking pot was suspended over an open hearth. Owen rubbed his hands together, and helped the shepherd start the fire.

After borrowing a woollen smock from the shepherd Owen changed out of his damp clothes and enjoyed the best meal he'd had since he left home. The shepherd was a man of few words, but that suited Owen, who passed the evening telling stories of life in the queen's guard.

The autumn evenings were drawing in and they went to bed as soon as the light failed. Thankful for his good luck, he went to sleep thinking this would do him nicely until the war was safely over.

Owen was woken by someone roughly shaking him and shouting. It took him a moment to remember where he was, then he realised the smallholding was full of Du warriors. One was demanding that he got them water and asking if he had any beer.

Another was plucking the now headless chickens he had noticed the previous day. The shepherd was nowhere to be seen and Owen had to think quickly. It was clear they thought this was his home and didn't suspect that he was a soldier of the Gwyn.

He grabbed an old wooden bucket and went to the spring, wondering if he should try to run. There were too many warriors, with big black war horses and he had heard what the Du did with their prisoners, so decided it was best to see what happened and trust that the shepherd did not give him away.

He cleared the previous night's ashes from the hearth and busied himself with making a fire to boil the water. He was listening all the time to the booming voices talking loudly in the old language then froze when he heard the name of their tattooed leader. Warlord Vorath.

The warriors ate heartily of the chickens they had slaughtered, then turned the attention to the stone house and outbuildings, looking for anything of value and arguing about where they were going to sleep that night.

Owen was playing the role of dumb shepherd, speaking only when spoken to and trying to stay out of the way of the warlord. He was thinking it had gone quite well when he heard loud curses and noisy commotion from inside the house and one of the warriors appeared at the doorway brandishing Owen's ceremonial sword in one hand and carrying his uniform of the queen's guard in the other.

Vorath moved swiftly, snatching the highly polished sword and holding it to Owen's throat. 'What can you tell me about the strength and position of the Gwyn... shepherd?' He stressed the last word, leaving Owen in no doubt his cover was blown.

The sword had never been used but Owen had kept it sharp and he could see from the look in the warlord's dark eyes that he was in no mood for clemency. All Vorath's men dropped what they were doing and gathered round to hear Owen's answer.

For a desperate moment he considered making up a story about stealing the sword and uniform from a dead soldier, but instead started telling Vorath all he knew about the number of men at Caerphilly. He also explained how the garrison from Pembroke had recently marched to reinforce the Royal Llysoedd at Pennard.

Vorath wanted more and made it clear that Owen's life depended on his answers, so he found himself admitting that the men at Pennard were poorly led and even that the queen was somewhere in the relatively unprotected west.

The tall shepherd had not emerged from his hiding place until several hours after he was certain the warriors of the Du had left. He had looked around his ransacked home, seeing chicken feathers strewn over what had been his garden, the theft of his only cooking pot, all his earthenware pots and plates had been smashed.

He still counted his blessings. It could have been very

different if he had not been such a light sleeper, waking at the first sound of the unwelcome visitors, or if the Gwyn soldier had not appeared from nowhere and been mistaken for him. He put the last stone in place and stood back to admire his work. It was shallow for a grave but he had taken great care to spell out one word in light stones on the dark earth. Owen.

CHAPTER 16

hile King Gwayne and his archers returned to the castle at Caerphilly to a triumphant hero's welcome, Vorath was angrily brooding at the loss of some of his best men and being forced to retreat.

He gathered his warriors around the fire and the blazing logs shot sparks high into the sky as they drank the dark ale favoured by the Du and argued into the night about how best to defeat the soldiers of the Gwyn.

They had all seen how the range and accuracy of the Gwyn longbow meant they would not even see the men they were fighting until it was too late. One of the older warriors regaled them with stories of how Lord Llewelyn had always favoured stealth and cunning over charging at the enemy.

Vorath knew he must to do more than simply rely on his reputation for courage and ruthless bravery. Some of his followers argued that they should make hit and run raids on the villages to the south, gradually demoralising the people of the Gwyn.

They could attack at night and it would force the king to stretch his resources, defending a much wider area. Others argued that they should wait for the reinforcements to arrive from the north, then storm the castle at Caerphilly and take it by force.

If they could capture or kill King Gwayne the war would be won. The castle would also be ideal to defend against any attack from the Saxons. Warlord Vorath knew the value of considering all the suggestions but he was not one to wait or to strike only under the cover of darkness.

One of his warriors, a fierce fighter but an intelligent man, had listened carefully to the arguments then reminded them how easily they had mistaken the Gwyn soldier for a shepherd, only discovering his cover through his own carelessness.

They had been lucky, as he had overheard much that would have been of value to the Gwyn. The disguised soldier had provided useful information about the leadership of the men who had marched from Pembroke, suggesting a very different tactic. The men fell silent as they realised he was suggesting they could infiltrate the leaderless soldiers and find those who were willing to fight for King Gethin.

The idea appealed to Vorath and he produced a leather purse, carefully opening the drawstring to show his men a handful of tiny nuggets of pure Welsh gold and small diamonds that sparkled brightly in the firelight.

King Gethin had given the purse to him to fund his campaign in the south, so he decided that each warrior would take a share to bribe the soldiers of the Gwyn. Vorath thought he would be too easily recognised and had to remain in the hills, but the rest of his men changed their black tunics for undyed wool and slipped into the taverns and gambling houses of the town. They carried their knives but left their swords with Vorath, as their main weapon was the gold, carefully shared from the leather purse.

It was risky work, as the Du were outnumbered more than a hundred to one, but the men in Abertawe were bored and many had no particular loyalty to the tax raising king of the Gwyn. Some were quickly persuaded to change sides, having seen the defeat of Sir Gwynfor as a sign that the war was already lost.

Others were prepared to fight as mercenaries, having been poorly paid by the Gwyn. A tiny nugget of gold or a single diamond would feed their families for many months and they were tempted by the promise of more.

A few followed the Du because they had secretly mourned the passing of the old ways and had been conscripted into the Gwyn army though no choice of their own. Before dawn, a good number of the soldiers who had marched from Pembroke were following Vorath's warriors back to their hiding place. They had become men of the Du.

The audacious plan was risky and could not go completely unnoticed by the Gwyn, so it was unsurprising that two of Vorath's men never returned. One had been set upon by a group of men once they realised he carried gold. He put up a brave fight but was stabbed in a dark alley, his lifeless body thrown unceremoniously into the fast flowing River Tawe, where it soon drifted out to sea.

Another unlucky warrior tried to offer his gold to one of the king's most loyal soldiers, who promptly had him arrested and thrown into the dungeons by the king's guard on a charge of treason. The king himself rode west to question the warrior but they learned nothing from him, as he chose to die rather than betray his fellow warriors.

Lord Vorath regretted the loss of the men but they had given their lives in exchange for several hundred fighting men, so he was in high spirits as he marched his new army to the safety of the hills. His plan had worked much better than expected so now he had a new problem, of how to feed and equip so many men.

He told his warriors to gather for their orders. One was sent on the long ride to meet with King Gethin at Flint. He was to inform the king what had happened and return with weapons and supplies. Vorath also wanted the king to unleash the warriors who had been waiting in Llewelyn's hill fort at Ynys Mon on the vulnerable west coast. Each of his remaining warriors was given command of a group of the former Gwyn soldiers to do what they could to train them to fight as men of the Du.

As well as the Du warrior, King Gwayne's guards had also managed to arrest several of the deserters, so the king decided it was necessary to make an example of them. They were lined up in front of the remaining soldiers from Abertawe while one of the officers explained the penalty for cowardice and desertion.

All of them were then executed by a swordsman but as he watched the king could see that his actions had done little to bolster the morale of his men. He had hoped for cheers from the crowd but his soldiers stood in stony silence, no doubt wondering what the future held for them.

King Gwayne returned to his rooms in the castle at Caerphilly deeply troubled. It was obvious that the warrior they had tortured to death was part of a much wider and well organised Du conspiracy.

Once again they had managed to take him by surprise and his picture of the Du as illiterate tribesmen was beginning to look very wrong. He immediately put his entire army on full alert and posted extra lookouts to be ready for any attack.

The king was at a loss to understand why his men would even consider deserting to join the warriors of the Du and he wondered if the loss of Sir Gwynfor had affected him more profoundly than he had expected.

Although he had never really liked the man, the loss of his champion was a blow that seemed to have sapped the spirits of his people. He consoled himself that he no longer needed to worry about Queen Elvina, but wished he had confronted the young knight about his behaviour and attitude to the queen. He realised that he had been glad when she left the Royal Llysoedd but now with Gwynfor dead and the garrison no longer in

Pembroke the west was vulnerable and he suddenly felt concerned for her safety.

~

King Gwayne would have been even more concerned if he had known that since Sir Gwynfor's death the mercenary Cadell felt no further obligation towards him and was now fighting for King Gethin. Cadell had risen to a position of some importance in the hill fort at Ynys Mon but it seemed a long time since he had seen any action and the isolation of the island meant it was difficult to follow the events of the war.

He was saddened by the news of the death of Lord Llewelyn, as he had liked and respected the old warlord, but apart from that one victory it seemed that the Gwyn had barely ventured from the safety of their fortresses. If the stories brought back by traders and travellers about the battles of Lord Vorath and his army of warriors were true, then Cadell knew he would do well to prove his allegiance to the Du.

Cadell had also taken on Lord Llewelyn's loyal former servant Bryn. Although Bryn knew the old warlord had achieved the warrior's death he had wished for, his own life had suddenly seemed without purpose, so he was glad to have a new master.

Bryn was proving a useful assistant to Cadell, as he had extensive knowledge of the ways of the Du and was happy to frequent the ale houses in the town that were becoming the main sources of news. It was in one of these that he had asked to meet Cadell about a private matter. He found the big unruly man waiting for him in a quiet corner of the tavern and paid for two large tankards of dark frothy ale.

'So what's the mystery Bryn, it's not like you to be so secretive?' His new servant was not his usual jovial self.

Bryn looked around cautiously before answering to make sure they could not be overheard. 'When I was Lord Llewelyn's servant we would often visit the queen. One of her servants was sent all the way to see me with an unusual request,' said Bryn. 'She has asked if I can persuade you to undertake a special mission, in secret, for the sister of the queen.'

Cadell had heard the queen had a sister, although he had never seen her himself it had been said that she was very wealthy in her own right, as attractive as Queen Rhiannon and was yet to marry. 'Well I am interested Bryn, but why me?'

'It was my idea to ask you,' admitted Bryn, drinking nearly half his beer in one gulp to hide his embarrassment. He grinned awkwardly and wiped the froth from his beard before looking at Cadell seriously. 'She said I was to find someone they could rely on.'

Cadell was touched by Bryn's words despite himself. 'What does she want me to do?'

Bryn explained Rhiannon's decision to go to the lodge near the border and how the guards had returned to report that the queen been taken in the night, with the guard on duty at the time found drowned. The only clues to the queen's disappearance were a sighting of an old monk, who had been watching the lodge, and the discovery of a meat cleaver apparently dropped on the floor in the kitchen.

The guards reported that the queen's bed did not appear to have been slept in but the candles had been lit, so it seemed she had been taken against her will in the early evening. Bryn also told Cadell about the letters the queen sent the night she disappeared.

Her sister was desperate for one last search or she would have to send the second letter to the king. Cadell's mind was working quickly, as he realised this could be a good opportunity to prove his loyalty and win a place close to the royal family of the Du.

'What do you know of the queen's sister Bryn?'

'Her name is Ceinwen,' said Bryn. He looked round again to

see that no one was listening. 'She fears the queen may have been taken by the Gwyn.'

～

Cadell wasted no time in leaving for the border, taking one of the best of Lord Llewelyn's fine black Welsh Cobs. He was impressed by Queen Rhiannon's bravery but the risks she had taken were significant and he hoped he could reach her before she was captured by the Gwyn.

Her sister Ceinwen was right, that could put the king in an impossible position. From what Bryn had told him of the queen, she was resourceful and well educated, so should have been able to look after herself, but he was not optimistic about finding her.

One thing that troubled him was that he'd spent time living with the Gwyn and knew the way they worked. If the Gwyn had succeeded in capturing the Du queen they would have already demanded King Gethin's surrender.

As he rode he pondered the drowning of the guard. He knew the area was home to all manner of thieves and robbers, so there was a chance that this was nothing to do with the Gwyn. When he arrived at the lodge Cadell was surprised to find it unlocked and deserted.

He felt the ashes in the stone hearth and they were cold, so it had been unoccupied for some days. The stables were empty and there was no sign of the guards, so he decided to ride up into the woods and search for the queen. He was wary of ambush and travelled as silently as he could.

There was no trail to follow and although Cadell had experience as a tracker, there was little else he could think of to do. There were only a few hours of daylight left and he knew it would be impossible to search at night, so his best hope was to reach a good vantage point on the higher ground above the valley.

The path was narrow, so it took longer than he expected and the light was fading when Cadell reached the highest point. He dismounted and looked all around but could see or hear nothing other than the evening calls of birds settling down to roost.

Cadell flinched as the peace of the early evening was shattered by the hissing scream of a barn owl in flight. Beautiful and mysterious, he watched the white and gold owl hunt silently until it vanished into the dusk. He smiled to himself, the owl had startled him but the old warlord Llewelyn had trained his horse so well it took no notice.

Glancing down the narrow path into the valley, he could see the hunting lodge far below and was pleased to see the yellow light of a candle flickering in the window. The guards must have returned, so at least he would have some help with his mission and be able to question them more closely about the night the queen disappeared. Cadell mounted his horse and carefully picked his way back through the gnarled old oak trees in the failing light.

He opened the wooden door of the lodge and found a large man on his knees lighting a fire in the stone grate. He was not one of the queen's guards, as he was dressed in the rough woollen habit of a monk with a large hood hanging down his back. Unshaven, with unruly grey hair, the stranger looked round at Cadell as he entered the lodge. He immediately realised this must be the man the guards had reported seeing and drew his sword.

'Who are you? Cadell noticed that the man was using a heavy iron poker to prod the fire into life and realised it could be used as an effective weapon.

'My name is Cledwin,' answered the stranger. He hesitated, then added as an afterthought 'Bishop Cledwin.' He laid down the poker and stood with his hands raised palms outward to show he meant no harm.

Cadell had heard of Bishop Cledwin of the Gwyn but never met him. He knew the bishop was a wealthy man and owned vast areas of land in the west. The figure before him looked more like a poor pilgrim but his voice was unexpectedly well educated and Cadell recognised the subtle accent of West Wales.

'What are you doing here?'

'I came to capture Queen Rhiannon,' Cledwin said in a matter of fact tone. He looked at Cadell, who was still holding his sword ready, but clearly struggling to understand.

'Where is she?' Cadell instinctively knew the answer from Cledwin's demeanour.

'The queen is dead. I am afraid she killed herself rather than be taken by the Gwyn.' The truth of the words hung heavy on the air, as did the sadness Cadell could see on the bishop's face.

Cadell sheathed his sword, deciding Cledwin was not a threat to him. 'I was sent here to find the queen.' He shook his head. 'I suppose I knew that something like this must have happened.'

'I wish I could have stopped her,' said Cledwin. 'She was determined not to be my prisoner.'

Cadell suddenly remembered what Bryn had told him in the tavern. 'I heard that one of the guards was found dead?'

Cledwin told him how the guard had died. 'The guards were mistaken, he didn't drown. It was an accident… I never meant to kill him.' Cadell could see that the Bishop was telling the truth. He seemed a good man and in different circumstances would have liked him, but Cledwin was now his enemy.

'I am afraid I must take you back with me,' he said. 'You are my prisoner now, Bishop Cledwin. You can tell your story to the sister of the queen.' He looked out of the window. 'It's too dark to travel through the woods now. I need you to give me your word you will not try to escape?'

The bishop nodded. 'There is no escape for me now.' He looked like a beaten man.

Cadell believed him but decided to shut him up in the stable until the morning, as there was something unsettling about the coldly factual way the bishop had described the murder of the guard. Cadell had lived a hard life as a mercenary and learnt to trust no one.

The stable had no lock, so as an extra precaution he dragged a heavy log across the outside of the stable door that would be virtually impossible for the bishop to move from the inside.

He woke at first light, with a good idea forming in his mind. His decision to side with the Du meant he would be in a vulnerable position if they lost to the Gwyn. The bishop's actions seemed to have been well intentioned, so he decided to help him safely reach the border in return for a promise that his support would not be forgotten.

He walked over to the stable and was relieved to see that the heavy log was still in place, so Bishop Cledwin had been as good as his word. Cadell dragged the log out of the way and opened the door to the stable. The mercenary stood looking at the big man, slowly swinging from the wooden roof beam by a length of strong cord. He had forgotten to ask the bishop what he had done with the body of the queen.

CHAPTER 17

*B*ethan noticed a worrying change in Queen Elvina. After they received the news of Sir Gwynfor's death at the hands of the Du she had become withdrawn, staying in her room and hardly eating. Bethan was concerned, as it was difficult for her to know what to say to the queen. She listened at the door to the queen's room then gently knocked.

'Yes?' The queen answered. Her voice sounded sleepy, even though it was nearly noon.

'It's me, my lady.'

Queen Elvina opened the door. 'Come in, Bethan.'

Bethan noticed that the queen looked a little brighter and was glad to see the parchment map the king had given her was on the bed. 'It is time we were leaving this place, we are no longer safe.'

The queen looked out of the small leaded window. She had a view of the sea and could see it was a clear day. The sunlight sparkled on the water and herring gulls wheeled and called to each other noisily. She turned to Bethan. 'I don't understand. How can we not be safe?'

'Word has spread that you are staying here. It is the talk of the village.'

'You are right, Bethan. Let us pack our things and return to Pennard. The garrison from Pembroke is not far from there now, so it is as safe as anywhere.'

Bethan looked hesitant, as if she wanted to say something. Elvina had known her long enough to recognise the look.

'What is it? You are keeping something from me Bethan?'

'I have heard that the Du plan to attack the garrison, my lady. We should stay away from there. It will be dangerous for you if there is fighting so close to Pennard.'

'I am sure the garrison are capable of seeing off the Du.' She sensed there was something more that Bethan was not telling her. 'Where would you hear such a thing? Has there been a message from the king?'

'No, my lady. As far as I know the king is still in Caerphilly. I am sure he will send a message to you soon.'

Elvina looked back out of the small window. She missed Sir Gwynfor and wished they had been able to meet. Her sadness was turning into anger at the people of the north. It would take her a long time to get used to the realisation she would never see him again. 'Where do you think we should go?'

'I know a remote farm close to the border where we could be safe, my lady.'

'The border? There is something you are not telling me.' She looked Bethan with concern in her eyes. 'There is more bad news?'

Bethan nodded. 'They say that the warriors from Ynys Mon are readying to take the west. They could be here any time.'

Elvina looked at Bethan again. Her handmaiden seemed to know a lot about the plans of the Du. The king had often spoken about how there were many Du spies in the south. She remembered teasing him about it and wondered again about Bethan's loyalty. She would have to take care. If Bethan was right and the war was turning against the king she would be useful to her, for now.

'That's decided then. We must leave today.'

~

The warriors of the Yns Mon hill fort had been crossing the narrow and dangerous straits of the Menai throughout the day in any boats they could find. Even the oldest could not remember ever seeing so many men on the opposite bank, shouting and calling encouragement to those yet to make the crossing.

The black Cob Horses and supplies took the largest barges, with the men crammed into small fishing boats. Inevitably some ended up in the water. For those who could swim there was a hope that they would be able to make landfall further down. Others who could not yelled in alarm and sank quickly into the dark fast flowing water.

Eventually they were all assembled and ready for the long journey south. The main body of men marched in groups, carrying spears and bows, with riders on Llewelyn's sturdy black Welsh Cobs acting as scouts to the front.

A second group of mounted warriors protected the rear. Many local people had turned out to see their army off and lined the old cobbled road, cheering and waving, shouting encouragement to those that they knew. Some women and girls gave their men last hugs and kisses, as it was impossible to know when they would see them again. Only a few would be remaining at the hill fort, including Cadell's servant Bryn, who would wait there for his master's return.

The king's orders were clear. He wanted as many warriors as possible to take the west from the Gwyn and claim it in his name. The goal was to reach the castle at Pembroke and take control before the alarm was raised and the garrison could return.

King Gethin knew it was a risk worth taking. Apart from the men with him in the east, the north would be left undefended but he was encouraged by the message from Vorath. His warlord had done well. With the supplies and extra men he had sent Lord Vorath would soon have control of the south and keep the garrison at Abertawe busy.

The men of Ynys Mon had been waiting for the order to advance and were eager for the chance to avenge the death of their leader, Lord Llewelyn. They made good time reaching the border, despite the shortening autumn days, and continued marching south into the territory of the Gwyn.

They had been warned by warlord Vorath to be vigilant for signal beacons on the high ground and sent riders ahead to deal with any that they found. The riders returned to report that the whole area seemed to be undefended but there was a sense of calm before the storm and the men kept their spears and bows at the ready, determined to honour the memory of their leader.

The scouts also reported a sizeable Gwyn village ahead of their path on the coastal road. The warriors needed a base camp from which to conduct their night time raids. It was decided they would seize the entire village in the name of the king and learn what they could about the strength of the Gwyn forces in the west. The only sound in the village was the barking of farm dogs as they stealthily scouted the layout.

On the signal, the archers lit arrows covered with pitch and fired them into the thatched roofs of the selected buildings. The road quickly filled with villagers, screaming women, angry men and crying, terrified children.

A few of the younger men of the village were armed with swords and knives. Others used farm implements to defend their property. They put up a good fight but they were no match for the trained warriors, who quickly disarmed them. The first Gwyn village in the west had fallen to the Du.

Elvina had slept lightly and was woken by the distant screams and the noises of fighting. She woke Bethan and they stood together in the cold night looking in the direction the shouts and yells were coming from.

The sky to the west was lit by the bright orange glow of flames. Her guards had already taken position around the little farm that had become their new home but the scale of the destruction they could see suggested a much larger force. Their sanctuary was in danger of becoming a trap.

Elvina's hand went to the handle of the ornate dagger the king had given her. She had asked Bethan to sew the white leather scabbard into a hidden pocket in her dress so that she could easily reach it. She found it strangely comforting to trace with her fingers the ancient Celtic symbols engraved deeply into the silver handle, as she did now.

'We left just in time. They must have been closer than I thought,' said Bethan.

'The Du?'

Bethan nodded, 'Where do we go now, I wonder?'

For the first time Elvina realised that her life was at risk. They had comfortably outnumbered the Du before but now she sensed they were in real danger. An idea occurred to her. 'You heard that the Du were heading south?'

'Yes, my lady, the warning was right,' replied Bethan, unable to take her eyes from the flames that were still lighting up the horizon.

'We will cross the border north, it is the safest place now.'

Bethan looked at her in amazement. 'We should send for more guards.'

Elvina shook her head. 'There isn't time, we should leave before they realise we are here!'

They hurriedly packed and set off into the darkness, taking only what they could carry on the horses and leaving the rest hidden at the farm. The guards were unhappy with the queen's decision, as they had strict orders from the king not to cross the border, but they had not relished the prospect of taking on the Du army.

Bethan found a dark woollen shawl for Elvina to wear over her white dress but it was difficult to ride quietly and their white horses seemed to glow like beacons in the night. Although they were now heading deep into the territory of the Du, they felt safer as they moved further from the flames on the western skyline.

～

The mercenary Cadell buried the body of Bishop Cledwin in the grounds of the peaceful hunting lodge. It was hard work, as he was a large man and heavy. Cadell was not religious but he marked the grave with a cross formed from two pieces of wood.

Kneeling in front of the fresh grave he did his best to remember the words of a Christian prayer he learnt when in the service of the Saxons. Cadell's divided loyalties meant he felt he somehow owed it to the old man, just as he owed it to Ceinwen to make sure that Cledwin's story was true before he returned.

He began a thorough search of the inside of the lodge, looking for any clue to the queen's disappearance. He found a purse containing several gold coins and some jewellery among the possessions she had left behind, which he decided were proof she was abducted and not robbed. He put the coins in his pocket, thinking they would do well as payment for his troubles.

After an equally thorough examination of the grounds of the lodge, Cadell decided to search the main path south they would have taken towards the border. It was unlikely that the bishop would have been able to dig much of a grave, so he hoped to see a cairn of stones or some form of marker. To make sure he missed nothing, Cadell led his horse by the bridle and stopped at any clearing or open area close to the path to search for any sign of disturbed ground.

~

Queen Elvina's guards had been chosen personally by the king from his most experienced men. Their mission to guard the queen on her journey had been unexpectedly eventful, with the killing of the Du warrior and now the lucky escape from what must have been a significant raiding party. It seemed strange to them that she wished to travel deeper into the territory of the tribes and they argued amongst themselves about what the king would say when they returned.

Two of the guards travelled well in front of the queen to make sure the path was safe. They had fought at the king's side in the last war with the Du, so knew, how important it was to be vigilant for any sign of their enemy.

It was easy for them to see ahead when they were on the open road but quite a different matter when they reached the hills. With narrow twisting tracks covered over with old and twisted oaks, the hills offered countless opportunities for anyone who wished to ambush them.

Their vigilance paid off when the guards crested the brow of a hill and could see a lone figure approaching. He was on foot, leading a black horse by the reins and wearing the black cloak of a warrior of the Du. It was too late to take cover, as he also looked up the hill and had already spotted them.

They drew their swords and charged, knowing he would raise the alarm if they allowed him to escape. The Du warrior's reaction took them both by surprise, as he simply raised his hands in surrender. It could be a trap but they slowed.

'My name is Cadell,' he shouted. His rich voice showing a trace of his West Country upbringing. 'I am a mercenary, paid by Sir Gwynfor of Picton to scout the Du strength and positions.'

The guards stopped and looked at him, undecided. One of them called back. 'Can you prove what you say is true?'

'I have heard Sir Gwynfor has been killed but King Gwayne can vouch for me.'

'Lay down your sword, mercenary!'

Cadell slowly unbuckled his sword from his waist and lay it carefully on the track in front of him. The guards approached him and one dismounted to pick it up and also took Cadell's dagger while the other kept his own sword at the ready. The mounted guard was still unsure of him.

'Where were you going?'

'On my way back to report,' Cadell replied. 'I have valuable information for the king.' He could see they were still undecided about what to do. 'I recognise your uniform. What are men of the king's guard doing in Du territory?'

'We crossed the border to avoid the Du army.' The second guard looked thoughtfully at Cadell. 'We are escort to someone of importance. Can you show us somewhere safe we can stay for the night?'

Cadell pointed back down the track. 'Nowhere is safe but I've been staying at a hunting lodge not far down the track. We would need to keep a look out but at least it is warm and dry.'

The mounted guard turned to the man who was holding Cadell's sword. 'Wait here. I will see what our orders are.'

Cadell knew that he could probably overpower the guard and escape if he wished but events had taken an unexpected turn and his curiosity had been aroused. He had been surprised to learn that Du warriors were already in the west but decided his story had seemed to satisfy the guards.

They waited in an uneasy silence until a group of riders appeared at the crest of the hill. He immediately recognised Queen Elvina, riding a beautiful white horse. Even though she was the last person he was expecting to see in the lands of the tribes, her long blonde hair made her unmistakeable.

She brought her horse to a stop to look at him. He seemed more tanned and athletic than when she had last seen him with

Sir Gwynfor. He now looked like how she had always imagined a warrior would be.

She remembered the intelligence in his dark eyes that were now looking at her with a confidence she rarely saw. 'That is Cadell, the mercenary,' said Elvina quietly to the guards. 'I have seen him before, when he visited the Royal Llysoedd.'

'At your service, my lady,' said Cadell, smiling.

'You can help us?' asked Elvina. She liked the look of the tough mercenary and it would be good to have an extra guard who knew so much about the ways of the Du.

'Of course, these dangerous woods are no place to be at night, my lady.' The guards were reassured by the queen's confirmation and nodded to Cadell, who mounted his black Welsh Cob and led them back down the track to the deserted lodge. He smiled to himself as he rode. He had been sent to find a queen of the Du and had instead found a beautiful queen of the Gwyn.

Bethan soon had a fire going in the stone hearth and made a soup from vegetables they dug from the garden on the lodge. They had carried with them a cured ham and a loaf of rye bread from the farm and Cadell produced a keg of good ale he found on his search of the store behind the kitchen. After their meal the guards went to patrol the grounds and Elvina invited Cadell to join her and Bethan to exchange news of the war.

He told them of his experiences at the hill fort of Ynys Mon and how he had managed to gain the confidence of the warriors of the Du, including the legendary Lord Llewelyn. Cadell made no mention of his search for the queen or the unfortunate suicide of Bishop Cledwin, but he could not resist telling them he knew the queen's sister, Ceinwen.

Elvina liked the handsome mercenary and was eager to learn as much as she could about their enemy. She had many questions about Ceinwen and was curious to learn that the baby prince of the Du was in her care.

Cadell was just as interested in Elvina's account of their

encounter with the lone Gwyn warrior and their lucky escape from the Du raiders in the west. Cadell knew these must be the warriors from Ynys Mon he had trained with and realised that the war was turning to the advantage of the Du. If it were not for his mission for Ceinwen he would have been with them, fighting his way down the coast to the castle at Pembroke.

When the queen and her handmaiden eventually retired for the night Cadell helped the guards stable the horses and followed them on a patrol of the grounds. He suggested that one of them should remain awake at all times to keep watch on the main approach the lodge and showed the other guards the servants quarters, where there was room for them to have some well deserved sleep.

Cadell told them he would sleep by the fire in the main room of the lodge and that they could rely on him to help at the first sign of any trouble. He lay wide awake listening to the noises of the night and wondering at the strange hand fate had dealt him.

In the small hours of the morning he heard the guards changing over and waited until the new guard was at the furthest point from the lodge. There was a full moon but the cloudy sky cut down its light and he had enough cover of darkness to creep up behind the guard.

Although they had not returned his sword and dagger, Cadell was skilled in unarmed combat. He expertly slipped his arm around the guard's neck from behind and quickly snapped it, killing him instantly. He dragged the guard's limp body into the bushes and returned stealthily to the lodge, closing the door silently behind him.

The hunting lodge was big enough for the queen to have a room of her own and Cadell had already made sure he was familiar with the layout. Easily finding his way around in the near darkness he stealthily opened the door and could see the shape of her sleeping. He crossed to her bed and placed one hand over Elvina's mouth, gripping her slender neck in a stranglehold with the other.

He could feel the soft warmth of her body as she woke and looked up at him with startled eyes. 'I don't want to kill you, but if I have to I will.' There was darkness in Cadell's voice that showed it was no empty threat.

Elvina nodded to show she understood and he moved his hand a little so she could breathe.

'We are leaving. Don't try anything if you want to live.' Cadell kept his voice low, which made it sound even more sinister.

Elvina wondered how he thought he could get her past her guards without being noticed then felt suddenly angry. Sir Gwynfor and King Gwayne had placed their trust in this mercenary and now he was betraying them all. She feared for her life if she let him take her but the strength of her anger gave her courage. 'This is my night dress,' she said quietly. 'It will be cold outside, will you let me put on my day clothes?'

'Be quick,' replied Cadell. He watched in the dim light as she slipped out of her night dress and was naked before him. This was not part of his plan, although the way she was looking at him earlier that evening had registered somewhere at the back of his mind. Elvina picked up her long white dress from the chair by the bed and was about to put it on when she turned and smiled at him.

'You know it is wrong to look at me like that, Cadell?' There was an unmistakable invitation in her voice.

He moved closer to her, his soldiers mind struggling against his aroused desire and losing. The light of the pale moon reflected from the exposed perfection of her soft white breasts as she moved towards him. Her lips came close to his and he felt a sudden sharp pain in his chest. Cadell looked down and saw the moonlight glint from the silver handle of an ornate dagger, engraved with Celtic symbols.

'A gift from the king,' said Elvina coldly as he died.

CHAPTER 18

*L*ord Vorath's warhorse Ddraig seemed to sense the impending battle and pawed the ground, kicking clumps of grass into the still night air. The back clad warriors stood ready, raising their spears in the air with a shout as the warlord rode to the front.

He looked at the rows of fighting men with pride. They had left the north as a band of riders but now he commanded an army. In addition to those who had joined them from the Gwyn, more men of the tribes had rallied to the flag as word of his victories spread.

Their orders were to crush the spirit of the Gwyn and take control of the king's residence at Pennard. They had learnt from their surprising defeat by the longbow archers of Caerphilly. This time Lord Vorath's warriors would attack at night and without warning. Their hands and faces were painted with a thick black mixture of soot and grease, so the whites of their eyes shone out in the dark.

Vorath's face was also painted black and he looked like a dark lord of the underworld as he raised his hand. He held the silence, savouring the moment and fixing it in his memory. This night would become one of the stories to tell his grandchildren. 'Show no mercy to the Gwyn!'

The warriors roared in response and followed him towards the town of Abertawe where the garrison of Pembroke lay sleeping. Vorath was aware he was leading his men against a well trained and much larger army, on its home territory, but one of the advantages of the enforced wait at their secret hiding place in the hills was that there had been plenty of time to plan the attack.

They would be outnumbered but the men who had joined him from the Gwyn had detailed knowledge of the town's defences and had helped Vorath to decide how best to use his warriors. On the warlord's signal, groups of warriors each ran silently for their targets, dark cloaks making them almost invisible in the night.

The greatest risk to Vorath's plan of attack was the ring of high wooden lookout towers the Gwyn had built around the town. If his men were spotted by the Gwyn sentries he would lose the element of surprise, so these lookout towers were the target for the first group of warriors.

Vorath's men swarmed up the supports of the towers and slaughtered the surprised guards before they had any chance to raise the alarm. The warlord had ordered his warriors to hold position in the lookout towers, so they threw the bodies to the ground and stayed, ready with spears to pick off any Gwyn soldiers who tried to escape.

Lord Vorath led the next group to the command post, the nerve centre of the garrison. The only entrance was to the front, so although it was high risk they had no choice but to storm the building, relying on the element of surprise.

Vorath's men had already described the layout of the building, so once they had dealt with the men in the guard's room he know exactly where to go. The acting commander of the Gwyn garrison woke just in time to look into the dark eyes of the warlord's black painted face as Vorath's sword slashed across his throat.

The warriors who were tasked with the raid on the main Gwyn barracks had fire as their weapon. The roof of the building was covered with slate but the walls were timber, sealed with pitch. Men who had once slept there knew that the adjacent stables were full of bales of dry straw, used for the bedding, so it was this that the warriors silently piled against the doors then alight.

The flames soon took hold but the men inside reacted quickly, woken by the thick grey smoke. Trained to sleep fully clothed with their swords by their sides, the Gwyn soldiers burst from the doors of the barracks, knocking the burning straw aside and attacking the Du warriors.

Vorath heard the yells of the violent battle that ensued and took the reins of his warhorse from a warrior outside the command post. He galloped to the burning Gwyn barracks to find that his men were outnumbered by the soldiers. Vorath charged into the mass of fighting men, hacking and slashing with his sword.

Acrid smoke from the burning barracks drifted towards the fighting men, causing them to choke and cough as it filled their lungs. The light breeze fanned the flames which finally took hold of main timber in the roof, lighting up the night with an eerie glow.

A barbed arrow from a Gwyn bowman flashed through the air and struck Vorath deep in the shoulder, nearly knocking him from the saddle. It simply seemed to strengthen his resolve as the warlord continued fighting, roaring at his enemy as he killed and wounded with relentless force.

The drifting smoke made it hard to see but he knew he was completely surrounded by Gwyn swordsmen. The agony of the arrow in his shoulder weakened him and he was expecting to die a warrior's death when he heard terrifying war cries and the sound of hooves clattering on the cobbled road. His riders had joined the battle.

The soldiers of the garrison fought on bravely but didn't stand a chance against the battle hardened mounted warriors. One by one, the soldiers from the barracks were cut down. With their commander dead, some of the less brave Gwyn started deserting, only to fall victim to the warriors waiting in the lookout towers, who used the advantage of height to impale the running men with spears and arrows.

As dawn broke over Abertawe the warriors of the Du were ensuring that not a single soldier of the Gwyn escaped alive. In Pennard, Lord Vorath was recovering from his wounds in the king's oak beamed room of the Royal Llysoedd.

The arrow was painfully removed from his shoulder and a deep cut to his sword arm stitched by one of the Du physicians. Vorath stood looking above the fireplace at the battered shield, once used by the old king, and vowed that he would not rest until he had forced King Gwayne's surrender.

~

Afon had never been far north of his home at Caerphilly and his work as a labourer on the building of the castle had kept him close to home. It seemed a sensible idea to sign up for the army when there was talk of war with the Du, and he had enjoyed the camaraderie of the training. He had not been promoted but he had unexpectedly become something of a popular spokesman, sticking up for the pay and conditions of his fellow soldiers.

Now the men were all talking about the defeat of the Pembroke garrison he wished he had stayed out of the army, as it was rumoured that the king was planning his retaliation.

Accounts of the battle were mixed but although the Du had clearly suffered casualties, with many men wounded, the soldiers of the Gwyn had been massacred. Sir Padrig was to be summoned back with his men but Afon knew it would be the

Caerphilly garrison that was likely to be sent to 'sort out' the Du in Abertawe and reclaim the Royal Llysoedd at Pennard.

The king decreed that the Du must never surprise them again, so the castle guards had been doubled both day and night, with patrols and checkpoints on all the main roads. At first the men accepted their new orders, aware that there was a real threat, but as the days passed more of them were complaining of the long hours of boredom. Afon found the night watch particularly challenging, as he would start to imagine black shapes moving in the trees and had twice woken the entire garrison with false alarms.

Kane had been promoted to the commander of Afon's watch, so when he asked for volunteers to act as an advance guard to the north of the castle, Afon was quick to put himself forward. Although he worked on the principle of never volunteering for anything, he quickly realised that he could do well to be safely out of the castle. He set off in good spirits, determined not to return until the threat from the Du had been resolved, one way or another.

~

To the west the warriors of Ynys Mon continued to seize every town and village in their path and eventually arrived at the most westerly point of St Davids. When word of Vorath's defeat of the garrison at Abertawe reached them, it was no longer necessary to continue raiding only at night.

They marched openly, living off the land and easily dealing with any Gwyn resistance. Warnings of their approach reached Bishop Cledwin's housekeeper Anwen, who realised it would be impossible to defend the bishop's property, as all the men of fighting age had long since been ordered to join the army. There had been no word from the bishop since he left for the north and no reply to even the message she had sent to the archbishop.

They had no choice but to pray that their lives would be

spared. Anwen had sewn black pennants, which the farm workers raised on long wooden poles to show there would be no resistance to the Du.

The warriors of Ynys Mon cheered when they saw the flags and rewarded the bishop's staff by deciding not to loot and burn the property, as they had done with many others on their journey south. They claimed Bishop Cledwin's lands in the name of King Gethin and Anwen invited the leaders to use the bishop's house.

She served them the bishop's best wine and arranged for a pig to be slaughtered and roasted, wondering how long she could detain them before they became suspicious. Unknown to the Du, Anwen had taken the risk of sending one of the farm workers to alert the soldiers at their final objective, the fortress at Pembroke. Although he had been deemed too old for military service Anwen hoped he would be able to ride quickly on one of the bishop's horses and reach them before it was too late.

When the exhausted rider from St Davids galloped in to the castle, the guards remaining there knew it was time to take action. The loss of the garrison at Abertawe shocked them. They had been expecting the Du, as accounts of their progress down the western coast had been reaching them almost every day, but now they were effectively cut off from the king and his reinforcements at Caerphilly.

There were still a good number of fighting men in the town, but they lacked experienced leaders. Some wanted to abandon the castle and others argued that they should barricade themselves inside the walls.

Neb was one of the original archers at Pembroke castle from before the war had started. He was a survivor but not a leader, and although he had the most experience, he had never fired a single arrow at the enemy so was not confident that he was the best choice to lead a group of archers to ambush the Du.

When the idea was first suggested it seemed to have a good chance of success, but the news from Anwen's rider from St

Davids made them realise they had underestimated the number of warriors heading in their direction. Neb gathered the archers in the courtyard of the castle.

He looked at the men around him. He had thought himself lucky not to have been sent to Abertawe but now the odds looked even worse. At least the garrison had the advantage of their numbers. 'The Du are on their way here soon,' he told them. 'It's time to put your training to some use.'

One of his men was concerned. 'We are never going to stop a whole army. It would take twice as many men!'

'We have a good supply of arrows and bows, but we are the only archers,' Neb agreed. 'We'll do what we can to slow them down then run for the hills,' he joked, secretly wondering if any of them were going to get back alive.

The bishop's housekeeper Anwen had done her work well, as there was time to choose a position with good cover where the road narrowed. Neb's archers took turns to keep a lookout for the warriors arriving and did not have long to wait, as the Du could soon be heard approaching.

The men of Ynys Mon had grown complacent with a string of easy victories. They had been told that the way ahead of them was poorly defended, so were not prepared for the hail of arrows unleashed by Neb and his archers. The entire first rank of the marching warriors fell before they even realised it was an ambush and the rest ran from the road in disarray.

Neb had made sure each of his archers had stuck a plentiful supply of arrows in the ground at their feet to increase the rate of fire. It was an old archer's trick for as well as making the arrows easy to grab, the dirt would do no good to any of the enemy they managed to hit.

Most of the archers could achieve at least ten shots a minute and they fired the arrows without waiting any commands or taking time to carefully choose their targets, sacrificing accuracy for quantity in an effort to make the Du think they were facing a much larger force. They had been lucky that the warriors did not wear armour and were taken completely by surprise.

The Du quickly retreated well out of range of Neb and his men, with many dead and even more wounded. The heads of the Gwyn arrows were barbed and attached with warm beeswax, so when the warriors tried to remove them by pulling on the shaft, the heads would fall off deep inside the wound.

The only solution was to cut deeper to retrieve the barbed arrow head then cauterise the wound with hot irons to stop the bleeding and reduce the risk of infection. The warriors were supposed to endure this without making a sound, but Neb and his men heard yelling and the occasional scream of agony and could only guess at the damage they had inflicted on the Du army.

As soon as they thought it was safe, Neb ordered his men to return to the castle, not realising that a group of Du warriors had already cut off their escape. Most of their arrows were now gone but they were all armed with swords and many also carried knives.

Nothing in their training had prepared them for warriors with spears. Neb was the first to die, with a Du spear in his chest, and two other archers also fell dying before they had even drawn their swords. The rest of his men put up a brave fight, as they had no experience of hand to hand fighting. It had been costly, but before long the Du were celebrating yet another victory.

~

King Gwayne rode out with Kane to the hills north of the castle. He had just received word that Pennard had fallen to the Du and was in an angry mood.

'I need Sir Padrig and his men,' he said. 'Send another rider. It would be good to have him here.'

'These are difficult times, my lord. I suspect that our riders are being taken by the Du, as there has been no word from the queen or any reply to your message to King Athelstan.'

'Athelstan has his own problems with the Vikings in the north, but I am worried about the queen. It was a mistake not to bring her here.'

'I have a suggestion, my lord.'

'What is it?'

'I know of a man named Cade. He's not a soldier but assistant to Archbishop Renfrew and has a good knowledge of the area. He travels in the name of the church so should be able to escape the attention of the Du.'

'Good. Have him track down Sir Padrig.'

'I was thinking to send him to find Queen Elvina?'

'Now that Vorath had control of the west it will not be long before he turns his attention to Caerphilly. We need Sir Padrig's men, so we will have to send someone else for the queen.' Gwayne knew the long haired man was right. Elvina was in real danger now but so were they all. She would have to look after herself.

~

Cade had no idea the Archbishop was dead. All he knew was that Renfrew had gone to see the Bishops of the Du to see if he could shorten the war. He was often away for weeks at a time and it was a long journey to the northern coast, so he didn't expect to see him back again for some time.

As an employee of the church, he was surprised to be summoned urgently to the royal rooms at the castle. He waited apprehensively outside the king's meeting room, wondering what the king would require of him. An elderly servant appeared in the doorway and ushered him in.

Cade entered the king's room, surprised at how dark it was. The window had been shuttered against the autumn rain and the only light was from an oil lamp, burning brightly but inefficiently. The rest of the room was sparsely furnished, with simple oak furniture and wool rugs on the floor. There was little to indicate it belonged to the king.

The king was seated alone by the hearth and did not look in a good mood. He did not ask Cade to sit but looked at him seriously. 'I have been told you know this area well. Is that true?'

'Yes, my lord, I work for Archbishop Renfrew as an assistant and messenger,' replied Cade.

The king looked at him. 'Where is your master the archbishop?' He realised that he had not seen his advisor for some time and Renfrew was an important link to the Saxon court.

'He is visiting Bishop Elfred, my lord. I am sure he will be back soon.'

'You know the knight Sir Padrig?'

'Yes, my lord.'

'I need you to take him my order that he is to return. Our victory in the war with the Du could depend on it.'

'Of course, my lord. I will leave right away.' He was relieved to have such a simple request.

Gwayne held up his hand to stop him. 'You need to know that the warlord Vorath has offered a bounty for the capture of messengers, to be paid if they are alive or dead. Take care, as my spies tell me that he has left Pennard and is camped in the hills to the west of here.'

Cade looed surprised. 'I will do my best, my lord.'

King Gwayne nodded. Cade was a good man and he could use a few more like him now.

After Cade left Gwayne sat staring into the dying embers of the hearth, wondering if he should have sent Cade to find the queen as Kane had suggested. He suddenly realised that his wife would now be Vorath's prisoner if she had stayed at Pennard as he had nearly insisted. The war had changed so many things. He missed Elvina and prayed for her safety, wherever she was.

Cade was used to taking messages for Archbishop Renfrew and knew the area well. He had decided to travel unarmed except for his knife, which he carried all the time. Riding one of the Archbishop's horses to make good time, he said a silent prayer that they would respect the protection of the church. Now he knew the Du had been ambushing riders who could be carrying messages.

The warriors who spotted Cade gave him no opportunity to explain that he was not a soldier. He rode straight into their ambush but nearly managed to escape, as he quickly turned and galloped back the way he had come. Cade could hear the warriors closing on him and realised their horses were faster.

They carried spears and at least one of them had a bow, so he was riding for his life, as fast as he dared when a warrior suddenly appeared to the side of him and pulled him from his horse. He was injured in the fall, hitting his head on a rock and saw that his wound was bleeding heavily before he lost consciousness. The warriors took his white horse and delivered him to Lord Vorath to claim their reward.

Vorath looked at Cade with interest. His instinct told him this man was not like the other messengers they had captured.

'Where are you off to in such a hurry?'

Cade knew he must not give away the fact that Sir Padrig and his men were so close. 'I have been summoned by my master, Archbishop Renfrew.'

'I don't believe you. You came from the castle?'

Cade realised the Du must be watching their every move. 'I often go to the castle with my work for the church.'

Vorath considered his answer. The bishops of the north advised the king on all matters and he had heard of Archbishop Renfrew, who was reputed to be under the control of the Saxons. 'You tried to escape from my men. I will give you one last chance to tell me the real reason for your journey.'

Cade realised his life was in danger and had heard tales of

what the Du did with their prisoners, but remained silent. He could not betray the king but there was no way he could escape now. His head was still bleeding and he found it hard to think.

On a nod from Lord Vorath a warrior tied Cade's hands behind his back held him next to the horses drinking trough while another held his head under the muddy water, only letting him up gasping for air when he was on the point of drowning.

Vorath disliked torture of unarmed men but was impressed by how long Cade endured this treatment before telling all he knew about the plans of the Gwyn. He was pleased to discover the location of Sir Padrig and his men and respected Cade's courage and loyalty but still had him executed, as the man knew too much.

CHAPTER 19

A powerful autumn gale swirled around the tall stone towers of Caerphilly castle. making the long white pennants of the Gwyn flap violently on their flagpoles. The wind loosened the iron catch fastening the heavy shutters of the room where King Gwayne lay dreaming. He dreamed of ghoulish black cloaked enemies that turned to smoke when he tried to kill them. He dreamed of his father, the old king, cursing him for failing to finish the Du and reclaim his lands they had stolen.

He also dreamed of his beautiful wife Elvina, desperately calling for him to come to her rescue. The wooden shutters banged hard against the stone castle wall, waking him and he lay in the darkness, thinking it was time to bring an end to this war.

In the morning he splashed his face with cold water and called for Kane to come as soon as he could. Kane was pleased to see the gloomy mood that had preoccupied the king in recent weeks was replaced with a new commitment he had not seen for a long time. He also noticed that the parchment map with detailed drawings of the Du defences was spread out on the table.

'Your orders, my lord?'

'I want every able bodied man ready to fight,' said Gwayne. 'First we will deal with this insolent warlord Vorath, then we will march to this castle at Flint,' he stabbed his finger aggressively at the mark on the parchment. 'I have a score to settle with their king!'

'I've learnt not to underestimate this Vorath,' said Kane calmly. 'Do we know where we can find him?'

The king looked pleased with himself. 'I have a spy in his camp. He can tell me where Vorath and his men are going to be and when!'

'A spy?' Kane looked interested. One of the advantages of being so close to the king was learning secrets few men of his position could expect to know. Vorath had been able to elude them by retreating quickly to secret hiding places in the hills, so a spy would give the Gwyn the advantage they needed.

King Gwayne smiled. 'He is one of our men Vorath bribed with gold to join him. I think it serves him right! He looked out of the window and was pleased to see that the wind had eased and it was turning into a fine clear day. 'When can the men be ready to march?'

'I will see to it right away,' said Kane.

A young drummer beat out the step as the men of Caerphilly garrison marched west down the long and well maintained old Roman road towards Abertawe. They were in good spirits, as they had waited and trained for a long time to be part of the war against the Du invaders. Some of them were fighting through loyalty to the king, others because their own lands were under attack and a few simply because they needed the good pay and rations that came with military service.

The king remained at the castle in Caerphilly, waiting for word from Sir Padrig about when he would be returning. Kane had also chosen to stay, as he had some urgent business to attend to.

He rode west on a fast horse from the castle, dressed in a grey cloak with a hood pulled low over his face, as he hoped his absence would not be noticed. Once out of sight of the castle he increased his pace to a canter, then a gallop, as time was of the essence and he had a long way to ride.

He was challenged by a warrior on lookout duty as he neared the Du encampment and asked to be shown to Lord Vorath, explaining that he had vital information for him about the Gwyn garrison at Caerphilly. The lookout seemed unimpressed but took him to a stone building guarded by two warriors, armed with vicious spears. He waited outside while the lookout went in and explained his request, then was shown inside and saw warlord Vorath for the first time.

At first he found it hard to see, as the room was dark and there was a smoky fire, but his eyes quickly adjusted to the poor light and he saw the black clad figure standing before him. Kane was surprised to see that Vorath was about his own age and build, with a dark beard and bare muscular arms, encircled with tattoos of sacred symbols.

The stories he had been told of Vorath's exploits had become so exaggerated in the retelling that he had expected someone much taller and older. He noted the bloodstain on a cloth bandage covering a wound on Vorath's shoulder and realised that this was a warrior as well as a leader of men.

Vorath had not expected to see that the Gwyn informer would look like a man of the tribes, with his long dark hair and Celtic tattoos on both arms, similar to his own. He also had the bearing of one used to command and showed no sign of fear at the dangerous situation he was in.

'You are a warrior?' asked Vorath, his deep voice booming in the sparsely furnished room.

'My father was,' replied Kane.

'Was?'

'My family lived in the north, a fishing village on the coast. We were raided by Vikings when I was a boy. My father was killed protecting our land, as were many other good men that day. It was too much for my mother and she took me south. I have been here ever since.'

Vorath liked the calm and controlled way the man spoke, showing no emotion even when taking about what must have been very difficult times. He forced himself to focus on the newcomer. 'You said you had important information for me?'

Kane hesitated for a moment. He was about to change his life forever, betray the trust of the king, all the men he had trained and the people of the Gwyn. Then he realised that he was now a man of the Du, so he told himself it was no longer treachery.

'You have a spy in your camp, Lord Vorath.'

'What is his name?'

'All I know is he is one of the men who joined you from the Gwyn. He is passing information about your movements to the king.'

'There are many spies,' said Vorath. 'We will find him.'

Kane looked Vorath in the eye. 'It is not the spy I came to tell you about, Lord Vorath. I came to warn you that the king has ordered the entire Caerphilly garrison to march on your camp. These are well trained and experienced men. You would be heavily outnumbered.'

'When are they leaving?'

'The men are marching as we speak so there is not much time.'

'How do I know I can trust you?'

Kane looked at him. 'I risked my life to bring you this information.'

～

King Gethin was pleased with the accounts he had received of Lord Vorath's success in the south and decided it was time he was rewarded. Vorath had asked for reinforcements, so he would send the warriors of Flint castle to Vorath's growing army and help him to finish the Gwyn for good.

Vorath needed the reinforcements to reach him as quickly as they could, so he ordered the longest march ever undertaken, even within the memory of the oldest living warriors. It would be over two hundred miles to Lord Vorath's camp, taking the fastest route through the mountains.

The men travelled light, carrying only what they needed, with supplies on pack mules rather than wagons so they would not be slowed down on the hills. They made good progress on the first day, covering nearly forty miles over the rough ground before darkness fell.

Once in the mountains the pace slowed and they formed small groups, each competing with the other to have the glory of being fastest and not wanting the humiliation of coming last. During the day they relied on the position of the sun to guide their way once the path became less distinct, keeping it to their left in the mornings and to the right as it began to set.

If the sky was clear they were also led by men who could read the stars and find the pole star, a rare skill that helped them make up the extra miles they needed by marching on in the darkness.

The warriors rested at night but only had a blanket or their cape to shelter from the cold and damp of the wilderness. They were lucky that the nights were mild and free of frost but some of the men grumbled.

They had been given strict orders not to light fires that could alert the Gwyn, so the only food was eaten cold, washed down with freezing water from the mountain springs. Most of the men were unused to marching such long distances and many were soon suffering from blisters on their feet, with others simply exhausted by the relentless pace over the uneven ground. Fights broke out between some of the men from rival tribes and the older warriors had to threaten them with a beating to keep up the challenging march.

Lord Vorath's message to the king had also told them to be vigilant for men of the Gwyn ready to light warning beacons on the hill tops, as it was important that they kept the element of surprise.

As a precaution they sent some of the younger warriors up to reconnoitre the highest ground and posted extra lookouts whenever they rested. When they crossed the border and entered the territory of the Gwyn there was a call from the forward lookout that riders had been seen approaching.

The warriors of Flint melted into the bushes as they had been trained to do and waited. The riders stopped and identified themselves as warlord Vorath's men, come to guide them to his camp in the hills. There was a cheer from the men of Flint as it had been a gruelling march and their objective was finally in sight.

Lord Vorath welcomed the warriors to his camp and congratulated them on their impressive achievement, telling them they had written another chapter in the stories of the tribes. He ordered that every man should have a hot meal and sat with the most experienced warriors to discuss the battle he had been planning.

'We can win this war if we defeat the garrison of Caerphilly,' he told them. 'If they had stayed in the castle we would have needed to starve them out, but I have been able to draw them into the open for you. Now you have a chance to make the king proud of you.'

'Do you know where the Gwyn garrison is now, Lord Vorath?' One of the older warriors asked the question they had all been wondering about.

'Yes. I've had men watching them since they left the castle.' He grinned. 'They are camped in a valley near Abertawe, a few miles south of here. There is high ground overlooking their camp so you must get your men into position without being seen.'

'We have a lot of men. It will be hard to avoid being seen by their sentries?' It was one of the younger warriors, a practical man who showed great promise.

'My men will take care of the sentries and your attack must be made at night. We have learned to watch for the Gwyn longbow men. They are good but they can't hit you if they can't see you!' He laughed, lightening the sombre mood and called for a jug of the dark Du beer. They all raised a tankard in the air to their victory against the Gwyn, although some of them wondered if it would be their last.

As the night approached the warriors of Flint prepared for battle and smeared their skin with the traditional mixture of soot and fat. As well as striking terror into their enemies, the black war paint made it harder for them to be seen, especially under the cover of darkness. They all wore warriors black capes and tunics, paid for by the king as a mark of their status, with many of them carrying the long sharp Du spears, as well as their swords and knives.

They were silently led to the high ground overlooking the Gwyn camp by some of Vorath's men and lay in the long damp grass, out of the view of any lookouts, waiting in the clear night for the signal. The sudden piercing screech of a hunting owl was the only sound in the valley. If any of the Gwyn lookouts had still been alive they would have thought nothing of it but the men of Flint knew it was Lord Vorath's signal that the sentries were all now dead.

The men of Flint cautiously approached the ridge over-looking the enemy camp and could see the flickering light of fires below. A few men were walking around in the camp but most were sleeping, unaware that the battle was only moments away.

The commander of the Caerphilly garrison had chosen to camp deep in the bottom of a steep sided valley, close to a stream that ran parallel to the road. There were a lot of men in the garrison and unlike the warriors of Flint, they were well equipped with tents of canvas that shone in the moonlight like dozens of white sails. As warlord Vorath had suggested, the warriors had agreed to divide into two groups and stealthily approached the sleeping soldiers from the road in both directions.

A second owl shriek rang out into the darkness and was replied to with another, the signal that both groups were in position. With a roar the warriors of Flint charged into the peaceful camp, killing some men as they emerged from their tents and others before they were even properly awake. Some of the warriors had been trained to throw their spears with deadly accuracy and many soldiers fell to the ground with the heavy shafts sticking from their lifeless bodies.

Others held their spears like a fighting staff, with their right hand near the end and their left a shoulder's width apart, quickly thrusting the deadly iron tip at the heads and necks of their enemy while keeping themselves well out of range of the slashing Gwyn swords.

One group of warriors had sharpened iron blades on the edges of their spears and swung them low at the legs of the soldiers, cutting swiftly through muscle and bringing them to their knees for the final killing thrust.

The commander of the garrison was a light sleeper and quickly realised they were under attack. Wondering why his sentries had not raised the alarm, he called his men to him. He sent a group of his best archers to climb the high ground on the sides of the valley and ordered them to fire at any Du they could see.

He organised the rest of his men into lines, swords and buckle shields at the ready. They had based this technique on a development of the Roman way of fighting and trained for months although this was the first time they had used it against a real enemy. The commander made them wait for the warriors to come closer to them and said a silent prayer that he would live to see another day.

Several of his men fell immediately to vicious spear throws but the others closed ranks and pushed towards the warriors, slashing and cutting as they went, deflecting the Du swords and spears with their shields.

The men of Flint were not trained to deal with this technique, being more used to hand to hand fighting, and it soon became clear that the battle was turning in the favour of the Caerphilly garrison. Encouraged, the soldiers started taking a heavy toll on the warriors, killing with ruthless efficiency.

The archers had taken a while to find good positions on the high ground in the darkness but were now ready. Many were armed with powerful longbows and although they found it hard to see their targets, they risked killing some of their own men as a hail of deadly iron tipped arrows rained down on the Du.

One of the older warriors was struck violently by an arrow that hit him with such force it almost passed right through his body. When the Du realised what was happening, one of them called for a group of men to follow him up the steep sides of the valley.

They made short work of the archers, who had not even carried their swords and were running out of arrows, but had left the men in the valley outnumbered. Some warriors found they were fighting two or three Gwyn soldiers at once and paying the price as swords slashed and stabbed into their unprotected bodies.

Some of the Gwyn soldiers had found time to pull on their chain mail vests and armoured breast plates for protection, but the commander of the Gwyn had not and was suddenly hit full in the chest by a well aimed Du spear.

He died instantly, thrown on to his back with the force of the throw and his men panicked with their leader suddenly lost. The commander's well organised rows of men quickly broke up as some tried to run for cover and others took the battle into their own hands, swept up in the violence of the fighting.

This suited the individual fighting style of the men of Flint, who quickly took advantage, yelling their blood curdling battle cries and forcing the soldiers of the garrison back onto the defensive.

By the time the first signs of dawn were creeping into the valley the battle was over and the only sound was of dying men. The garrison of Caerphilly was no more and the warriors of Flint had delivered another victory for the Du.

CHAPTER 20

Q ueen Elvina was glad to be leaving the hunting lodge in the woods. Bethan had listened in astonishment to Elvina's description of how Cadell's treachery had nearly cost the queen her life.

Elvina had been troubled by the violence of her reaction and the way she had been able to kill a man, even if it was in self defence. Her conscience was eased a little when they found the body of her murdered guard in the bushes. They had all been taken in by Cadell's charm and Elvina realised she'd had another lucky escape.

As the guards dug two deep graves in the clearing at the rear of the lodge, Bethan and Elvina discussed what they should do next.

'We could stay here,' said Elvina. 'It is comfortable and good to have a dry roof over our heads but I don't want to sleep in here another night.'

Bethan looked concerned. 'Are you thinking we should go back the way we came?'

Elvina shook her head. 'We did well to avoid the Du raiders. We can't risk it again.'

'You could send one of the guards with a message to the king.'

'We would need to tell him where we are, which could be dangerous if the guard was captured.'

'What do you think we should do, my lady?'

'Do you believe in destiny, Bethan?'

'I suppose… yes, sometimes it seems we are being led in this direction.'

'You remember what Cadell told us about the Du queen's sister?'

'Yes. I think her name was Ceinwen?' Bethan looked confused.

'She is looking after the young prince, the king's only son. If I could take him hostage we could force the king to surrender.' Elvina looked thoughtful. 'Gwayne will become king of all Wales.'

'The risks are great,' said Bethan. 'Cadell said they were living on the northern coast. Is that really where you want to go?'

'We must travel in disguise, can you help me look like a woman of the tribes?'

Bethan laughed, happy to forget the danger they were in for a moment. 'You could cover your hair with a black shawl? I saw black dresses and a black cloak in your room. We could try them and see if they fit you?'

Elvina was pleased with the good quality of the black dresses. She was a little slimmer and taller than the person who owned them but Bethan pointed out that it was better for riding any distance than if they were too tight. The problem was how to hide the queen's blonde hair, which could draw unwanted attention to her.

'The Du make their black dye by grinding old acorns and oak galls, mixed with rust from iron,' suggested Bethan. 'We could dye your hair black?'

'No!' said Elvina quickly, 'I will tie it back and you can cut up some of this black material to make me a headscarf.'

Bethan did so and laughed at the effect, as she had only ever seen the queen wearing white but had to agree that it helped. 'Your eyes look very blue, for a lady of the north!'

Elvina smiled. Bethan had been a perfect travelling companion for her and her mood was lifting now that she had a plan to bring an end to the war, however risky.

The guards were unhappy as they left for the north but knew better than to say anything. The king could have them thrown in the castle dungeons for their failure to protect the queen. Elvina was now wearing a black dress, with a scarf over her hair and rode Cadell's black Welsh Cob to help complete her disguise.

The guards had also removed their white cloaks and chain mail, with just grey woollen smocks and grey wool blankets to protect against the cold. One of them led Elvina's fine white mare by the bridle, as there was no certainty if they would ever pass that way again and the thoroughbred horse was too valuable to abandon.

The tree lined road to the north was strangely quiet and deserted but as they rode towards the coast they started seeing a few other travellers. Elvina realised they must be people of the tribes, her enemies. She pulled her black cloak around her and avoided looking in their direction.

There was no sign of any Du warriors but their disguise would not stand close scrutiny, so it was important not to attract attention. Queen Elvina looked across at Bethan and wondered if she was willing to be part of the plan to kidnap the prince. It would be a real test of her handmaiden's loyalty and her life could depend on the outcome.

～

They had wondered how they could find the queen's sister once they reached the coast but it proved to be surprisingly easy. Elvina sent Bethan to ask the way at a bakery in a nearby village and one of the bakers was happy to help. As well as giving her directions, he presented her with a freshly baked loaf and asked to be remembered to Ceinwen.

The stone built house where she lived was a short distance from the sea in a pleasant but isolated spot. The queen told two of the guards to go the rear of the house and be ready to stop anyone who tried to escape. She ordered the others to wait for her call, a short distance from the entrance to the house, while she went to the heavy oak door with Bethan and knocked. The door was answered by a shy but pretty servant girl.

'Is your mistress Ceinwen at home?' asked Elvina.

The girl nodded and asked them to wait.

Ceinwen was putting Prince Evan to bed in his wooden crib and not expecting any callers, so was curious.

'Did they say what they want?'

'I am really sorry my lady,' said the servant girl. 'I forgot to ask their names.'

'Never mind. Please ask them to come in and I'll see for myself.'

The servant returned, followed by the two women. Ceinwen had never seen either of them before but was shocked to realise they were both wearing her sister's black dresses. It was possible that they were just similar but she was fairly certain, as she had spent many hours carefully sewing them for her. Her mind raced as she tried to smile in welcome. Something had gone terribly wrong and she had to discover what it was and how.

'You are in great danger from the Gwyn,' said Elvina, keeping her voice low so that only Ceinwen could hear. She looked at the baby prince in his crib, who smiled back at her. 'How many guards do you have here?'

Ceinwen looked at the women, trying to think quickly. 'I have no guards now, only servants.' She longed for Hywel and was worried about Rhiannon. 'Who are you? What are you doing here?'

Elvina removed her headscarf to reveal her long gold hair. 'I am Queen Elvina. You are our prisoner now, Ceinwen.'

Ceinwen looked alarmed and sat down in her chair, amazed at how quickly everything had changed. 'My sister, Queen Rhiannon?'

'She will be brought here when we find her.' She turned to Bethan. 'Tell the guards to secure the house please Bethan.'

Ceinwen looked tearful. 'What are you going to do with us? What about the Prince Evan?'

'As long as you do what I say, I will make sure no harm comes to you or the prince.' Elvina found it easy to sound convincing. It was the truth but the threat in her voice was clear.

'We are going to write a letter to your king, demanding his surrender.' Elvina looked at Ceinwen with conviction in her deep blue eyes. 'We want a quick end to this war and you are going to help me to achieve it.'

~

The castle at Flint was a very empty place now the warriors had left for the war in the south. King Gethin was almost alone and wished he could have gone with them. The news from Vorath had been encouraging but there had been no word for several days, so he was relieved when a messenger finally arrived.

It was not news of the war, but he carried a letter with the queen's royal seal, so the king took it to his rooms, expecting to see Rhiannon's familiar handwriting. He broke the wax seal and opened it, surprised to see it was written in fine Latin by a hand he did not recognise.

He read the letter through several times in astonishment. There were some parts he had difficulty understanding but the message was clear. The Gwyn had captured his son and at the bottom was the signature of the queen's sister Ceinwen, confirming it was true.

Gethin felt anger surge through him as he realised what the letter meant. He had been foolish to commit his entire army so far away in the south and leave his wife and son undefended. He sent a rider to summon Bishop Deniol, as the entire future of the Du was suddenly under threat.

Deniol was interrupted from his prayers by the urgent knocking. He had hoped to quietly wait out the war, studying the old religious texts in his library but now the king was demanding to see him. The messenger was insistent that he should leave right away.

Hastily packing his things, Deniol set off with the king's rider on the short journey to the coast. A cold wind was blowing from the south and chilling him to the bone. Despite his dislike of superstition he sensed it could be a bad omen.

The king was in a troubled mood when Deniol arrived. He showed the bishop the letter and waited while he carefully read it through.

Deniol looked at the king with concerned eyes. 'I regret that this looks genuine,' he said. 'The Latin is perfect. It has to be written by the Gwyn, as Bishop Emrys is the only other person I know other than Queen Rhiannon who can write as well as this and it is not his hand.'

'You are right,' said Gethin. 'The letter bore the queen's seal, which means the Gwyn have probably captured her as well as Prince Evan.'

'I wonder why it is signed by the queen's sister, rather than the queen?'

'I was thinking about that. It may mean she has been able to escape.' He clung on to the hope that his wife was safe but in his heart he was already preparing himself for the worst. He crossed to the window, looking out to the windswept estuary as he struggled to control his emotions. His world had been turned around by that one letter.

Deniol waited in silence.

The king turned to him. 'You know I can never surrender to the Gwyn.'

Deniol shook his head. 'There must be something you can do?'

'Even if I could find enough men to come with me, any rescue could put their lives at risk.' Gethin paced the hard stone floor, thinking. He looked up at the bishop. 'Any day now I should hear we have control of the south, so I need you to write a reply that will buy us some time.'

~

By the time the wounded soldier reached Sir Padrig's camp he was so weakened by loss of blood he could hardly talk. Padrig's men tended to his injuries as well as they could and gave him a strong drink.

Padrig had been out hunting for red deer in the hills and was in good spirits, having killed a good stag with a lucky shot from a longbow. He was told of the injured man when he returned and asked to be taken to him at once.

'Good God man, what's happened?' Sir Padrig had followed his orders diligently and was certain that no Du warriors had passed him.

The soldier looked up and recognised the big man. 'The garrison is lost, Sir Padrig. The Du surprised us, in the middle of the night.'

'Which garrison? You mean Pembroke?'

'Caerphilly, Sir Padrig. Not many of us escaped.' Seeing Padrig's reaction the soldier hesitated to tell him the rest of the bad news. 'The Pembroke garrison is also defeated and the Du have taken Pennard.'

Sir Padrig looked shocked. 'The king?'

'As far as I know the king is safe at Caerphilly castle sir.'

'Why did he not summon me?' Padrig didn't expect the soldier to answer but another question occurred to him. 'I expect the men of your garrison gave the Du quite a beating?'

'Yes, we did,' recalled the soldier. 'I saw many dead and injured Du warriors before I was knocked out.' He saw Sir Padrig's enquiring look. 'They left me for dead. I don't think they were interested in taking any prisoners.'

Padrig whirled round and yelled for his commanders. 'Stand to men, we have a chance to win this war if we can be quick!'

Within the hour Sir Padrig and his men were on their way to find the Du warriors who had massacred the Caerphilly garrison. Padrig was riding his new battle horse and wearing his brilliant white breastplate with a flowing white cape. He may not have been born to be a knight of the Gwyn but he knew how to make sure he looked the part.

Behind him was the entire surviving army of the Gwyn, men he had trained personally and could rely on in a fight. He knew of the valley the wounded soldier had described as the scene of the garrison's last battle. The Du army had suffered a lot of wounded men, so they were likely to be taking refuge somewhere in the hills above the valley.

They arrived in the late afternoon with the autumn sun dazzlingly low in the western sky. They had approached the valley from the north and luck was with them, as they could see the thin columns of grey smoke of camp fires rising into the still air ahead.

If the Du were on the opposite side of the valley it would have been much harder for Padrig's men and if they had gone to Abertawe it may have been impossible to find them. He silently thanked the brave survivor of the battle being able to alert them in time. The Du did not seem to be expecting a counter attack and probably thought they now had full control of the area.

Sir Padrig called his commanders to the front. He would lead the main group in a frontal attack on the Du camp, while the two commanders would each take a group of men to the flanks.

Although Padrig was normally jovial and made light of even the most challenging situations, his men could see he was stern faced and serious about this battle. The Du had invaded their homeland and murdered their friends and comrades, so this was more than just another battle. They would kill or be killed.

He turned to face the waiting men. 'For the King and for the Gwyn!'

They charged towards the smoking fires, covering the ground so quickly that the Du lookouts saw them too late to warn the warriors. Sir Padrig swung his heavy sword viciously left and right, killing a man with each blow, then rode hard into a third who was about to throw a spear. The iron shod hooves of Padrig's powerful white horse smashed into the warrior's chest and he was trampled before he knew what had happened.

One of the men behind Padrig shouted a warning and he ducked as a sharp Du spear flew past, grazing his shoulder. Shouting his thanks he stayed low in the saddle and rode hard at the man who had thrown the spear, slashing with his sword and cutting deep into the man's neck. Even as the warrior fell dead Padrig was attacking the next, oblivious to the swords and spears all around him as the Du tried to defend themselves against the sudden and violent attack.

As Padrig ordered, his commanders rode in with their men attacking on both flanks, trapping the Du warriors, as their only escape was the treacherously steep side of the valley. One of the commanders yelled out in surprise and pain as a Du arrow struck him in the ribs but even though badly wounded he continued leading his men into the mass of fighting warriors. The mounted soldiers of the Gwyn were slashing down on the men on the ground and showing no mercy.

Sir Padrig chose his own group of men in the centre from the toughest and most experienced fighters and they were spurred on by the knowledge that the Du were trying to take their lands. They charged a group of warriors who were ready with swords and the air rang with the bright clash of metal as men fought for their lives. Several of Padrig's men fell victim to spear throws, suffering terrible wounds that were likely to be beyond the ability of any healer, but the rest continued to fight on undaunted.

A group of warriors targeted Sir Padrig and pulled him roughly from his horse. He fell heavily but although he was quickly back on his feet, sword in his hand but completely surrounded by the Du warriors. One tried to disarm him by grabbing his sword but instantly regretted it as Padrig thrust forward, stabbing him in the throat.

He turned just in time to parry a second warrior's sword then reversed his swing and chopped into the head of a third warrior. His horse was well trained and remained close, despite the noise of battle, so Padrig managed to climb back into the saddle and swung his blade in a wide and deadly circle, killing one man and wounding another.

The battle was soon over, as the Du warriors were tired and many of them had lost their spears or had wounds and injuries from their fight with the garrison. They began to retreat from the relentless onslaught and were being driven closer to the edge of the valley. Sir Padrig's man pressed forward again, killing and maiming until every single warrior who had left Flint castle on the great march lay dead.

CHAPTER 21

*B*ishop Emrys had written a long letter, explaining in as much detail as he could recall the circumstances of the accident that led to Archbishop Renfrew's tragic death. He found writing down the traumatic events of that night also helped him come to terms with it, as he had been wondering if he could have stopped the archbishop returning into the building.

Emrys included a simply drawn map showing where Renfrew had been buried and signed it, satisfied with the result. His problem was where to send the letter and how. He knew the archbishop lived in the village of Llandaff but did not feel inclined to travel to the territory of the Gwyn while there was a war being fought.

He decided the letter would keep for now and headed back in the direction of his home, stopping at a remote old chapel in the wilderness on the way to pray for Renfrew's soul. He'd lost the few possessions he had brought on the journey in the fire but found some comfort in living the simple life of a pilgrim. He was in no hurry to return to his home in the north and was content with travelling from one chapel to the next, relying on the charity of the local priests and parishioners.

Before the archbishop was buried, Emrys had removed his valuable gold crucifix with the ruby at its centre. This decision troubled his recurring dreams, where he replayed the events of the fateful night over and over in his mind. He held the gold crucifix before him and could clearly recall the voice of Renfrew explaining how the church had to play its part in ending the war.

The archbishop was right but there were many ways to achieve that end. Bishop Emrys was a man of the north and could help to end the war by making sure his people won. He would do what he could to see that King Gwayne was treated fairly in defeat.

～

Padrig led his exhausted but victorious men back to the relative safety of their camp in the hills. He had seen to the proper burial of his dead and his men had done what they could for those who had been wounded.

Some of his soldiers were so badly injured that he sent them home, unfit to fight again, to be cared for by their families. Others had their wounds carefully stitched up and wooden splints bound over any broken bones, but they would need some time before they would be ready for a battle against the warriors of the warlord Vorath.

The greatest risk to them now was that their wounds would fail to heal and turn bad. Padrig feared little but had seen the bravest of men in tears, begging for someone to end their misery as a sword cut slowly turned blue, then black, a sure sign of a slow and lingering death through poisoning of the blood.

His physicians knew a great deal about the use of herbs and the importance of cleaning the wound of soil but they always had more failures than successes. Padrig had never been a particularly religious man but now he prayed for the quick recovery of his men.

Sir Padrig had luckily managed to escape serious injury to himself in the battle but he was badly bruised across his ribs by the fall from his horse. He wondered if one of them was broken, as he felt a stabbing pain and could no longer sleep on one side.

He would have liked to visit the king in person but instead decided he should stay with his men, in case Vorath attacked. He decided to send one of his riders to the king with news of their victory and told him to watch out for ambush by Vorath's men.

It was clear that there could be no peace until he had tracked down the warlord Vorath and found a way to defeat him, before it was too late. Instead of celebrating their victory over the Du, Padrig ordered all the uninjured men to organise a search of the area, checking with the remote farms and smallholders for any news of the location of Vorath's men. They knew the area well and soon located the Du camp just south of their own and dangerously close.

His rider returned the next day with important news from King Gwayne. Padrig was relieved to see him and greeted the man warmly.

'Good to see you back safely! How is the king?'

'The king is pleased with your victory, Sir,' said the rider. 'He has a spy in Vorath's camp. The warlord is preparing to move north to the border, so he asks that you have your men ready.'

'We found the Du. Their camp is very near here.'

The rider nodded. 'I was nearly caught by them but spotted their lookout just in time.'

'I knew you were the right man to send,' grinned Padrig. 'Our wounded are recovering well so we will hold this position.'

As the rider left to tend to his horse Padrig secretly wondered if it would really be so easy. From what he had heard, Vorath had luck on his side, so far.

~

Lord Vorath was sitting with his men enjoying a drink of dark ale by the fire when one of his warriors rode in to camp and asked to see him,

'I have bad news to tell you, lord Vorath. The warriors of Flint have been defeated by the Gwyn.'

Vorath felt suddenly saddened. He had known many of the good men from Flint all his life. 'What happened?'

'My brother was at the Du encampment...' The warrior struggled to find the words. 'They are all dead, Lord Vorath.' He was carrying a Du spear and showed it to the warlord.

Vorath examined the thick wooden shaft. It had been cleanly cut through by a sharp blade. 'This can only have been the knight Padrig. We knew he was somewhere close. We were going to find him but if he can defeat the men of Flint...'

He put his hand on the warrior's shoulder. 'I am sure your brother died a brave warrior's death.'

Vorath had been relying on the reinforcements of the warriors from Flint castle to help him with the final stage of his plan to take Caerphilly and the king of the Gwyn. Now he would need a different plan, and time to think. He suddenly realised that they were in great danger and turned to his warriors, who had been gathering round listening to the news of the battle.

'This Padrig will have his men looking for us. He is not like the other Gwyn soldiers and he can't be far away.'

One of his warriors stood. 'I will double the guards and warn them to be extra vigilant.'

Vorath agreed. 'We must move north, while we can.'

The Du were skilled at quickly breaking camp and before the dawn had moved to a new location closer to their own border, avoiding any contact with the Gwyn. It angered Vorath that certain victory had been snatched from him so suddenly. He had sworn that he would never return to his homeland until he had forced the king of the Gwyn to surrender but he was a patient man and knew his time would come.

~

Ceinwen's house on the coast was comfortable with room for them all and Elvina was learning a lot about the king from Ceinwen, who was still unhappy but seemed to have become resigned to her capture.

'Do you think he will try to rescue the prince?' she asked.

Ceinwen nodded. 'I am certain of it. He won't have taken kindly to the letter.'

'We need to move. There must be somewhere not too far from here?'

'I could see if there is somewhere we could rent,' suggested Bethan, 'You still have the Saxon coins.'

Elvina agreed. 'Take two of the guards with you but remember the location of it must be kept secret or we may as well stay here.'

Ceinwen saw a problem with their idea. 'How will you know if there is a reply from the king?'

'I was thinking about that,' said Elvina. 'Your servant girl can stay here and keep this house in order. One of the guards can call each day to see if there are any messages.'

Bethan left with two of the guards to find them a suitable hiding place a little further down the coast. It took all morning but she had a purse full of silver coins and was able to find a farmer who was happy to rent two slate roofed cottages. There was also a good sized stable for their horses. It was a little way off the main track but Bethan knew that would suit Elvina.

The young servant girl seemed happy with the arrangement and asked no questions about where they were staying or for how long. They moved to the cottages that afternoon, Elvina allowing Ceinwen to carry the sleeping prince, escorted by four of the guards. They passed no one on the road, so there was little opportunity for Ceinwen to raise the alarm, even if she had been inclined to.

～

Lord Llewelyn's loyal servant Bryn had become concerned when his new master Cadell failed to return. There were a number of possible reasons, as he could have easily met up with the warriors of Ynys Mon, or been drawn further south by his search for Queen Rhiannon.

Bryn was worried because he thought he knew his master well enough to be fairly sure that he would have first reported back to Ceinwen, the queen's sister. He waited another week but it was quiet at the hill fort with all the men away and he felt he had a responsibility to the queen's sister to follow the road his master had taken to the hunting lodge in the woods.

Bryn took the last of the Welsh Cobs from the stables and packed as much as he could carry, as he had no idea how long he would be away. The road was now completely deserted and he realised that he must be one of the few men of the Du army not already in the south fighting the Gwyn.

He reached the peaceful lodge by mid morning and could see that the shutters were on the window and the doors barred. Always resourceful, Bryn went round the back and tried the door to the kitchen, which opened easily when he put his shoulder to it. There was no food in the lodge but he could see that someone had been there recently, as there was a jug of fresh water on the table.

A search of the rooms told him little, although he did find the remains of a black dress that had been cut up and it looked as if the beds had all been slept in. He rested in one of them for a while then went to check the stables and outbuildings. Bryn stood looking at the two freshly dug graves. They were unmarked but their purpose was clear. He wondered who had died there and if it meant his search was over or just beginning.

～

The lone soldier Afon continued his journey far north of his home at Caerphilly, glad to be safely out of the fighting or the endless guard duties at the castle. He'd managed to catch a rabbit in one of the snares he set and roasted it over a fire the previous day. Now he was hungry again, so was glad to see the thatched roof of a small croft in the distance. There was a steady line of smoke coming from the chimney, so he knew there was someone inside.

'Hello,' he called. 'Anyone there?'

A man appeared at the doorway and studied him. 'You a soldier of the Gwyn?'

'Yes,' replied Afon, suddenly unsure of himself. He remembered the warning about the dangers of trusting the people who lived in the wilderness and his hand dropped involuntarily to the dagger he wore at his belt.

'Watch out for the Du,' warned the crofter. 'They're not far away. One of them stole from my neighbour.'

Afon looked at the crofter's house. He had been sleeping rough and was quickly running out of food. 'I need a meal and a good night's sleep,' he called. 'I will pay you?'

The man looked at him for a moment, as if making up his mind, then waved him to come in. It was dark and cramped inside the croft and smoke from the fire made Afon's eyes water, but the thick mutton soup was hot and tasty and he gratefully took a bed in the corner and fell quickly to sleep.

He woke with a start, wondering where he was for a moment as he looked around the old stone croft. There was no sign of the man but his boots had dried out by the fire overnight and he felt much better than he had for some days. The sun was high overhead as it approached mid day.

Afon was starting to enjoy the wild countryside and wondering what he was going to do for lunch when he spotted movement in the distance. Quickly hiding behind one of the few trees, he watched carefully, his heart beating like a drum in his chest.

This was no crofter. He could see it was a warrior, dressed in black and armed with a sword. The archer Kane had told him about this moment many times during practice at Caerphilly Castle. 'Kill or be killed,' he had said, his eyes dark with some memory of when that was what he had to do.

~

The man that Afon could see approaching was one of the few men who had not joined the long march from Flint castle. Dafydd had once considered himself a future warlord and Vorath's successor, but the young favourite Tristan had put paid to that. Now he thought himself lucky that he had not been made to go to reinforce the army in the south. He would have been even more certain if he had known that his friends now lay dead.

Dafydd had expected to be retained by the king to deliver messages and take his turn on the lookout duty bit instead had been ordered to the border as an advance guard. It would have been lonely work if it were not for the fact that the Saxon's had built their defensive dyke along the line of much of his journey to the remote outpost, so he had company of a sort from the bored Saxon lookouts.

The men seemed unsure of their role and were happy to have shouted conversations with the people of the Du. One of them even threw him a loaf of bread. It was a little stale but Dafydd was grateful as he needed all the supplies he could find.

As he approached the border with the Gwyn he realised that he must have somehow missed the outpost, as the countryside was changing and he must have accidentally wandered into enemy territory.

Dafydd had been wondering as he walked if some form of truce with the Gwyn would be such a bad thing. He had heard tales of how the southerners had become wealthy through trade with the English and thought perhaps it was time that the Du had the benefit of more modern thinking.

He decided that if he saw any Gwyn soldiers he would surrender rather than fight and see if he could negotiate with them. It seemed a better idea than trying to kill them and he had a new spring in his step as he walked further into the lands of the Gwyn.

CHAPTER 22

*S*ir Padrig was woken by the sound of arguing amongst his men. Buckling his white breastplate over his shirt he winced as his broken rib made a sharp stabbing pain in his side and he had to take a few deep breaths before he could go on.

This war with the Du was taking its toll and he wondered if he was getting too old to be living in the field. He splashed some cold water in his face then strapped on his sword and followed the raised voices.

'What's going on?' Padrig looked round at the faces of his soldiers and realised that it was the commander of the guard he had heard arguing with a young soldier, one of the scouts.

'We've located Vorath's camp,' the soldier answered. 'We need to strike now, before he moves again or goes after the king.'

'Our men are battle weary and many are recovering from their wounds,' said the commander firmly. 'It would be madness to attack Vorath until we are ready.'

Padrig was surprised at how quickly the discipline of his men was slipping away and how they now referred to Vorath. He could see both sides of their argument. His heart told him they should fight the invader but he knew the men needed time. He turned to the commander. 'How long?' He already knew the answer.

The commander shrugged. 'A week, maybe two.'

The soldier looked shocked. 'By that time they could have taken the king!'

Padrig shook his head and put his hand on the shoulder of the young soldier. 'I know how you feel,' he said. 'I would like to go now and take back our lands, but we need more men.'

The soldier looked disappointed. 'It was hard to count how many Du were in the camp but they are not so well trained as us and we know this ground well.'

Padrig liked the young soldier. He looked confident and reminded him a little of himself when he was younger. 'You and I will go and have another look at this Vorath, then we will decide.'

They set off as the earliest light of dawn was breaking. It was a risky venture and Padrig's broken rib was still very painful, but these were exceptional times and the kingdom of the Gwyn could be at stake.

They could not expect any mercy if they were captured, so had both replaced their white uniforms with the rough grey wool favoured by the local crofters. It would make them harder to spot and may even allow them to infiltrate the camp, as Vorath's army now included many deserters and local people who had simply switched their allegiance to the king of the Du.

'This way,' whispered the young soldier as they came close to the perimeter of the camp. They took cover under some twisted oak trees and Padrig suddenly made out the dark shape of a warrior armed with a spear.

It was one of Vorath's sentries, well positioned to have the widest field of view. Taking great care, they slowly crept around him in a large circle and ran to a hedge overlooking the camp. Padrig was glad they hadn't taken the soldier's advice, as he could see many men camped out in a large field that was well chosen and easy to defend.

He was about to suggest to the soldier that they should go when he spotted a possibility. 'See the Du horses?' He whispered, pointing to the next field.

The soldier nodded. 'I can only see a handful of men guarding them.'

Padrig counted at least thirty of the big black war horses and another twenty Welsh ponies, probably looted from farms as the warriors made their way through the Gwyn territory. Some were grazing at the short grass in the muddy field and others seemed to be sleeping standing up.

'Without their horses, the Du would have to travel more slowly.'

Padrig agreed. 'It won't be easy but if we can take them it would give us the time we need.'

They returned stealthily back the way they had come and Padrig explained his plan to the commander. Their best archers would deal with the warriors guarding the horses then a mounted group led by Sir Padrig would take as many horses as they could.

The commander was to take the walking wounded to a hideout north of the Du camp, the last place they thought the warlord Vorath would think of looking. The commander looked at their grim faces, knowing that if the plan went wrong they would all be killed, then saluted the knight and went to brief the men.

The archers left at midnight, led by the young soldier who knew the layout of the camp. He took them to a good vantage point with some cover where they silently prepared, sighting on the warriors guarding the horses and readying their bows for the signal.

It was a dry night, with a partial moon to help them but it also made their mission more dangerous. Unlike the Du, the Gwyn soldiers were not equipped for night fighting, although the archers had been allowed to replace their white tunics with brown capes that should help prevent them being seen.

Sir Padrig chose only skilled riders who were good at handling horses. It was important that they could keep their head in a fight, as all their lives would depend on the success of the raid.

They rode as close to the enemy camp as they dared, then dismounted and led their horses in the darkness as silently as they could in a wide arc out of view of any sentries. Padrig winced with the pain from his broken rib as he climbed down from his horse and hoped that none of his men had noticed.

Padrig waited until they were all ready and in position. 'Mount up men. Ready for my signal and remember my orders. We are not here for a battle this night, so if the Du come for us you are to make good your escape but be sure they do not follow you to our hideaway.' He nodded to the young soldier who had been waiting to relay his signal to the archers. There was no going back now.

The arrows flew silently in the night and struck with deadly force at such close range. One of the Du sentries fell wounded and started to call out for help but the hour was late and his yell of surprise went unnoticed. Sir Padrig swiftly rode to him and finished him with a single blow from his sword.

As they had planned, one group of riders took spare horses to the archers, while the rest followed Sir Padrig to ride between the horses and the camp, slipping the tethers of the black war horses and skilfully driving them north as a herd. Their hooves made little noise on the soft turf and the riders were careful not to panic the horses.

By the time Lord Vorath heard his men shouting and ran into the field the horses were all gone and Padrig was safely far north in his hideaway with his prize. The stolen horses included Vorath's own warhorse Ddraig and were worth a fortune in addition to their military value.

Vorath took one of the white-feathered arrows from the ground next to one of his dead sentries and held it in the air. 'This is why we need to finish the Gwyn! We will track down these cowards and show them what we do with horse thieves!' His men roared in agreement. There would be no mercy for any soldiers of the south from now on.

CHAPTER 23

*K*ing Gethin paced restlessly around the windswept battlements of the castle at Flint, desperate for news. The castle which had seemed so full of life was now empty, damp and cold. Several days had passed since any word of the war in the south and he found Bishop Deniol well meaning but poor company.

He looked to the path from the west and saw the small black shape of a single rider approaching. He was not riding with any sense of urgency that could have meant good or bad news but Gethin felt a strange sense of foreboding as he watched the man approach.

The king picked his way down the rickety wooden steps from the battlements to meet the rider at the gate. As he came closer Gethin could see the man was wearing the black tunic of the royal household and cursed under his breath. It must be another letter demanding ransom for Prince Evan.

He considered taking some men to free his son but the best warriors had left long ago with Lord Vorath, so all that remained were too young or old to fight. The rider recognised the king and dismounted, looking nervous. He produced a black leather case from his saddlebag and handed it to the king.

'There is a letter from the queen, my lord, and one from her sister which she respectfully requests for you to read first.' The man took a step backward, still holding tightly to the reins of his horse.

'You come from the queen?' Gethin had been concerned about the safety of his wife and could not conceal the hope from his voice.

'No, my lord. I carried the message on command of the queen's sister.' He had not wanted to make the long journey across the northern coast in bad weather and knew from the queen's sister that the king may react angrily to the contents of the letters.

Gethin told him to wait and went to his rooms to read the letters, ordering for Bishop Deniol to be summoned. He did not expect to have difficulty reading a letter from either Rhiannon or her sister Ceinwen but his hand was not as good as he wished and he could need some assistance with the reply.

One letter bore the queens personal seal and the other the royal mark. Ceinwen had also repeated her request that her letter should be read first on the front in stark black ink. He hesitated, looking at the small dark royal seal for a moment before breaking it and opened the first letter.

Ceinwen explained that she was a still held captive, a prisoner of the Gwyn, as was the prince, but they were both being treated very well and in good health. Her main concern was that there had been no reply to the original letter, so she repeated the demands of the Gwyn and Gethin realised that she had been made to do so under duress.

She then said she was concerned about the queen. The people holding her had been to the hunting lodge and there was no sign of her, apart from her black dresses. One of these Ceinwen knew the queen would not have left behind, as it was a special favourite. It was with great reluctance therefore that she was abiding with her sister's wish that the second letter should be delivered to him.

Gethin picked up the letter with Rhiannon's seal and remembered the last time he saw her. She had a look of sadness in her eyes that haunted his dreams for many nights, as if she had some premonition that she would never see him again. He ran his finger over the small black wax seal. It was from the Welsh gold signet ring that she always wore, a Celtic design from the old days. He opened the second letter and saw Rhiannon's distinctive handwriting.

Any happiness at finally hearing from her vanished as he realised she had taken too great a risk, sacrificing her safety for the good of her people. He had no way of knowing if her actions had any impact on the course of the war but, by her own admission, the fact that he was reading the letter meant that something had gone badly wrong.

Worst of all, she asked him to make sure that their son was kept safely away from the Gwyn until he was old enough to look after himself. Gethin sat back in the heavy oak chair in despair and his mood quickly turned to anger at the people of the south.

A timid knock at the door announced the arrival of the Bishop.

'Come in, Deniol. You need to see these and help me make sense of it all.'

Bishop Deniol entered and took the first letter from the king. After reading it carefully he picked up the second and read that through twice.

'If the queen is also in the hands of the Gwyn, my lord, I am sure we would have heard from them. The fact that they only mention the prince is indeed curious.' He looked at the king and for the first time had a sense of the pressure the man was under.

'I will have to find the truth of this,' answered Gethin quietly.

'I will ride to the nearest camp and find some warriors worthy of the name.'

'The closest is just south of here, my lord, but the best had gone to the territory of the Gwyn with the warlord Vorath...'

'I need you to find Bishop Emrys. If anyone knows where the queen could be hiding or where my son is being held, it will be him.'

'Of course, my lord. I will leave as soon as I can,' replied Deniol, retreating towards the door. He would be glad to be out of the damp castle and there would be safety in numbers by staying with Bishop Emrys. Even the Gwyn would hesitate to attack two representatives of the church.

Gethin folded the letters and stared at them for a long time, wondering what was for the best. It would be a short ride south of the castle, so he packed only what would fit in his saddlebag and ordered his servants to prepare for the journey west as soon as he returned.

Pulling his cape around him as some protection from the rain Gethin rode alone ahead of his servants, starting to form a plan. The letters which he carried inside the pocket of his black tunic nagged at his conscience. In his heart he knew he should be doing everything in his power to ensure the safety of his wife and his son and heir but for now he just had to have faith.

Bishop Deniol travelled south west, alone in his sturdy horse drawn cart towards the last known location of Bishop Emrys. He fixed a cover to guard against the rain but still he was glad to have relief from the biting cold wind when he called at a small chapel. He knew the garrulous old priest was the only person able to write and read in the village, so it fell naturally to him to gather the latest news.

As well as being a notorious gossip, there had once been a

question about him showing favour in the distribution of alms to the poor of the village. Priests were meant to behave better than the laymen but if they fell from grace they could suffer at the hands of the less privileged. The priest had asked Deniol to speak up for him and the bishop earned his complete loyalty in return.

The priest could hardly wait for him to stable his horse and be seated before he started telling the tale of the tragic death of Archbishop Renfrew.

'Slowly, please brother,' said Deniol, raising his hand to silence the man, his head whirling with too much information.

The priest ignored him and continued with the practiced ease of someone who has told a story many times. 'There was a terrible raging fire,' he explained excitedly. 'Some say the Lord has punished his servant for his sins!'

Deniol disagreed but decided to leave it and watched in silence as the priest poured them each a generous goblet of good red wine. 'Bishop Emrys escaped unharmed?'

The priest shook his head. 'His body is unharmed but they say the whole event has turned his mind. He has taken it on himself to see a proper end to this war, although I don't see how...'

'What of the Gwyn?' asked Deniol, mindful of his discussion with the king.

The priest looked pleased with himself and drained his goblet of wine with enthusiasm. 'The war is all but won! I heard we have routed the armies of the Gwyn. Just one knight and his retainers are left and the king of the Gwyn will run to the Saxons.'

Once again, Bishop Deniol chose to privately disagree but also chose not to share his concerns with the talkative priest. As far as he was concerned, few people would ever learn of the ransom of the prince or the disappearance of Queen Rhiannon.

As he listened to the old priest's gabbling his mind was on higher matters. With the archbishop dead and Emrys apparently suffering from some form of shock, the way was clear for him to be considered as the new archbishop of all Wales.

Deniol had never thought himself ambitious and had merely become the king's advisor through the accident of proximity. Recent events had suddenly opened a window through which he could glimpse a very different future for himself.

~

King Gwayne was aware that his rooms at Caerphilly were the finest of any castle in the land, yet he missed the comfort of his home at Pennard. He realised he missed the guidance of his father, the old king. He was also surprised to realise that he missed his beautiful young wife, particularly on the long cold winter nights.

Unaware that Queen Elvina was now living on the northern coast, he was thinking of her to be safely in the sanctuary of the church at St Davids. It was only when he overheard his servants discussing rumours that the Du had taken Pembroke that he began to be concerned for her.

He went to the window and looked out to the western hills. The lush green was now just a memory and had long been replaced with the dull tones of approaching winter. Gwayne had been reassured by Sir Padrig's victory and was confident that the knight and his men would keep the warlord Vorath occupied, but he had stayed too long in the castle.

He summoned Kane but his servant returned within the hour to report that the archer was nowhere to be found. He felt the stubble on his chin and an idea formed in his troubled mind. Kane had deserted him in his time of need. Gwayne felt anger at the archer's disloyalty but knew in his heart that he had expected as much.

'Fetch my horse, and tell my escort to be ready!' he shouted, more aggressively than was really necessary.

As his nervous servant scuttled off to make the arrangements, Gwayne realised he wasn't sure where he would be headed. He had always planned as a last resort to escape over the border to the east and find Elvina's brother, King Athelstan. To do so would be to admit defeat, something he knew his father would never have done.

Gwayne considered risking a journey to join Sir Padrig, but he was way off to the north and it would mean passing Vorath's army to reach him. Reports of the fate of the garrison suggested that if any men survived the massacre he would be lucky to find them. King Gwayne said a rare prayer for luck and left the castle with his escort, taking the path west, to find the survivors.

~

The Du camp had been moved as close to the castle as possible without being seen and a whole sheep now roasted on a spit over a fire pit. The deep core of hot, glowing hardwood embers were the remains of a big roaring fire and gave an intense heat without flame that could have burned the meat. A young warrior had the job of stirring the ash covered embers with a spear. His face was slick with sweat from the hot fire pit which glowed brightly in the failing evening light.

Lord Vorath watched with little interest, still angry and mourning the loss of his fine black warhorse Ddraig to the thieving Gwyn. They had fought and won many battles together and he vowed he would not rest until his horse was returned.

He had taken a small group of warriors on the few remaining horses and set off in rapid pursuit of the Sir Padrig's men but the Gwyn had too much of a lead and had vanished into the misty mountain air. Reluctantly, he had called his men to a halt and been forced to concede that the pursuit was futile.

The men knew better than to speak to Vorath but one of his most trusted warriors knew how to tempt him out of the black mood.

'The man Kane was here, asking for you again, Lord Vorath.'

Vorath looked up with keen interest in his dark eyes. 'Where is he now?'

The warrior pointed to a temporary stockade they had built from saplings to safeguard their remaining horses. 'We have him prisoner, for his own safety. The men have a score to settle with archers of the Gwyn.'

Vorath grinned. 'Bring him to me. We will see what he knows.'

Kane was led to him rubbing his wrists to restore the circulation where they had been bound too tightly with twine. He looked defiant and could barely be distinguished from the hardened Du warriors.

Vorath took his knife from the leather scabbard at his belt and cut a slice from the roasted mutton. 'Eat with us,' he ordered, handing the hot meat to Kane.

The archer took it gratefully. 'Thank you Lord Vorath. There has not been any time to eat since I left the castle.'

Vorath nodded and made space for Kane to sit by the fire. 'Are you with us, Kane?' He watched the man's face carefully but there was no clue to his allegiance.

'I am with the victors of this war,' Kane replied. 'Right now, that looks like the Du.' It was a dangerous tactic but he knew the Du respected loyalty, however misguided it may be.

Vorath was busy eating but his eyes never left Kane's as he considered his response. He carefully wiped his hands on a cloth and looked Kane in the eyes. 'Our scouts sighted a group of Gwyn riders leaving the castle this morning.'

'Where were they headed?'

'West. Could your king be with them?'

Kane pondered this. 'He could. He has not forgiven you for taking Pennard. My guess is that's where he is headed.'

Vorath grunted. 'It was undefended. Just a few farmers and servants.' He offered Kane more of the smoking meat and signalled one of the warriors to pour them both some of the dark Du beer. 'They surrendered when we arrived.'

'He may have sent the riders as a distraction while he heads east to the Saxon king,' suggested Kane. He drank deeply from the tankard of Du beer. It was warm and strong, with the rich flavour of malt and roasted barley. He needed to keep his head clear but the salty meat had made him thirsty and he wondered if Vorath's unexpected hospitality was a plan to loosen his tongue.

'We have all roads covered,' replied Vorath. 'If he does go east he will never make it to the border!'

Kane remained silent and took another swig of his beer.

Vorath threw a bone into the fire pit and watched as it flared into flame in the intense heat of the glowing embers. 'We ride tomorrow to finish this.' He raised his tankard in the air and called to his men. 'To victory over the Gwyn!'

The warriors roared in response and despite himself Kane felt proud to be accepted by the people of the north.

~

King Gwayne was exhilarated to be leading his men further west, towards his home. They had set a pace to reach Pennard after nightfall and he knew the path so well he was happy to ride under the welcome cover of darkness. As familiar landmarks loomed out of the night his thoughts turned to his wife.

He would have loved to find her waiting to greet him but knew instead he would find armed warriors of the Du guarding his home. He said another silent prayer that Kane was right and they could not have captured her without using her as a hostage.

The king and his escort stopped briefly in Abertawe and tried to track down any soldiers of the garrison but had no success. Instead they were seen by Vorath's spies, who hastened to notify the warlord.

Gwayne was saddened to realise that so many good men had given their lives to defend his vision of freedom for the people of the south. He was encouraged a little to see that his escort had doubled in number when they left the town, as farmers and traders still loyal to the cause had armed themselves with whatever weapons they owned.

~

Bishop Emrys of the Du saddled a borrowed horse and followed his calling, heading to the south west. He was not given to visions and disapproved of superstition but felt compelled to do what he could to see the war resolved in a fair and proper manner. There was no one to see him leave, or to wish him well but he was unconcerned, as the tragic end of Archbishop Renfrew had given him a new perspective on his life.

His life as bishop to the queen seemed far off now. He had enjoyed the challenge of teaching Queen Rhiannon to read and write in the language of the tribes, as well as Latin and a little Anglo Saxon.

He had hoped she would ask him to tutor the young prince but he had received no word from her since long before the fire that changed his life, so it seemed his work was done. He was unaware that his decision to travel south placed the king of the Gwyn under a new threat and had triggered a sequence of events that could only have one outcome.

~

King Gwayne and his escort took the back road to Pennard and watched his former home from the safety of the trees. There was a Du sentry at the gate as expected but few lights in the windows, suggesting that Vorath had decided not to leave many men to guard it.

The irony of the situation was not lost on Gwayne, as he waited in the darkness like a Du warrior, outside his own house, with only a handful of Gwyn soldiers left to support him while Lord Vorath roamed freely through the lands of the south.

He turned to his men. 'I need an archer, the best amongst you.'

A young soldier stepped forward, already fitting a white feathered arrow to his bow. 'My lord?'

'Are you certain you can take the sentry from here?'

The soldier nodded. 'I can, my lord.'

Gwayne beckoned the other soldiers to him. 'Be ready once the sentry falls. We need to check every room for the Du and quickly, before they know what's going on.'

The men looked grim faced, knowing the risks but loyal to the king. He nodded to the archer, who carefully sighted on the sentry standing just in the shadow of the entrance to the Royal Llysoedd.

The arrow flew straight and true, thudding deep into the chest of the Du warrior and killing him instantly. Gwayne drew his sword and led his men in a run to the entrance and put his shoulder to the heavy oak door. It was not barred and opened to reveal am empty courtyard. He silently gestured for half his men to check the queen's apartments and let the rest into the main building.

The Du looked up in surprise as King Gwayne and his men burst into the main hall. Empty wooden casks of the kings finest wine lay all around and it was clear they had been drinking. Without hesitating, Gwayne slashed the throat of the nearest and his men did the same to three others but not before one gave a yell of alarm, his last act for the warriors of the Du.

Two black clad warriors appeared in the doorway and took in the scene. One carried a spear, which he threw at a Gwyn soldier, piercing him mortally through his unprotected neck. Gwayne yelled in fury and hacked at both men with his sword, killing the spear thrower and opening up a deep gash in the face of the second. Undeterred, the Du warrior fought back bravely, with the blood running freely down his tunic, but he was outnumbered and soon lay dead on the cold stone floor.

Gwayne stood back panting with the exertion of the fight. It seemed so much more violent in the familiar surroundings of his home and he realised it was the first time he had actually killed a man for many years.

He sent the soldiers to check the other rooms but stayed alone in the blood spattered room with the dead. Looking up at his father's battle shield that still had pride of place on the wall above the fireplace he vowed that he would never surrender his lands to the Du. Whatever the cost.

CHAPTER 24

*T*he sturdy cart driven by Bishop Deniol ground to a
halt on the muddy track leading west and he wished he
was back at home, reading in the comfort of his library of
Basingwerk. He looked up at the brooding sky and wondered
what he had done to deserve such poor luck, then noticed that a
man who had been following at a distance would soon catch up
with him.

The bishop felt the weight of the silver coins in the leather
purse he carried at his waist. He would only part with them as a
last resort so attempted a forced smile. As the man came closer
Deniol could see he was a strong and hardy type, more than
capable of helping him out of his predicament.

'Good day to you, sir. I am the Bishop of Flint,' he called.
'Would you be so kind as to lead my old horse out of this mud?'

The man looked at him suspiciously. He had little time for the
church and the cart looked substantial but it would block the
road if it was left there, so he reluctantly took the rein of the
horse and encouraged it to pull the cart from the deep rut. At
first it seemed too much of a challenge for the tired horse but the

man persevered and with a final squelch of mud the wheels of the cart began to turn once more.

The Bishop was grateful. 'There is plenty of room if you would care to ride with me? I would be glad of the company.'

The man answered by climbing up onto the cart and taking his place at the reins. He seemed to know what he was doing. What happened next took the bishop completely by surprise. The man produced a sharp dagger which he held to Deniol's throat.

'Your money?' His voice was dark and threatening.

Deniol remembered the warnings he had been given of the lawless men of the wilderness and knew he had no choice. He nervously handed over his purse, fairly sure that the blade had already nicked the skin of his neck. 'It's all I have. There is nothing else of value.'

The robber relaxed a little and grinned as he hefted the purse in his hand. It was more wealth than he had ever had in his life. He put his dagger back in its scabbard and loosened the draw string of the purse to see the contents.

Something snapped in Bishop Deniol's mind. He was not a violent man but he felt a surge of anger at the man's impudence. He grabbed the handle of the dagger and quickly held the blade to the robber's neck. Now the situation was reversed he felt quite pleased with himself.

'I'll have that purse back now!'

The man pulled back suddenly but there was not much room on the seat of the cart and he slipped, falling heavily to the ground. He lay there unmoving, so Deniol hastily climbed down after him and was shocked to see that the man was unconscious and bleeding profusely from a head wound where he had hit his head on a large rock. There was nothing the bishop could do but to leave him to take his chances by the side of the road.

For the rest of his journey south Deniol was in turns elated at his own surprising bravery and wracked with guilt over probably causing the death of a man, even though he was a robber who preyed on innocent travellers.

As he neared the church of St Davids his luck changed. The keeper of an inn where he had stopped for some rest told him Bishop Emrys was staying in a chapel a few miles further down the road. Deniol was pleased to find Emrys after such a long and dangerous journey but was shocked at the change in the bishop, who seemed to have aged beyond his years.

Once he had seen to his horse he sat with Bishop Emrys in the modestly furnished vestry, a room attached to the chapel used to store the records of the parish. As with many chapels in Wales, the vestry was used for the serving of tea when the congregation returned to the chapel after the burial or cremation, so now it also served as a convenient temporary home for Emrys.

Bishop Deniol was glad of the warmth of a log fire which flickered in the hearth and accepted a small goblet of wine. 'I heard what happened,' he said. 'Archbishop Renfrew was a good man.'

Emrys nodded. 'He made me realise I could do more to bring an end to this war.'

Deniol was surprised. 'The church must do what it can to end suffering, but I don't see what we can do about the war?'

'The fact that we are both here in the south means we are already changing the course of the war,' replied Emrys. 'We have priests in every village of the south and they make it their business to know what is happening in their parishes.'

'Of course,' agreed Deniol. 'But surely they are loyal to the Gwyn king?'

'I have learned that they are loyal to the church first,' said Emrys. 'You need to know that the men of Ynys Mon have control of the west and Lord Vorath moves freely in the south.'

'Then there is something you need to know,' said Deniol. 'We need to act quickly as the Gwyn have Prince Evan held hostage.'

Now Bishop Emrys looked shocked. 'It may be the Lord's will

is that we work to save him,' he muttered. 'We must get word to the warlord Vorath.'

Deniol found himself being drawn deeper into what he now realised was only going to lead to more deaths and wondered if he really would have been safer staying in the empty castle at Flint.

~

Encouraged by the ease with which he had retaken Pennard, King Gwayne resolved to recruit more men to his cause in the west while the army of Lord Vorath remained in the east. After the best night of sleep he'd had in a long time, Gwayne and his men took the weapons and horses of the dead warriors of the Du and rode to the market town of Carmarthen.

It was a fine sunny morning for the ride, although the bitingly cold wind could not let them forget that winter was now upon them. Gwayne looked at the pure white clouds that filled the sky for as far as he could see. A heavy fall of snow would make it hard for the Du and could buy him the time he needed to rebuild his army.

Their arrival in Carmarthen was very different from the last time he had visited the town. Instead of being greeted by cheering throngs of people lining the streets, the king and his small band of soldiers pulled grey cloaks around them to avoid drawing attention and took the back way into the town.

They found a stable for their horses and made their way quietly to a tavern where they hoped to find men still loyal to the Gwyn. The tavern was poorly lit and smelled of wood smoke and stale beer, but the man Gwayne had sent in advance had already been able to assemble a dozen young men who were ready to fight.

'It is good to see you well, my lord,' said one of the older men. Gwayne could see the glint of silver chain mail through holes in his rough cotton tunic and realised that the man was either one of the few survivors of his army or a deserter.

Gwayne raised his hand in acknowledgement. 'You may have heard rumours that I'd been slain by the warlord Vorath?' Some of the men looked uncomfortable and he knew it was true. Gwayne smiled. 'Well as you can see I am very much alive!'

The man in the chain mail stepped forward. 'My lord, you know that there is a large Du army to the west?'

Gwayne nodded. 'I do, and I know many men have turned their allegiance to the Du, but we will fight on while I still draw breath.'

The men cheered and Gwayne held up a hand to silence them. 'We must act with stealth, as we need time to prepare for the last battle.' He gestured to one of the soldiers who had travelled with him from Pennard, who handed him a heavy leather saddlebag. Gwayne opened it and produced a handful of bright gold coins which he held high for everyone in the room to see.

'I have a secret weapon, the royal treasury of the Gwyn. With this gold we will buy the best weapons and horses, recruit good men to the cause and hire as many mercenaries as it will take to drive the Du from our lands.' The light from the poor quality candles in the tavern glinted on the gold, which made a satisfying chinking noise as the king let it fall back into the saddlebag.

Despite his warnings, the men could not resist another cheer. The king called for the landlord and ordered drinks all round. Many of the men who had secretly thought the war was well and truly lost suddenly found fresh hope.

Some were happy to know that the Du would finally be shown how badly they had underestimated the people of the Gwyn. Others were motivated more by self interest. Just one of those gold coins would keep them in comfort for many years and the king had more than any of them could count.

As they were all looking at the king and his treasure, none of them noticed a man slip quietly from the back of the room. He had a fast horse ready and galloped into the mist which had silently drifted over the town from the sea. If he rode hard, he could reach his master in two days. The gold had really tempted him and for a moment he had wondered if he would be better off following the Gwyn. Then he remembered what Lord Vorath did to traitors.

~

Vorath listened carefully to his spy's account of the king's arrival in Carmarthen and asked many questions before he let the man go for a much needed rest. He wished now that he had stayed at Pennard and simply waited for the king to arrive, instead of allowing himself to be drawn into a fight by the knight Sir Padrig. He called for his warriors and ordered them to break camp. They would have to leave for the west right away to stop the Gwyn before it was too late.

The Du were on the road within the hour but once again Vorath cursed the loss of their best horses. He had sent out raiders to all the farms in the area and they returned with a mix of ponies and farm horses, as well as several strong oxen to help pull carts carrying weapons and equipment.

Many of the horses were past their best and unused to the demands of war or the need to travel long distances quickly. Vorath had chosen a good black stallion for himself but still missed his faithful warhorse and hoped that the thieving Gwyn were taking good care of it.

It was good that they no longer needed to travel under the cover of darkness and could use the best roads, rather than the overgrown tracks they had been used to. As they passed through one of the Gwyn towns on the way, Vorath was surprised to be approached by a Gwyn priest with a message from the bishops of the Du.

'The church wants an end to the fighting, my lord,' said the priest. 'Too many good people have died.'

Vorath had not realised that both bishops of the Du were in the south and looked at the priest. The man seemed sincere and had the air of authority that came from a good education. He had never expected help from the church but it was welcome, as communication had been one his biggest problems in the south. Although he knew the old warlord had died a warrior's death he had received no word at all from the Lord Llewelyn's men of Ynys Mon.

'I'm pleased your people no longer run from us,' he said. 'They still fear my warriors but they seem to accept the right of the Du to travel freely in the south.'

The priest nodded. 'The bishops are working for a truce with King Gwayne. Those that support him will listen to the words of their priests, and the bishops of the Du have the authority of King Gethin, as well as that of the church in Wales.'

Vorath grinned at the mention of King Gethin. A lot had happened since he had left the fort at Flint and he missed his king, who was also his best friend and a fine warrior. 'You can get a message to King Gethin?'

'There are priests in chapels and churches in every village and town in Wales,' he replied. 'You must know that news travels faster within the church than by any other means.'

'Then I have a message for the bishops. Tell them if they can secure surrender from the Gwyn king my men will let him leave the country unharmed. If he will not, he will face the might of our armies.'

The priest turned to go, a little overcome by the significance of the task ahead of him, on which many lives could depend. Vorath called him back.

'I would also be glad if you can arrange for the good bishops to let King Gethin know we now have control of the south.'

~

Gwayne looked at the priest in disbelief. If it had been anyone else he would have struck them down for their insolence, but he knew the man in front of him was simply a messenger.

It was the worst possible blow to his plans to know that the warlord Vorath was already in the west, poised to attack, but even more shocking to learn that the church had turned against him.

'Where is Archbishop Renfrew when I need him?'

The priest looked anxious. He had been chosen to relay the message because of his skills in diplomacy but this was different. King Gwayne was a desperate man and there was more bad news to tell him.

'With regret, I must inform you that the archbishop is dead.'

'Dead?' It took a moment for the significance of this to sink in. Archbishop Renfrew had been his main contact with the Saxon King Athelstan, as well as the architect of his marriage to Queen Elvina. An idea occurred to him.

'Do you know if Queen Elvina is safe?'

The priest shook his head. 'I could ask the bishops to help you locate her?'

Gwayne's heavy boots thumped the hard stone floor as he paced up and down, deep in thought. He could not believe his future could depend on his reply to the bishops of the Du. The priest waited in silence, aware that the future of the country was about to be decided.

'Tell the bishops I will never surrender.' His words hung in the air and he was surprised to see sadness in the eyes of the priest.

'If that is your wish, my lord.'

'It is. I would also ask that they find Queen Elvina and ensure her safe passage to King Athelstan. She is one of the many innocent victims of this war.'

Even as he said the words, he realised that he was defeated but there was one last hope. As soon as the priest was gone Gwayne rallied his men and rode as hard as he could for the abandoned castle at Pembroke.

~

Vorath's army was poised north of the castle but were tired and battle weary, waiting for a break in the weather. The swirling mist had been replaced by gales and a relentless rain that lashed at the thin tents of their camp and turned the paths to rivers of mud.

Vorath was with two of his warriors, discussing a parchment map of the land around Pembroke, when he was interrupted by the sentry. The man was dripping wet and shivering with the cold.

'A visitor, Lord Vorath. Bishop Deniol wishes to speak with you.'

'Deniol?' Vorath had never liked the scholarly bishop and was suspected that it had been him who advised the king to stay in Flint when he could have been helping to defeat the Gwyn. Then he remembered that he was only in the west because of the bishops, so he was intrigued to see what Deniol had to say.

'Show him in.' The warriors made ready to leave but he gestured for them to stay. 'I think you will be interested to see what it is the bishop needs to discuss.'

Bishop Deniol entered the damp tent trying to hide his fear of the warlord. He removed his wet cape and braced himself for a difficult meeting. If he was ever going to become archbishop of Wales he would have to learn to work with men such as Vorath. The warlord stood as a mark of respect then grasped the bishop's arm firmly in a warrior's greeting.

'It is good to see you, Bishop Deniol. I am grateful for the service you do for our cause.'

Deniol felt his confidence grow in that instant. He worked for a greater Lord than Vorath and had now held the future of the country in his hands.

'Thank you, Lord Vorath. You fought bravely for our people and it is good to see you are well.'

Vorath grinned and pulled back the shoulder of his tunic to reveal an ugly scar where his flesh had been roughly stitched.

'A Gwyn archer had me,' he explained. 'The arrow was nearly too deep to dig out but it is healing well enough now.'

'I was nearly killed by a robber on the way south,' admitted Deniol. 'I managed to fight him off and he is one who will never trouble travellers again.'

'A man after my own heart!' Vorath was starting to like the studious Bishop. 'Well done, well done.'

He gestured for Deniol to join them at the table where the map was spread out on the table. Deniol looked at it with keen interest. He had never seen such an accurate map and quickly revised his understanding of the local area.

He turned back to Lord Vorath. 'I have come to tell you King Gwayne has refused your offer of clemency.'

If Vorath was surprised he showed no sign of it. 'Your work is done then Bishop. No one could do more to see a peaceful end to this war. Now we need to plan how to end it as warriors.'

Deniol appreciated that Vorath was effectively dismissing him but he had come too far to leave now. He looked back at the map and placed his thin finger on the neatly drawn symbol representing Pembroke castle.

'The river is wide and forms a natural defence of the castle at Pembroke. We are on the wrong side of it, so unless you can find suitable boats, your men face a long march?'

Vorath nodded in agreement. 'My men have marched far and by the time they reach Pembroke the Gwyn would have plenty of warning of our approach.' He looked at the Bishop with renewed interest. 'The church is in communication with King Gwayne?'

'It is, my lord.'

'I need you to find a way to persuade him to leave the castle and travel east, where I can arrange a welcome for him by the men of Ynys Mon. They have been waiting for this chance, so between us we will give it to them.'

King Gwayne had managed to find enough men to guard the castle but little else. He had recruited a few mercenaries but wondered how much he could really depend on them in a battle against the much stronger army of the Du. The rain stopped at last and as he stood on the high battlement looking out across the water at the high ground he knew that it was now just a matter of time.

The faces of those he had lost seemed to float on the misty river. His father, still angry and demanding revenge, the knight Sir Gwynfor, as confident as ever, and the Archbishop who would have been such an asset to him now.

His thoughts were interrupted by a sentry. He had been so lost in reminiscence of the past he had no idea how long the man had been waiting to speak to him.

'What is it?'

'A priest, my lord, with communication from the bishops of the Du.'

'I will see him in my rooms.'

The sentry looked troubled.

'There is more?'

'My lord... the men no longer trust the priests and don't want them to see how few men we have.'

Gwayne nodded. 'The men are right. Have the priest blind-folded before he is allowed into the castle and make sure he hears nothing.'

The sentry seemed satisfied with this solution and went to do the king's bidding. Once again, Gwayne cursed at how his lands seemed to be ruled more and more by the church.

The terrified priest had been well and truly bound by the over zealous guards, who had even tied his hands behind his back as an extra precaution. The king ordered him to be untied at once and told the guards to leave them, as he did not want anything the man had to say to be overheard.

'Welcome to Pembroke castle.'

The priest looked at him in silence, still in shock at his treatment, then recovered his composure. 'I have come to warn that you are in great danger. The armies of the Du are ready to attack and plan to hold you in siege here for as long as it takes.'

King Gwayne shook his head. 'You came here to tell me this?'

The priest looked him straight in the eyes. 'Bishop Deniol himself has sent me to suggest that you have one chance to escape before Lord Vorath's men can march around the river.'

'They have no boats?'

'Not enough.'

King Gwayne had heard Renfrew mention Bishop Deniol of the north and knew that he carried the authority of the Du King as his spiritual advisor. There was a chance that the Bishop was covering his bets to ensure his safety whichever side won.

'Have the Du started marching here yet?'

'No, my lord, they are still camped north of the river.'

'Then there is time for us to return to Pennard.' Gwayne was talking to himself now, oblivious to the priest. If he had to make a stand, it would be better than being trapped in the damp cold castle until they ran out of food. Somewhere at the back of his mind was also an idea about escaping by sea, to rebuild the army of the Gwyn.

He led the priest to a side exit from the castle. There was no need for a blindfold now they were heading home. Before the priest went the king put his hand on the man's shoulder.

'Thank Bishop Deniol for me and tell him if there is any way to reach my knight Sir Padrig he is to meet me at Pennard as soon as he can.'

'I will do that my lord.'

'Thank you.' As the king watched him go he remembered too late that he had forgotten to ask if there was any news of his wife, Queen Elvina.

The men were glad to hear it was time to go, as none of them relished the idea of a fight against overwhelming odds. They travelled light, taking only what they could carry in saddlebags, and left at first light on the coast road. King Gwayne was filled with new hope as the fresh sea air filled his lungs.

The warriors of Ynys Mon were in high spirits and sang an old marching song sang as they made their way to the river crossing. They had been a long time away from home and hoped this would be their last battle in the south.

They also knew that the army of Lord Vorath was close behind them, ready if needed. The one thing that had not turned to their advantage was the weather, as the first flakes of snow were already settling and those who claimed to know had foretold a harsh winter.

King Gwayne also saw the early snow falling and smiled, glad to be heading back to Pennard before it was too late. He looked back at the small column of loyal men of the Gwyn behind him, all that remained of a vast army apart from Sir Padrig's soldiers. He wondered if Sir Padrig was still alive and if he would ever know what had kept him far away when he was so badly needed.

Safely over the rickety wooden bridge that spanned the river, the Du warriors picked up the pace, as the scouts who had been sent ahead returned with news of sighting the King's men on the coast road.

The snow began falling harder and was accompanied by an

icy wind that stung their faces and froze exposed fingers. The warriors were used to snow but it made the path harder to see and this was no time to be losing their way. The horses also had to slow, as their hooves skittered on the frozen ground and for the first time rumours began to spread among the men that the Gwyn may escape after all.

Gwayne was thinking the same as his men made good time despite the snow, which was lighter near to the coast and melted more quickly in the salty sea breeze. He also had the advantage of knowing the path even when it began to disappear under a few inches of snow, as he could easily pick out familiar landmarks.

He was looking for the familiar peak of a hill when he spotted the first of many dark shapes standing out sharply against the snowy background. He wheeled round to face his men and shouted for them to stop.

'The Du are on the ridge!' He pointed north where the men of Ynys Mon could now be clearly seen.

'Do we stand or run?' It was one of the mercenaries, recruited in Carmarthen.

'We stand!'

There was little cover on the exposed coast road, so all they could do was wait with their backs to the crashing waves and watch as an entire army approached.

'Archers to me!' King Gwayne clearly had no intention to surrender and was acting as if this were an evenly matched battle.

The small group of archers were well trained and stood ready in line in the deepening snow.

'On my command I need you to take out their leaders, if you can see them,' Gwayne's voice was calm and authoritative now. He turned to the remaining men.

'No quarter is to be given or expected. We have the advantage that the Du have marched a long way and must be tired.'

The men nodded, grim faced.

When the end came it was brutal and quick. The men of the

Gwyn fought bravely but for every warrior they cut down, another ten stepped forward to take his place. King Gwayne looked down at his hands and saw that they were slick with the blood of the Du.

He glanced to his right and was just in time to save one of his young archers by deflecting a viciously slashing sword but then found he was fighting two Du warriors at once. One warrior cut him so deeply on his arm that he staggered back with the pain and the other saw his chance to end the war.

King Gwayne's last thought as he lay dying in the softly falling snow from a mortal blow was that the old king, his father, would surely have approved.

EPILOGUE

$\mathcal{T}$he victory celebrations of the Du lasted right through a hard winter and many stories were told around roaring camp fires by those who had fought on both sides.

King Geraint charged Bishop Deniol to negotiate the safe release of his son, Prince Evan, which the bishop achieved within one month and was rewarded with appointment as Archbishop of all Wales.

His first act as effective head of the church was to reunite Queen Elvina with her brother, King Athelstan, thereby gaining favour with the Saxon court which was to prove very useful to them both.

King Athelstan ensured Elvina was quickly married to a rich young Saxon Prince and by all accounts she was better for her experience in Wales, for which she always had a great affection. Elvina also persuaded Bethan, her handmaiden, to join her in England and they would often converse in the language of the Gwyn to the bewilderment of the Saxons.

No trace was ever found of Queen Rhiannon, which fed the legends of her selfless action. The myth of Rhiannon even found its way into the medieval Welsh manuscripts that became the heroic stories of the Mabinogion. Rhiannon's sister Ceinwen was made responsible for the good upbringing of the young prince and never married, which led to rumours of a very close relationship with the king.

Sir Padrig and his men escaped across the English border and were thought to have made their way to Brycg Stowe, where they found passage on a ship bound for Ireland, although no one can be certain.

Lord Vorath's reward was to be granted the former lands of the Gwyn which he ruled like a king in all but name and became well loved by the people of the south. He would often speak of the courage of King Gwayne, calling him a true warrior, and ordered a monument to be raised in his memory overlooking the sea at Pennard.

I remember being fascinated by the chess pieces coming to life when I read *Alice in Wonderland* as a child. It was many years later when I began exploring the early history of Wales and saw the parallels to a game of chess. The idea of writing this book came to me when I realised that the whole of Wales could become the 'chess board' with kings and queens, bishops and castles – and the people becoming pawns in their civil wars.

I began with a list of all thirty-two chess pieces and started creating the characters, drawing on ancient Welsh legends and folk lore, as well as the evocative place names. I realised there were only two roles for women in my 'cast of players', so created more as wives and sisters, handmaidens and housekeepers.

My next challenge was to find a worthy game of chess and study all the moves, which would drive the narrative. I chose what is known as the 'Game of the Century', played between Donald Byrne and the thirteen-year-old Bobby Fischer at the Rosenwald Memorial Tournament in New York on October the 17th 1956.Fischer was playing black and Byrne white and, after a standard opening, Fischer made his famous 'queen sacrifice' move. Although Byrne takes the black queen, Fischer goes on to taking many other pieces and achieves a checkmate.

As a writer, it was fascinating to have to work out how, for example, a bishop could take a queen, or a pawn 'kill' a knight. It was also fun to visit the locations mentioned in the book, including the enchanting island of Ynys Mon and the magnificent castle at Pembroke, close to where I was born and now live. '*Queen Sacrifice*' became my first historical fiction novel – and inspired me to dig deeper into the amazing story of Owen Tudor, which led to my best selling Tudor trilogy.

Thank you for reading this book, which I hope you enjoyed as much as I did writing it. For more information about my other published work please see www.tonyriches.com

Tony Riches, Pembrokeshire.

OWEN - Book One of the Tudor Trilogy

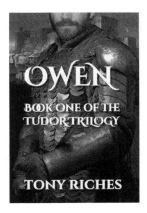

England 1422: Owen Tudor, a Welsh servant, waits in Windsor Castle to meet his new mistress, the beautiful and lonely Queen Catherine of Valois, widow of the warrior king, Henry V.

They fall in love, risking Owen's life and Queen Catherine's reputation, but how do they found the dynasty which changes British history – the Tudors?

This is the first historical novel to fully explore the amazing life of Owen Tudor, grandfather of King Henry VII and the great-grandfather of King Henry VIII. Set against a background of the conflict between the Houses of Lancaster and York, which develops into what have become known as the Wars of the Roses, Owen's story deserves to be told.

Available as paperback, eBook and audiobook

JASPER - Book Two of the Tudor Trilogy

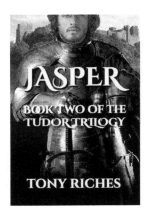

England 1461: The young King Edward of York has taken the country by force from King Henry VI of Lancaster. Sir Jasper Tudor, Earl of Pembroke, flees the massacre of his Welsh army at the Battle of Mortimer's Cross.

When King Henry is imprisoned by Edward in the Tower of London and murdered, Jasper escapes to Brittany with his young nephew, Henry Tudor. With nothing but his wits and charm, Jasper sees his chance to make young Henry Tudor king with a daring and reckless invasion of England.

Set in the often brutal world of fifteenth century England, Wales, Scotland, France, Burgundy and Brittany, during the Wars of the Roses, this fast-paced story is one of courage and adventure, love and belief in the destiny of the Tudors.

Available in paperback, eBook and audiobook

HENRY – Book Three of the Tudor Trilogy

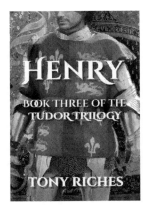

Bosworth 1485: After victory against King Richard III, Henry Tudor becomes King of England. Rebels and pretenders plot to seize his throne. The barons resent his plans to curb their power and he wonders who he can trust. He hopes to unite Lancaster and York through marriage to the beautiful Elizabeth of York.

With help from his mother, Lady Margaret Beaufort, he learns to keep a fragile peace. He chooses a Spanish Princess, Catherine of Aragon, as a wife for his son Prince Arthur.

His daughters will marry the King of Scotland and the son of the Emperor of Rome. It seems his prayers are answered, then disaster strikes and Henry must ensure the future of the Tudors.

Available as paperback, eBook and audiobook

The Secret Diary of Eleanor Cobham

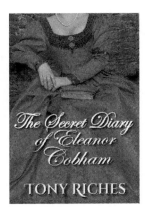

England 1441: Lady Eleanor Cobham hopes to become Queen of England before her interest in astrology and her husband's ambition leads their enemies to accuse her of a plot against the king. Eleanor is found guilty of sorcery and witchcraft. Rather than have her executed, King Henry VI orders Eleanor to be imprisoned for life.

More than a century after her death, carpenters restoring one of the towers of Beaumaris Castle discover a sealed box hidden under the wooden boards. Thinking they have found treasure, they break the ancient box open, disappointed to find it only contains a book.

The mysterious book changed hands many times for more than five centuries, between antiquarian book collectors, until it came to me. After years of frustrating failure to break the code, I discover it is based on a long forgotten medieval dialect and am at last able to decipher the secret diary of Eleanor Cobham.

Available as paperback, eBook and audiobook

WARWICK - The Man behind the Wars of the Roses

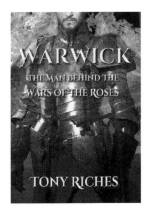

Richard Neville, Earl of Warwick, the 'Kingmaker', is the wealthiest noble in England. He becomes a warrior knight, bravely protecting the north against invasion by the Scots. A key figure in what have become known as 'the Wars of the Roses,' he fought in most of the important battles.

As Captain of Calais, he turns privateer, daring to take on the might of the Spanish fleet and becoming Admiral of England. The friend of kings, he is the sworn enemy of Queen Margaret of Anjou. Then, in an amazing change of heart, why does he risk everything to fight for her cause?

Warwick's story is one of adventure, power and influence at the heart of one of the most dangerous times in the history of England.

Available as paperback and eBook

24424913R00167

Printed in Great Britain
by Amazon